sunday love

kj lewis

Sunday Love
© 2017 by Kj Lewis Books

ISBN: 978-0-9976414-5-5

Editing by Anna Esquivel
Cover Design by Regina Wamba at maeidesign.com
Interior Design by Champagne Formats
Proofing by Monique Tarver

To all my girls looking for their Sunday Love.

sunday
love

chapter one

Elise

Will I ever learn? I'm a smart, organized, efficient woman. You'd think experience would have taught me by now to allow for a visit from that bitch, Karma. Man, she can hold a grudge. How long must I continue to pay for yelling at a kid on a bike? In my defense, I was sixteen, and I didn't know he was handicapped until I had already shouted for him to get out of the middle of road.

Evidently, I am a slow learner, despite being top in my class, and Karma's a sadistic whore who seeks pleasure in the little things that trip up my day. I should know better. The cues were all there. If I had just gone back to the hotel and my bed after I spilled cranberry juice down my blouse I could be asleep right now.

It was a full night of work that ensured I was up till the wee hours, which ensured I overslept this morning. Then she caused a run in my hose when I tripped and broke the heel on my sensible pumps. The only ray of sunshine she bestowed on me today was that all of this happened only steps from my hotel, so I was able to run back and change. Of course, I am out of stockings, and the only dress shoes I have are my 5 inch Louboutins that I brought for a formal dinner. Now I am running late to a meeting where I am about to fire people. Not only are they being fired today, but I can't even show them the respect to arrive on time.

Having adjusted my wardrobe malfunctions at lightning speed, I'm rushing into the twenty-floor skyscraper in downtown Philadelphia when I run chest first into a wall of a man in front of me, causing him to drop the folders he's carrying, losing his papers like a ticker tape parade, and me to land on my ass. By the time I make my apologies and help him gather everything, I am officially ten minutes late.

Exiting an elevator of wall-to-wall people, I am greeted by a young woman who shows me to a conference room where the meeting has begun without me. Par for the course, I am the only female in the room. I take the first open seat I find, only to see that Harold Smith, the current CEO of the telecommunications company our client recently acquired in the hostile takeover, is seated across from me.

"Miss Donovan. Glad to see you decided to honor us with your presence. Always looking to make an entrance." His eyes rake over me with idle disdain. If they were claws, I swear I would be gutted where I sit.

Harold and I have not seen eye-to-eye on much these last few weeks. Beckett Enterprises, who purchased the company a few weeks earlier, had hoped to leave the CEO in place, but my time here has only solidified what I assumed all along. A company in this shape doesn't get there by accident. It was achieved by poor leadership and fragmented decision-making processes from the top. Not only is he threatened because I am a woman– hear me roar and all that comes with that- but he doesn't appear to appreciate me as a person in general. Go Figure. I happen to be absolutely lovely.

"My apologies, gentlemen," I offer to the men in the room. I'm familiar with Harold's team whom I have been working with, but to my right are three men I haven't met before today.

"I was just filling in the team from Beckett." Harold passively motions to the three unfamiliar men. I turn to greet them with a nod, and am not prepared for the irritation I am met with from the good-looking man sitting closest to me. The mouth-watering, wet your lips, crawl to him, if he asks, kind of good-looking. His obvious displeasure is enough to halt my wayward thoughts and return my focus to Harold as he begins his slideshow of the changes that have occurred over the last four weeks.

"As you can see," Harold concludes, "we have made great strides thanks to our *home* leadership. I believe the information you gentlemen have been given is more than a little exaggerated. I consider that is to be expected given the nature of the reporter, if you understand what I mean." Harold looks at me. A monkey could understand his slam about my gender.

"Thank you, Harold. Everything looks in order," says one of the men from Beckett.

"Happy you're pleased. If there's nothing else?" Harold asks. The men move to stand before I stop them.

"Again, gentlemen, I apologize for my tardiness and if I am asking a question that was previously answered." Begrudgingly they take their seats again. "Harold, who provided you this presentation?"

"Excuse me?" He makes no attempt to hide his enmity at

my question.

"Who provided the data for this presentation? Did you pull these numbers on your own or were they provided to you?" My voice is a sugar-coated firmness.

"Let me educate you on how a company works. There's a CEO, *that's me*," he says with an effective pause. "Then you have a CFO, a COO, CMO, the list goes on and on. I ask for numbers and people deliver." The bulk of the men in the room snicker at his comments. "As a team we pull the numbers and go over them. Normally, we have a secretary put it in a presentation format, but since we have you on the team now, we thought you could make yourself useful and" with a wink, "clean it up."

"Oh, it's been cleaned up enough." I address the men flanking him. "Who participated in this collection of information?"

I wait. After no response, I ask again.

"If you are part of the team Mr. Smith is referring to, please raise your hand."

"They aren't school children Miss Dono…"

"Raise your hand if you support this presentation," I ask more forcefully. His entire staff raises their hand in what I assume is a show of defiance.

"Is there anyone on the team who does not agree with this report?" I wait about three beats. "Last chance to withdraw your support."

I pull some papers out of my folder and pass a copy to each person at the table.

"I'm disappointed, gentlemen. Not one of you has the moral character to stand up for yourself or this company." I stand and start sliding manila envelopes with individual names across the table to their respective receivers. Their hands shoot out to stop them. "Mr. Smith, you and your team are hereby relieved of your duties. You will find your separation papers in your respective envelopes."

"Who the fuck do you think you are talking to?" He raises his voice while coming to his feet. Strains of red climb from beneath his dress shirt collar to his face.

"Your misrepresentation of this company and these numbers are proof that you either have no idea what you are doing or that you are a thief. I believe it's the latter. You have been falsifying financial reports, and I have the evidence to prove it."

"You have shit." He starts walking around the table, and I brace myself for what I am sure will be a verbal beat down.

I nod through the conference room window to an assistant assigned to work with me. He enters with several investigators from the SEC.

"You stupid bitch! Who the fuck do you think you are?" he spits and lunges for me but draws up short when one of the Beckett associates pushes him face down on the conference room table, pinning his arms behind his back. I'm holding my breath, not out of fear, but out of disorientation. There's a hand splayed across my stomach and a hard body molded to mine from behind me. His breathe tickles the spot just south of my ear and his scent wraps around me. Clean with a little bit of spice. He shifts me to his right as he leans over to say something to Harold. The man nods to his associate and Harold is released. Standing, he buttons his suit coat, runs his fingers through his hair, and glares at me. "You haven't seen the last of me."

"One can only dream," I counter with sarcastic sweetness.

"Thank you," I tell the man who, to my disappointment, has finally released me. I motion to shake his hand and when our skin touches, a current dives through me, pausing my eyes to linger on his for a moment. His eyes are like a two-sided coin reflecting both harshness and a softness to them.

"Elise." The head investigator from the SEC pulls my attention and asks me to sign some papers.

"Of course," I answer him before turning to the three men from Beckett. "Elise Donovan, I apologize; I didn't know Mr. Beckett was sending a team today. I'm actually headed to a retreat where I'll see him. If you speak with him before I do, please share the numbers I provided and let him know I don't feel the company can be salvaged. He should move with the contingency plan my team has designed. Break it off and sell it in pieces. I believe he should make a tidy profit."

"Sign here and here." The investigator is back with papers in front of me, peppering me with questions. When I finally look up again, it's been almost forty-five minutes and the team from Beckett is gone.

It takes me another thirty to wrap up and when I finally call Theo from the taxi, I have just enough time to grab my things from the hotel lobby where they are holding my luggage and make my flight.

"How was the meeting?" Theo asks.

"Informational. I'll fill you in when I get there."

"Don't go to your flight," he says as I hear him thanking someone in the background. When he comes back to me, I hear the inside of a car dinging.

"Where are you?"

"Picking up a few supplies. Listen, Beckett sent a team today..."

"I know. They were in the meeting."

"He said you might as well take his plane since it has to come here for him, anyway. His team is going to fly back on their own."

"That was nice of him. How did he know I was here?"

"I told him."

"Is he there yet?"

"No. When I talked to him this morning he said he was making a stop and wouldn't be here until this evening. I have a car waiting for you when you land to drive you here. The two of us can have dinner before I go to meet him at the airport."

"What about the team?"

"What about them? I haven't seen you in six fucking weeks. You're mine first."

"Sounds perfect to me. I need a little debrief time."

"Have a safe flight. I love you."

"Love you, too."

My boss, childhood friend, and CEO of Jacobs Inc., Theo Jacobs, accepted the challenge to turn around a fledging telecommunications company in four weeks. I have been living out of a suitcase for the last six having jumped from one client to another to be onsite to put in place new strategies and business plans. But mostly to problem solve. I figure out how to get fresh blood into a broken company that should be thriving. This is what we do. We fix things. Companies, people, images, you name it. We are the best in the business. Our team is a mixture of education and street smarts.

Theo and I have been partners since we were five. Every day he would pick me up at my door and we would ride the school bus together. He was the first boy I kissed and the first boy I showed my "juice box" to in a six-year-old's game of "You show me yours, I'll show you mine."

Theo is a man's man. A guy's guy. Football and basketball captain in high school, he twice led our school to a state championship. Everyone wanted to be Theo. We attended the same schools before choosing different universities, both in the same city so we were never far apart.

It was our freshman year of college when Theo finally admitted aloud what I had known since we were ten. He struggled with having feelings for other guys. He had never been with a guy or girl, and in true Theo fashion, didn't think he could know for sure without exploring all the options available to him. So, like Theo and I do in everything, we handled it.

We locked ourselves in Boston's Ritz-Carlton for a weekend (courtesy of his parent's emergency credit card) and lost our virginities to one another. As far as sex goes, it was not what I expect most people's first times to be like. Ever the Boy Scout, Theo came prepared with a game plan. It felt natural to share another first together. Neither of us expected it to lead to anything, but it was a safe way to learn and explore what we liked. By the end of the weekend, we were having some hot, explosive sex for being newbies, but we both knew it was only sex. Our own little sex-ed class.

That next weekend I introduced Theo to Ross, and Theo declared without a doubt that he is gay. They have been happily married three years.

Throughout college, Theo and I were fixers. Having always been level-headed, see-the-forest-through-the-trees kind of thinkers, we realized we were always pulled into situations where others needed someone to shape the narrative. To put a play in motion, to move something or someone forward. Theo used these tools to create Jacobs Inc. We have been working together for the last seven years. With Theo's connections at Harvard and my connections at Boston College, we had an instant clientele.

No time has been more challenging for Jacobs Inc. than these last two months. Business has expanded faster than either of us can maintain, and our teams are stretched to capacity. It was this momentum and sheer volume of clients that drove Theo to accept a deal with a friend from Harvard to merge with his company so that we could grow and expand our business. Have the ability to try some new things.

With our current crisis keeping me out of the office for the last few weeks, I haven't participated in the merger meetings. I've been communicating through emails late at night once I make it back to my hotel room. Normally, I would have already researched about the company we are merging with, but I trust Theo and know he has done his homework. That's why I didn't know who the Beckett men were at the meeting. My plan was to get up to speed at our company retreat this week.

Two years ago I implemented a company retreat for our team. While Theo trusts me implicitly, he's not as quick entrusting decisions to others. Despite my talents, I have yet to master cloning and therefore cannot be in six places at once. I had thought some time out of the office and away from the daily grind would help his comfort level and communication with the team. Since our first retreat, we have grown our yearly revenue from 3 million to 30 million in two years. Some of it by luck and being in the right place at the right time, but most of it has been strategic. That and some of our wealthier clients have been in some pickles that they paid a great deal of money to have fixed or to have disappear.

My next stop is our retreat in Colorado. I give the taxi driver the terminal information Theo passed along. Thirty minutes later, we pull up to the plane on the tarmac. I've flown in a company jet often enough that this isn't a special treat, but the thrill of not having to go through security and deal with all the layovers is never lost on me. I am so glad I packed a change of clothes in my travel bag.

"Miss Donovan," the captain greets me.

"Hello," I smile back.

"Just you today ma'am?"

"Just me."

"Have a seat and we'll get going. All the pre-checks are done, and we're ready for departure."

"Thank you." I snag the first seat I come to and greet the steward, who introduces himself before disappearing to the front of the plane.

The captain signals that we are taking off, and after a smooth transition, we are in the air. Shawn, the steward, informs me lunch will be served in two hours. It's a little more than a four-and-a-half-hour flight. Standing, I get my first real look at the jet. It's stunning. There are multiple seating areas with four doors along the wall at the rear of the plane. Two are marked "lavatory." The second opens to a personal office that is obviously used by Reid Beckett himself, and the fourth opens to a bedroom.

I enter and close the door. What I wouldn't give to lie down and sleep till we arrive. More than exhausted from six weeks of short nights and long days, I sit on the edge of the bed for a minute and think about the meeting this morning. In our line of work, you would think I wouldn't still be shocked by people's callousness, but it never ceases to amaze me. Things people will do for money and fame. Standing, I stretch and remove my jacket, which thankfully covered my earlier cranberry incident. *This shirt will never recover from this stain*, I muse as I roll it in a ball. My bra choice this morning was based on the see through shell I was wearing, but wasn't the most comfortable choice. Right now I just want a tank top. I have been dressed in work clothes every day for the last six weeks. I don't know what I am looking forward to more this week, my sweats or sleep.

Stepping out of my skirt, I grab the lotion out of my bag. The Philadelphia climate wreaked havoc on my skin, and in my haste to get ready this morning I didn't follow my daily moisturizing routines. Taking my time, I apply the crème onto each arm and my stomach, giving myself a light massage as I go. My eyes close and I take a minute to enjoy working the warm lotion into my shoulders and chest. It feels heavenly. With a deep sigh, I finish circling each breast and smooth the lotion over my nipples, elongating them as I go.

I open my eyes to grab my tank before moving onto my legs- "*What the fuck?*" I yell. Shocked and maybe a little aroused, because damn if this man isn't delectable.

"Watch it," he snarls, and looks none too happy to find me in here.

"I don't think so. Who the fuck are you?" I quickly pull on my tank and grab my leggings only to realize I still have on my 5 inch heels. Great. I can imagine what I must look like in lacy underwear and five-inch fuck-me pumps rubbing my tits. I will never be taken seriously by this man again.

Gathering what little dignity I have left, I finish pulling on my leggings and place both hands on my hips in a move to take control and turn the tables on him.

"Do you make a habit of being a perv and watching women dress?"

He seems surprised by my tactic and raises a brow at me in challenge. "Really?" He cocks his head to the side. "Would we call that dressing?" The sexiest, slow smirk dances across his lips. Karma. Bitch.

"Well?" I ask not to be deterred in my line of questioning.

"I didn't realize anyone would be in *my* private quarters."

"I was told I was the only one on the plane," my voice drifts off. "Your private quarters? I thought this was Reid Beckett's plane."

"That's correct."

"Then how is this your private quarters? Reid gives you your own room on the plane? Oh I'm sorry," I say, just hiding my disappointment, when it finally hits me. "You're Reid's boyfriend? Partner? I'm sorry. Are you his husband? I never know what the preference is. Theo and Ross used partners till they were married." I ramble like someone who wasn't just showing her bouncing Buddhas to a perfect stranger. I tie a plaid shirt around my waist and pull my chestnut hair out of the bun holding it on top of my head. It falls long over my shoulders and down my back. I look into his eyes and am struck again by how beautiful they are and it hits me, I never felt threatened by his presence. If anyone else had walked in here I would have been screaming, kicking, and clawing them out of my space, but my guard is not up with him. Probably because he's gay.

"So have you two always worked together? Is that how you met?"

"Who?" he asks with a dip to his brows.

"Are you practicing to be an owl?" I laugh. "You and Reid."

"I'm..."

"There's a call for you, sir. Theo Jacobs." Shawn announces from the office doorway. "They're patching it through."

"Oh he's calling for me," I respond. "Thanks, Shawn. Do you mind?" I motion towards the office. "I'm Elise, by the way."

"By all means." He steps back, allowing me to enter. "And it's nice to meet you, Elise." He smiles and I detect a bit of humor in his eyes.

"Hey, babe." I lean against the desk and look at Theo on the large screen built into the wall.

"Hey, gorgeous. Aren't you a sight for sore eyes," he smiles. Theo has a beautiful smile. In fact, everything about him is beautiful. He's always had the stunning boy-next-door features that draw the looks of everyone everywhere we go. He has blond hair with smooth dark eyes that are offset by his chiseled features. His 6'2", two-hundred-pound frame of solid muscle makes it easy to see why he is so athletic and comfortable with his body.

"So are you. I cannot wait to see you. Did you need something?"

"No, I was calling to get the take on the meeting this morning. I got an email that you decided the company should be broken up, and I heard the CEO got a little rough with you."

"No one got rough with me. You know how it is, no one likes to be fired. Much less by a girl." I lift myself to sit on the edge of the desk.

"What are you wearing?" Theo leans closer to his laptop.

"Don't start. I've been in a suit 24/7 for six weeks. I'm not going to fly four-and-a-half hours in one. Don't worry. I'll be presentable tonight."

"I'm not worried about tonight. For Christ's sake put your shirt on if you aren't going to wear proper undergarments."

"Why? It's just him, and he could care less what my marshmallows look like." I hitch my thumb to the now occupied chair behind me.

"Sir." Shawn answers a buzz.

"Do we have any marshmallows on board?" he smirks when I turn around. "I have a sudden craving."

I roll my eyes and turn my attention back to Theo. I fill

him in on the meeting and the numbers I came across last night before our final meeting this morning. I explain how I knew Smith was cooking the books and what lead me to suggest we advise the company be dismantled.

"I agree with you, Elise. I'd still like to get his take on the meeting."

"Why?" I ask scooting to the side giving full view to the chair behind me. "I'm your guy. Not him. He's Reid's guy. The only assessment you need is mine and eventually Reid Beckett's."

He frowns. "I know."

"Then don't insult me by going to him. No offense," I say over my shoulder.

He lifts his hands in a brief wave. "None taken."

"So what was your take?" Theo still asks him. I'm too pissed to interrupt as he deftly breaks down the meeting. I have to give it to the guy; he's giving me all the praise for figuring out what plenty of other people couldn't and for how I handled the confrontation.

"Good job, Elise," Theo says when he finishes his assessment.

I roll my eyes.

"What?" Theo asks, knowing full well what the eye roll means.

"I thought we had worked through this. You *have* to learn to manage people, Theo. You just sat here and told me that my and Reid's opinion are the only ones that matter and yet you still ask him." I point to the boyfriend.

"And?" When I don't answer, he adds, "Have you been hitting the giggle weed?"

"Theo, I'm serious. I don't like it and this conversation isn't over."

"Fine. Let's table it until you get here. Maybe in person I'll be able to understand what the hell you're talking about. Six weeks apart and I've lost the ability to speak Elise. I don't know what the hell is happening."

"Fine. We land," I look at my watch, "at three-thirty Colorado time."

"Great. I was going to have a car waiting for you, but I'll be there to pick you up. I've missed my girl."

"Don't worry about it. I'll take the car. Save you from having to make the drive to the airport twice."

"Why would I have to make the drive twice?"

"You said you were picking Reid up tonight."

"That was before I knew he was with you."

"He's not with us."

Theo runs a frustrated hand over his face and busts out laughing. "Baby, *that's* Reid." He points to the guy behind me.

I feel a tap on my left arm. Looking down I see Reid is handing me something. It's his driver's license. It says "Reid Garrison Beckett."

"You're Reid Beckett?" I slide off the desk and turn to look at him.

"I am."

"Why didn't you correct me? You lead me to believe you were Reid's boyfriend."

"No, I didn't."

"Yes, you did."

"No, I didn't. You weaved that craziness all on your own. I just didn't course correct."

"Oh my God, it's official." I look at Theo. "I need a vacation."

"Babe." Theo is laughing to the point of tears. "It was like watching 'Who's on First.'"

"So there is no boyfriend?"

Reid Beckett shakes his head.

"You saw my boobs," I frown.

"That I most definitely did." He smiles like a kid who's won a prize.

"And you aren't gay?"

"That I most definitely am not." His eyes move to my chest and he pops a marshmallow in his mouth from the bowl that Shawn delivered moments ago.

"Elise, cover the fuck up," Theo bellows from the screen. "Eyes up, dickwad."

Reid leans forward and hits a button on his desk that disconnects the video call.

"You could have told me."

"And missed all this? I don't think so." He pops another marshmallow in his mouth.

chapter two

Reid

Elise's eyes watch me before her shoulders finally shrug to suggest that she can't be bothered with it anymore. She grabs a marshmallow and my cock jumps when her plump lips wrap around it as she heads to the main door of my office.

"I'm going to eat lunch. Hungry?" She waits for my answer in what I think is an attempt at some dignity.

"Start without me. I have a call to make first."

She nods and closes the door behind her. I reach down to adjust the hard-on I've sported since I walked in on her in my bedroom. Watching her massage the lotion into her skin, I nearly lost my shit. All I could do was hope she would move from her shoulders to her breast. Fuck me when she did it. I'm a business tycoon for Christ's sake, and in mere seconds she reduced me to a 14-year-old kid who almost shot his load watching her touch herself. My cock twitches again, and I groan trying to bring my body under control.

"Get a grip, Beckett," I tell myself in the bathroom mirror and splash some water on my face. "She's just a girl for fuck's sake." But I don't feel the conviction of my own words.

Having brought my body to heel, I head into the main cabin. Shawn is serving our meals, and I'm struck by the frustration I feel when I see Elise smiling at something he has said. They have obviously been laughing and enjoying each other's company. It irritates me. It irritates me that I'm irritated.

"Thank you, Shawn. That will be all." I excuse my wayward staff and take a seat across from Elise.

"You're awfully dismissive," she comments, buttering a roll. I think she is chastising me.

"I have staff and they have a role. I thanked him for our meal and let him know we had everything we needed."

"You dismissed him."

"Tomato, tom-ah-to." I take a sip of my water.

"No. Apple, orange. We aren't describing the same thing in two different ways, we are describing two different things."

"Did you want me to ask him to join us?" The derision in my tone is blatant.

"That's not the point."

"What is the point?" I raise a brow and make no attempt to hide my annoyance at her trying to school me on handling my own staff.

"You were short when it wasn't necessary."

I don't like that she seems disappointed by me. *Where did that come from?*

"Eat your food, Elise."

"I am," she says, showing me the parts of a roll she has in each hand.

We eat in a comfortable silence. She really is beautiful.

She has long, reddish-brown hair that flows freely down her back. Her skin is flawless with just a hint of olive coloring. She has round cheeks with a cute nose. She's adorable, but it's her eyes that elevate her to another level. Gold specks set off large, gray discs that appear to take in everything. Based on what I know about her, she is 27 like me, but she looks like she might be 22 at the most. How commanding she must be in the boardroom to be taken seriously? The thought intrigues me.

All I have heard Theo talk about other than Ross is Elise. When we were at Harvard, he would spend a fair amount of time with her at Boston College. I was surprised to learn he was gay. I really thought he and Elise were a couple. I never crossed paths with Theo when she was visiting, but several of our mutual friends did and I recall they always spoke fondly of her.

Theo and I met our freshman year. We had identical schedules our first semester of business school and were matched as study partners. It proved advantageous for both of us, and seeing as how we were studying for the same degree, we stayed study partners for the reminder of our time at Harvard. We also both rowed for Harvard all four years, albeit for separate boats.

"How did you find out that Smith was falsifying his numbers?" I offer her my carrots. I don't like them and she has eaten all of hers.

"I made friends with the neglected kid on the finance floor. I was eating in one of the break rooms and we struck up a conversation. It became a ritual of sorts to meet up for a midday snack. I had a feeling something wasn't right and asked him to pull the numbers for me."

"If you are going to do that again, I'd prefer you to have

someone with you. What would you have done today if I hadn't been there?"

"I would have handled it."

"With what? Your karate kid moves?"

"I think it was you that had your karate kid moves on display." She takes a sip of her water. As if to placate me she gets serious. "I didn't discover it until last night. There wasn't time to get someone from our team there. He wasn't going to hurt me, and if he had laid a hand on me, I would have pressed charges. But thank you for stepping in. Saved me the paperwork. What did you say to him?"

"I told him I was already going to bankrupt him by selling his company off piece by piece and did he really want to add assault to his list of problems."

"What made you decide to merge with Theo?"

Her question catches me off guard. "How much has Theo told you?"

"Theo tells me everything," she says, matter-of-factly.

"How long have you known Theo?"

"Since we were five. We lived two doors down from each other. He was the first friend I made when I moved in with my family."

Her comment halts my fork full of salmon in midair. "Where did you live before you moved in with your family?"

"I was in the foster system. My mom died during childbirth, and my biological father gave me to the state when I was three."

"Why?" I know it's a personal question, but I can't stop myself from asking. Why would a father give up their child after caring for them for three years?

"I asked him the same question when I was ten. He said he never wanted to be a father and he didn't love me."

Even though she says it like she's spouting off a score from last night's baseball game, I can see the flicker of pain in her eyes. Surprised by my feelings of protectiveness over someone I met only hours ago, I steer us back to a topic where she feels safer.

"So, Theo tells you everything?"

"He does. I know what the plans are with the merger and how far along you are in the process. I know you plan on announcing it this week to the rest of the team."

"Does the team know?"

"No, they don't. Theo felt like it was better for them to meet you in person first."

"And will you continue to run the office in Chicago, or will you make the move to New York?"

"Ross has another year of residency in Chicago, so Theo plans to stay put and commute back and forth. I will be opening the office in New York."

"He really does tell you everything," I frown. He's broken about eight privacy clauses I have built into our deal.

"Is it really that big of a deal? You haven't told anyone on your team?"

"Other than my CFO, who happens to be my brother? No. Not yet. I told my mom because she has a soft spot for Theo and I knew she would be excited."

"Same thing," she shrugs. "Only I'm his best friend, and not his mom." She motions to the last of the salmon I've left on my plate and spears it with her fork when I nod.

"Not really. You work for him, and you are his number one asset. It muddies the waters."

"It shouldn't. Theo trusts me. One-hundred percent. Don't you have anyone on your team that you trust?"

"At that level outside of family, no." I lean back in my

chair and place my hands on my thighs. "I find in my line of work, most people have their own agendas."

She nods her response but doesn't say anything. I'm disappointed. I wanted to hear her thoughts.

Shawn enters and clears our plates, leaving us each with a bowl of chocolate ice cream.

"Thank you, Shawn, but I wouldn't care for any." I move to hand mine back.

"I'll take it." She intercepts the bowl and sets it beside hers before giving Shawn a full on smile.

"How many days has it been since you've eaten?" I ask and she laughs.

"I didn't have breakfast since I was running late, and I eat more when I'm sleep deprived. Plus, you can never have too much ice cream. I don't know how you could even send ice cream back."

I laugh at the look of confusion on her adorable face.

"Well, I have work to do before we land."

"Anything you need from me?" She licks the back of her spoon.

"Nope."

"Perfect," she purrs. "I plan on watching a movie and relaxing. What the...?" She drops her spoon and looks down like something has surprised her. I catch the wag of a tail.

"Nova, Elise. Elise, Nova." I motion between the two of them. She turns to my Pit Bull and pats her legs. Nova lifts his front paws and I watch Elise fall in love with one glance.

"Where have you been?" She gives him a big kiss on his snout and rubs his ears. He's in heaven.

"He's getting up in years. He usually sleeps on a bed under my desk for the whole flight." I look at him with his head unashamedly in her lap. Is it wrong to be jealous of a dog?

"He likes you."

"Of course he does. What's not to like?" She runs her fingers over his head, and I swear I've never seen this look of bliss on his face before.

"I'm not sure I have an answer to that question." It pleases me when I'm rewarded with a blush.

"How long have you had him?"

"I rescued him about six years ago when I was home visiting my parents. The vet said he thinks he was already a couple years old when I found him. He had been abandoned and was in bad shape. We weren't sure if he was going to make it. But you did, didn't you, fella?" My eyes move from Nova to Elise. She's watching me with a tenderness I'm not accustomed to. "What?" I ask in response.

"You're sweet." Her smile is genuine and it pulls at something unfamiliar in my chest.

"Enjoy your movie." I stand and make my way across the plane to my office whistling for Nova to follow. He looks at me as if he has no idea who I am and lays down at Elise's feet. This tickles her and I shake my head leaving them in the cabin.

I try to accomplish some work, but frustrated I close my laptop. I can't seem to concentrate my thoughts on anything other than the woman on my plane.

This won't do, I think as I head to the en suite to brush my teeth. I don't have the time to be distracted by a woman, much less one that will soon be my subordinate. Not to mention that, as a rule, I don't do relationships. I have fuck buddies and that gets me where I need to go. Why am I even thinking about this? It's not like I can screw her to get her out of my system. Can I? Technically, I'm not her boss yet. Maybe she would be in to simply hooking up. She seems like a girl who can detach herself from the emotional side of things. She is a fixer, after all. One of the best in the business. I've done quite a bit of research on her. If there's a problem, she's who you want running the show. She doesn't need Theo. She could have gone out on her own already, making Theo's company the second best. Theo has admitted as much.

That's why I went to Philadelphia today. I wanted to see her in action, see what I was really getting in this deal. Never did I expect her to walk in the door. Hips and legs that go on forever. And her breasts. God, her breasts. I close my eyes and remember how I caught her rubbing them earlier. The thought is all it takes to get me instantly hard, my balls aching for relief. I can't walk around in this condition and am forced to take matters in my own hands- irritated I can't control my body's errant response to Elise. Increasing the speed of my hand, I feel the electricity shooting down my spine and landing in my balls as I come hard, stroking myself through my orgasm. *Fuck!* That was fast. Cursing my lack of control, I clean up and change into a pair of jeans and a t-shirt. We have about thirty minutes before we start our decent. Thinking about the draw I feel to her, I enter the cabin in hopes of getting a drink. Plus, I'm curious to see what movie she has chosen.

"I see you found my Har…" I stop talking when I realize there's no one to listen. Elise is sound asleep with her head on the arm of the leather couch. Her legs are pulled up and Nova is laying curled into her behind her legs with his head on the crevice of her knees. I watch her for a solid minute. Locating a blanket in the console, I bend to cover her. Her eyelashes fan across her cheeks, and I notice she isn't wearing makeup. She really is beautiful. Stunning even. I place an errant lock of hair behind her ear before I run my finger over her lobe, and

I can't stop myself from placing a kiss to her temple. Her hand comes up to caress the side of my face and I freeze like a deer caught in headlights, but she's still fast asleep. I smile at her choice of movies and head back to the office to try to work again while Harry and Malfoy fight on screen.

I wrap up my emails and exit the office when the captain signals that we are preparing to land. Elise has her legs curled under her and is petting Nova.

"Thank you," she says lifting the blanket on her lap.

I shake my head like I don't know what she is talking about. "Must have been Shawn. Buckle up," I instruct and take a seat opposite to do the same. It's a smooth landing, and it's no time at all till we taxi to a stop.

Elise exits ahead of me. She thanks the flight crew and gives Shawn a thank-you hug on her way to exit the plane. I roll my eyes at his confused smile. He has no idea that she is thanking him for the blanket. *That fucker got my hug*, I grumble to myself.

We take the seven steps to the ground, and I have to stop to help Nova down. When I turn back around, Elise is in a sprint towards Theo, and I watch as she propels herself at him. He must have been expecting it because he doesn't falter. His head is thrown back in laughter when she wraps her arms and legs around him and peppers him with kisses all over his face.

"I missed you, too, sweetheart," I hear him say, and I see complete love on his face for this girl.

"Give a man a chance, will ya?" he says, taking his arms off her, laughing when she tightens her grip to keep herself in place. Elise places another kiss on his cheek before she slides down his body and wraps her arms around his waist.

"Reid." He leaves one arm around Elise and offers the

other one to me.

"Theo." I shake his hand.

"God, I missed you," she tells him.

"Never again," Theo says. "Six weeks is too long." He kisses the top of her head. "Need help with your bags?"

"Nah. Coop will bring them with him." I gesture to my right-hand man. Coop's main responsibility is security for me, my family, and my businesses. He also handles the day-to-day items.

"Was he on the plane the whole time?" Elise asked. She must recognize him as the man who put Harold Smith in an arm lock.

"Yes. It's his job to be discreet." For some reason my comment causes her to blush.

"Hungry?" Theo asks.

"We ate on the plane," she answers climbing into the back of a large Tahoe. "Come on, boy." She leans forward to help Nova up. I lift his hind legs and he settles in the seat next to her. I slide into the front passenger seat next to Theo, who is driving.

"I didn't mind sitting in the back," I say to Elise.

"It's about an hour to the resort. I'm going to take a nap."

"You just had one."

"And I'm going to have another. I've had about three hours of sleep a night for the last six weeks. I'm exhausted and I plan on getting some much needed rest this week."

Her honesty is refreshing. If she were a man in her position, she would never admit she was tired. It's not long before we hear her slow even breathing, and I turn to see she is out.

"Dude. No," Theo says.

"I have no idea what you are talking about." I face the road.

"Yes, you do. And I'm saying no."

I turn to face him. "It doesn't bother Ross how close you are?"

"Why should it? Our relationship is completely platonic."

"You're telling me you have no sexual feelings for her."

"No, dipshit. I'm gay. Elise is like a partner I don't have sex with."

"So Ross gets your dick but Elise gets your heart."

"What the fuck? No. Ross is my soulmate. *My heart*. Elise is my best friend. She will always have a place *in* my heart only for her. Ross understands and wouldn't want it any other way. He adores Elise. Why are you trying to define my relationship and place parameters around it?"

"You told her about the merger. Do you know how many legal clauses you broke by doing that? I am purchasing *your* business. Not hers."

"So sue me." His I-couldn't-give-a-fuck attitude makes me want to punch him.

"All I'm saying is I am about to take this business to the next level, and I'm not convinced of her loyalty. Does she work with the intensity she does now because she wants to please you? What if you think one thing and I think another? I will have controlling interest. Will she be able to fall in line? It's just muddies things is all I'm saying."

"Elise is loyal to a fault. And not just to me. If you treat her right, you will never have a more trustworthy ally."

"I guess we'll see."

"I think you are pushing back because of what I saw on the conference call today. And I'm telling you, no."

The forcefulness of his voice pulls my chin up. "I don't know what you're talking about. That said, I'm not so sure you would be okay with anyone."

"If someone proves to cherish Els' heart the way I do, I would gladly hand over the reins."

"You really are a chauvinistic son-of-a-bitch." I laugh at his highhandedness.

"I'd advise you not to talk about my mom like that." He turns onto a secluded highway leading into the mountains. "Look, I can be arrogant about Elise, because I know Elise. Better than I know myself. You won't have any problems with her loyalty."

I don't offer a response, and we sit in silence as we make our way along the curve of the mountains. It's beautiful here.

"So, where is this place we're staying?" I attempt to bring us back to a conversation we are more comfortable with.

"It's a luxury team retreat owned by a former BC classmate of Elise's. Corporations use it all the time for team building and helping their people think outside of the box. This is our third time to come. The team is already there. You two are the last to arrive."

"Please tell me we aren't in tents in the middle of the woods."

"I told you it was a luxury resort. There are several campsites, each with their own penthouse chalet and several smaller chalets. There was a mix-up with the booking and we are short a chalet, so Elise has to bunk with us."

"Us?"

"Yes. I had us in the two-bedroom penthouse chalet. No one likes to bunk with Elise, so I drew the short end of the straw and she's staying in my room."

"Why doesn't anyone like to stay with Elise?"

"She hogs the bed and sleeps like an octopus: eight limbs and suctioned to you," he laughs and pulls to a stop outside of a large two-story building. "We're here." He turns off the car.

There's another SUV like this one in the drive. "Elise, baby." He wakes her. "We're here."

"What cabin am I in?" she asks, stretching.

"We were short a room, so you are bunking with me."

"Ugh. Really?"

I'm amused she seems so put out by the news.

"You don't want to stay with me?" Theo laughs climbing out of the Tahoe.

Elise catches my glance and rolls her eyes. "He hogs the bed," she whispers to me. Theo opens her door to help her out and then lifts Nova down. "There ya go, buddy." He pats Nova's head.

The outside of the building looks like a standard chalet, but entering through the double doors I can see what Theo meant when he said luxury. The rounded chalet is built into the mountain, and the sixteen-foot ceilings offer an unobstructed picture of the hills surrounding us. The view is breathtaking.

We enter into a large open area that has a state-of-the-art kitchen, a dining area for twelve, and a living area that is large, but made cozy by the furnishings. From here I can see a wraparound balcony. There are two doors off this room on opposite sides of each other.

"That's the hallway to your wing." Theo points to the left. "Elise, you and I are on the right."

"Ross doesn't care that you sleep together?" I raise a brow as Elise walks to their wing.

"Does she have a dick?" Theo tosses back with a growl.

"I wouldn't know."

"No, but you know how to be one." I can tell he is over my pettiness about his relationship with Elise. And frankly, I have no idea why I care, other than I'm not sure it is the best situation for our business.

"Our room is amaz—" Elise is cutoff as she walks back into the living area.

"Brace yourself," Theo tells her as the front door opens and a swarm of folks enter.

"Elise!" Several of them yell and charge for her. The volume level rises several notches. I take a step back and watch. I know from the employee files who everyone is and their role on Theo's team. She greets each of them with a kiss and an embrace, and I'm taken with the way she makes each one of them feel special. It's telling. About her. About Theo's team.

The girls continue to talk a mile a minute as she is passed around from person to person. Some of the guys lift her off the ground as they hug her. It's obvious that it's been a while since they have seen her, and it's clear that they respect her. The commotion settles and Elise is left standing with Ryan's arm draped over her shoulders. Gabby is on her right holding her hand.

"Guys, I'd like you to meet our friend, Reid Beckett. He's going to hang with us this week."

I greet them and they respond in kind. It will be interesting to see how this team performs this week. A close knit team can be great for a business or it can be disastrous. This week should give me a pretty good idea which way this seesaw balances.

"Please tell me you're cooking tonight," Fran asks. "I haven't had a decent meal since you left."

"Fran," Theo scolds. "Let's give her a night to rest. I have the staff cooking for everyone."

"I don't mind," Elise offers, smiling at Theo. Theo firmly mouths the word "no" to her.

"I'll cook tomorrow night guys," she promises and leans

over to place a kiss to Fran's temple.

"All right," the guy I recognize as Blake says. "Let's re-convene for dinner at seven. And then…"

Everyone shouts, "Drunk Jenga!"

chapter three

Elise

"I don't know about that, guys. Drunk Jenga on our first night? I'm still recovering from the last time we played."

"Six weeks, Elise," Gabby says. "You've been gone six weeks. I don't care what Theo says, we are spending time with our girl tonight."

"Fine. We have an hour and a half before dinner. Let me rest and I'll be ready." My smile must satisfy them because they file out one-by-one and give me a few minutes to myself before jumping into a night with my work family.

"Drunk Jenga?" I look over my right shoulder at the voice.

"It's exactly as it sounds," I laugh and shake my head at Reid. "Welcome to Jacobs Inc."

I head into my room. Even though I've napped an hour on the plane and an hour in the car, I am still exhausted. If tonight is like the last time we played, it will be a while before we are in bed.

"Everyone leave?" Theo asks, coming out of the closet.

"Yes. They'll be back in time for dinner."

"I'm sorry our dinner plans got changed. I didn't think it was right to leave Reid on his own with the team while we went to eat. Plus, I had to promise the girls dinner so I wouldn't have to take them to the airport with me."

"It's alright. The team would have been disappointed we weren't all together anyway."

"Want to go for a run?" he asks, sliding into his tennis shoes. He's wearing shorts and a sleeveless t-shirt.

"Your body." I shake my head. No other words are necessary.

"You're a darlin'." He gives me his mega-watt smile. "I missed you." He wraps his arms around me, and we stand for a couple of minutes just enjoying the feel of one another. This is the land of comfort for me. Solace. It's like being held by my dad or Knox, my brother. Like no matter what is going on in my day, I am safe and loved.

"Ready?" There's a knock at the door. Reid is standing there.

"Reid and I are going running. See you when we get back." Theo kisses the top of my head and they leave. I take a few minutes to unpack my bags before pulling off my leggings and climbing into bed. I hit the shades to send the room into darkness. I have really missed everyone. I wonder how they will handle the news that Theo is selling control of Jacobs Inc. to Reid.

I trust Theo and I know that he is trying to position himself so that he and Ross have more time to start a family. This is the path he thinks will get him there. Ross' career has taken the backseat to his for the last seven years, and Theo wants him to have his chance at building his practice. With the sale of the company, Theo wouldn't have to work ever again, but his intention is to stay on as President with a lighter workload.

Releasing a long breath, I close my eyes and try to relax into the heavenly encasement of luxury bedding. The one thing my friend Owen knows how to do is run a luxury resort. This bed is dreamy.

I replay today's meeting in my mind again. I mentally catalog the items we need to learn from to make sure it never takes us so long to find the hidden bomb we found with Harold Smith's company. It worked out for us this time, but we won't always be that lucky.

I think about the way Reid's hand felt on my stomach and the jolt I felt when he shook my hand. The way he looked when I caught him watching me apply lotion on the plane. The way it felt when he covered me with a blanket and kissed my head. His skin under my fingers when I caressed his face. I can still smell him after his shower, clean like the outdoors. A moan escapes me. I giggle thinking about the funny look he gave Shawn when I hugged him for the blanket Reid denied giving me.

I think idly of the soft, dark curls that frame his angular face. *He could use a trim,* I think. Where Theo is prep-school pretty, Reid is handsome in a powerful way. I had to stop myself from staring at him while we were eating, wondering what it would be like to lick his one and only dimple. Another soft moan escapes me and my heartbeat quickens. I was so lost in my thoughts about Reid, I wasn't focused on the fact that my fingers have been between my legs working my clit into a hard bud.

I bring my free hand up to massage my breast while

moving my exploring fingers under my panties to find myself soaked at the thoughts of Reid. Shit, this man is going to be my boss. What the hell is wrong with me? But even as I ask it, I can't stop. My hips are already undulating on their own and my body is in control. My mind has taken a back seat.

Giving into it, I imagine Reid's hands on me. What it would feel like to be taken by him. Knowing I am alone, I don't censor my cries when an orgasm rips through me causing my body to bow off the bed. My chest moves at a rapid rate while my hand rests on my breast and the other rests against my sex. I do the only thing I can at that point: roll over and sleep. If I stick my head in the sand and ignore it, it'll go away, right?

"Hey, babe." I hear Theo's voice from a distance. "Els." It comes closer and I hear a chuckle. "Baby, it's time to get up. The team will be here soon." When I don't respond, he brings his lips to my ears and kisses my earlobe. "I'm turning on the lamp," he warns before filling the room with light.

"Ugh," I say before rolling over and squinting up at him.

"Why don't you just stay in here and sleep? Reid and I can hang with the team. You have all week to be with them."

I kick the covers off of me. "No, the girls will be disappointed. Plus, this is my last week with them. I move to New York next week."

"Are you sure?" he asks.

I sit up and he starts to stand. My fingers curl in his t-shirt to stop him.

"How am I going to tell them?" My eyes water as I look into his.

"Elise, people move. It doesn't mean you won't still be close with everyone. You will always be my girl, no matter where you live or who you are with. They are big boys and girls. They will understand." He runs a thumb over my cheek. "I told you, I don't mind being the one to tell them."

"No, I'm going to tell them."

"You don't have to move. I can make this work with you staying in Chicago."

"No, I want to move. It's the right thing for the company, and it's the next natural step. My family is ready for me to be back in New York. Just seeing them all again reminded me how hard it's going to be."

"One step at a time, babe. One step at a time." He waits for my nod. "Up. Everyone will be here in a few minutes. I let you sleep as late as I could." He walks into the bathroom, and a minute later I hear the shower running. I get ready and head into the living area. Reid is already in there, watching the staff set up our meal in the dining room.

"You two are like a married couple," Reid says as I turn to get a drink from the bar.

"Who?" My brows dip in confusion.

Reid rolls his eyes. "You and Theo."

"I told you, we have been together our whole lives."

"Who kiss, hold hands, and sleep together."

"We kiss like family would. You make it sound like we have our tongues down each other's throats. I hold hands with lots of people. I'm a hand holder. It's one of my favorite things. And we sleep together just like I sleep with Gabby or Fran if we were staying in the same room. You don't have any girls that are just friends? Totally platonic?"

"Not that have the kind of power you two have over each other."

What is his problem? I set my glass of water down harder than I intend.

"Look. I don't have to justify my relationships to you or

anyone else. I'm sorry if you are so unemotionally available that you can't comprehend loving someone for who they are and not because you stuck your dick in them."

He moves closer to me and I have to tilt my head back to look him in the eyes. Damn him for being so fuckable!

"It is my problem when I'm about to drop a small fortune for a company and build it around a woman whose reputation is unmatched by anyone in the business. Your reputation supersedes you, but your actions today paint a different picture."

I square my shoulders and take an even closer step towards him. "Listen. And I mean listen good because I plan on saying this only once. I won't apologize for the way I love people or the way I handle my team. I don't have to be a raving, detached bitch to be accomplished or to lead this company and this team. You can care about people and still get the job done. Something you could stand to learn a lesson in."

"What does that mean?" he bristles, crossing his arms over his chest.

"It means there's a reason why you can't break the top 10% of companies with the highest retention stats." There's a heat in his eyes, and I know instantly he is not used to being challenged.

"There's a difference between running a corporation that is responsible for tens of thousands of people and running a fun little team of college kids who are never held accountable."

His assessment of my team has me seeing red. "I agree with you that there is a difference between running a corporation that has to have checks and balances in place to ensure the lights stay on and the business grows. That's not what I do. My team gets called in to fix shit. And we're good at it. Really good at it. And not just business shit. Personal shit. Shit they make movies about. But in the end, it's about people and how to bring out the best in them. Whether it's a team of ten young kids or a team of thousands. People need to know they are working towards something. That they are part of something bigger than themselves. That they are making a difference. When you give them that, you tap into someone who would sell their left nut for you."

He leans into me, his beautiful green eyes boring into mine. "But what good is it if they give up who they are to give you that nut? Why do you play second fiddle to Theo? You could be the one making millions?"

"I don't care about the money."

"Bullshit. Everyone cares about money."

"I imagine in the crowd you associate with, it is that way. As long as I have a roof over my head and I can eat, I honestly don't care."

"You didn't answer my question. If you and Theo weren't so attached, I would be buying your company, not his, and you know it."

"I thought you and Theo were friends. Why are you acting like this?"

"Never mind. You just answered my question," he says with a finality that I am working to understand. "This is business, Elise. Theo understands that. I understand that. You're the only one who doesn't. That's a problem for me. I'm investing in a Pit Bull, not a soccer mom." He turns to walk away. "Nova, let's go out." He whistles for his dog.

Reid leaves me here trying to figure out what landmine I just stepped on and where it came from. Adding to my frustration, I totally got wet arguing with him. I wanted to jump him and ride him till the wheels fell off.

"We're here!" The crew enters carrying all kinds of alcohol.

"What is it?" Fran and Gabby are in front of me. These are my girls and nothing gets past them.

"Nothing. I'm tired," I lie.

"Mmmhh." Gabby looks at Fran.

"Could this have anything to do with Love Potion No. 9 and the way he was watching you today?"

"What are you talking about?"

"Yes, girls. What are you all talking about?" Blake joins us, hoping to get in on what I am sure he perceives to be the latest gossip. "Reid," he shouts seeing him enter with Nova. "Join us."

"Thanks. I will in a few." He takes Nova with him to his wing, never giving me a second look.

"Told ya." Fran gives Gabby a knowing glance.

"I'm going to change. I'll be right back." I excuse myself before I reveal more than I want to.

It's the end of June, so it's warm during the day but still cool at night. Throwing on a pair of jeans and a cardigan over my tank, I grab a vintage Hermes handkerchief I picked up on a trip to London and wrap it around my head like a headband.

When I enter back into the main area, everyone is seated. There are two fireplaces, one inside and one outside, and they are both on. The balcony doors are open, music and drinks are already flowing. Theo and Reid are sitting at each end of the table. I take a seat on the side in the middle between Ryan and Fran. Gabby is across from me. There are twelve of us, total.

At the beginning of each retreat, Theo opens with a line from *Game of Thrones* and I open with lines from *Dumb and Dumber* and *Coming to America*, encouraging the team to think outside of the box.

"Let the games begin!" Theo lifts his glass into the air and we all follow. The chefs have placed the food in the middle of the table. Tonight's meal is being served family style. Conversation, like the atmosphere, is light, and it feels good to all be in the same place.

"Knock-knock," Owen, my friend and the resort owner, says as he enters the dining room.

"Owen!" Everyone cheers and raises a glass to him.

Owen and I spent a lot of time together at school. We lived in the same dorms, and I was his coxswain on the rowing crew. I stand and make my way to him.

"Hey you." I reach my arms up to hug him. His arms fall around my waist, and he pulls me to him with his hand placed on my lower back. With a kiss to the cheek, he releases me.

"I swear you get better every year. You look fantastic."

"Thanks. You look great, too. I guess mountain life is agreeing with you. Sounds like business is good?"

"It's booming. Sorry about the mix up with the rooms. I figured you would end up with Theo. After last year, I know Gabby said never again."

"That's for damn sure!" Gabby says from her side of the table.

I give her the stink eye over my shoulder. "It's no problem. Everything on schedule?"

"Yep. We'll get started after lunch tomorrow. Give you all time to get settled in."

"Sounds perfect. Thanks again, Owen. Want to join us?" I turn towards the table and am surprised to find Reid watching us. He blinks and goes back to passing food.

"Thanks, but I have other guests to look after."

"But we're your favorite," Fran decrees, filling her plate.

"Definitely," Owen answers, his eyes skimming over me.

"So, we'll see you in the morning?" Theo stands and drapes his arm over my shoulders.

"Yep." Owen looks up at him and smiles a shit-eating grin. "I scheduled myself to be your leader tomorrow. See you then." He leans down and kisses my check before he turns to leave. "Bye, everyone."

"Bye, Owen." The team lifts their glasses again.

"Really?" I look at Theo who shrugs his shoulders before taking his seat again.

I review the schedule for the week with everyone, noting when and where they are expected to be. The remainder of dinner is spent catching up on what has been going on in each of their lives. There've been engagements, home purchases, and baby announcements that have all taken place in the six weeks that I have been gone. We have several interns who graduate this year, and they are all taking on full-time placements with the team.

"Ryan, how's Emily doing?" I look down the table.

"She's good. Dad is still in Indiana keeping the farm going. Mom is staying with her in Memphis while she finishes her treatment at St. Jude. We won't know anything until this round of chemo is done. Hopefully, it will shrink her tumor so she can have surgery. She's loving your packages, by the way."

"If anyone can buy for a thirteen-year old girl, it's Elise." Theo chimes in.

"Fran and Gabby have been helping me with ideas."

"Well, she loves them," Ryan says. "She has on a different tattoo every time I FaceTime with her, and the place looks like a sparkle bazooka went off." Ryan stops eating and looks at me with what I think is tenderness. "Emily says you call her a few times a week."

"Emily and I are buds," I wink at him. As conversation continues around the table, we hold our gaze for a minute until I nod and he goes back to eating. When you are with people who know you, words aren't necessary when your heart is being ripped out. Anyone can see that Ryan's is.

Sensing we need a little goofiness, Blake tells the group a story. He's a magical storyteller. Blake is the kind of guy who always has you asking for one more. Ninety-nine percent of his stories are true. I don't think anyone will ever know which ones fall into the other one percent.

"So, did you see Robert while you were in Philadelphia?" Ryan asks when Blake finishes his story.

"Who?" I look up from my plate confused.

"Robert."

"Don't you read your emails?" Fran takes a drink of her water. "Robert is no more."

"What?" Several utensils stop in midair.

"Since when?" Ryan probes.

"I don't know. Since we stopped dating and he moved," I answer like they should know this.

"But I thought you were still hooking up?" someone asks, and I catch Gabby and Fran making faces at each other.

"Leave her alone," Theo censures from his end of the table.

"We just thought you might light the flame again while you had six whole weeks of nothing to do but…"

"Run a company in Philadelphia and my team in Chicago?" I counter.

"Good. I hated that guy," Blake says from beside me.

"Here, here," Ryan says.

I stand and grab a bottle from the bar. "Let's go get drunk on Jenga."

Fifteen minutes later everyone is on the balcony ready to play. I take a seat on the circular cushioned bench that encircles the round table. Gabby assembles the tower in the middle at an equal distance away from each player. Fran is to my left. Theo is to my right. Directly across from me is Reid. I'm actually surprised he's participating, especially after our earlier conversation. Next to him is Gabby.

Gabby starts. "Every block has a directive on it. You have to do what it instructs then take a drink. If you don't do it, you have to take five drinks, unless the block directs otherwise. Salute." She lifts a shot glass and we all follow in kind, each taking our first drinks.

"I set it up, so you start," she says to Ryan on her left.

"Alright, let's get it started." Ryan claps his hands together and choses a tile. "First one out of the gate." He pulls his tile and reads, "Voyeur. Give two drinks to everyone you've seen naked." He looks up. "Blake. Drink Up. You nearly got your thing bitten off skinny dipping in the lake last year." His eyes move around the table. "Boss, take two."

"When have you ever seen me naked?" Theo arches a brow.

"Not Daddy boss. Mama boss." Ryan points to me.

"Really, Elise," Theo chastises.

I roll my eyes and attempt to explain. "It was when his mom invited me to the farm for the weekend. I had an unfortunate interaction with the wrong end of the cow I was milking. I thought Ryan was in the field with his family, so I stripped on the porch so I wouldn't take the smell in the house. When I went into the kitchen, Ryan was inside."

"With…" Ryan smiles, waiting for me to finish his sentence.

I exhale loudly. "*With* the family Pastor who came by

to check on his sister," I respond meekly, taking my second drink.

"Shit. That's worth everyone drinking two," Blake says and knocks his back. "You went to the farm over a year ago. I can't believe you kept that story to yourself." He raises a glass to Ryan.

Ryan smiles. "I knew it would come in handy."

We make our way around. Everyone has worked themselves into a slight buzz, and we're only six plays into the game. Theo draws his piece.

"Lick a neck." I look over to see that the arrow on the tile is pointing to the left, toward me.

"When did this game become all about sex?" he frowns.

"It's always been that way. You are just usually drunk by now," Fran says. Theo leans down and places a light kiss to my jaw line.

"No, sir," Blake says. "That is not a lick."

Theo holds up his left hand and wiggles his fingers, showcasing his wedding band. "Married."

"So, you can share a bed but you can't lick her neck?"

"Yes, Blake. That is correct," Theo answers. "There is nothing sexual going on in the bed. Licking someone's neck is sexual, no matter your sexual preference. The only neck I will be licking is Ross."

"We're not talking about *that* neck. We're talking about the one between your head and shoulders," Reid says drawing laughter from everyone. I can't help but finally look at him.

"He actually made a joke," I say to Theo in disbelief.

"Ignore him," he says.

"My turn." I pull a block from the middle. "Truth. Answer a question from the jar or drink five."

Gabby pulls out a piece of paper from the jar labeled "girls."

"Have you ever taken a dip in the lady pond?"

"No." I drink my drink.

"Four more drinks," Fran says. "You take five if you don't answer."

"Why? I answered the question."

"No, you didn't."

"Yes, I did."

"No, you didn't. You and Gabby have kissed."

"How deep is a dip?" I ask. "More than first base right?"

"Any toe in the pond counts," Fran says.

"Fine." I start on the remaining four drinks.

"Hold on." Blake looks at Fran. "Elise is the most straight-laced person I know. She won't even fuck a guy until he's a couple of months in, and you're telling us she kissed Gabby?"

"You make me sound like a prude." I'm looking anywhere except at Reid. I can feel his eyes on me.

"Look," Blake begins his campaign. "I know we tease you about sleeping with Theo, but aside from the cow incident, you are as straight-laced as they come. You never talk about sex like the rest of us. You never have one night stands. You take five drinks just so you don't have to answer certain questions. You're vanilla at a table full of coconuts. It's just surprising to hear that you, Elise Donovan, have kissed a girl."

"If you must know," Gabby says, thinking I need support, "I had very strict parents and was really sheltered. When I got to college, I was awkward and not very knowledgeable. I had a date one night and I had never kissed anyone before. I really liked him, so I asked Elise to teach me how to kiss. She did." She shrugs like, 'end of story'.

"That's right. I did my friend a solid. It wasn't a big deal.

It was like…I don't know," I gesture with my hand, thinking. "Like, thirty minutes of kissing."

"Did you know this?" Blake asks Theo who gives him an I-know-everything look. "I can't believe I never knew." Blake shakes his head.

Fran pulls her block. And because Karma has pulled my name today, the block has big red lips on it with an arrow to the right.

"Yes!" Fran gives a little fist pump.

"You are so weird," I say, turning to face her. "Why are you excited?"

"Because Gabby got to make out with you and I haven't. I always felt a little left out."

I roll my eyes and lean in to plant a quick kiss on her.

"Make it good, Donovan. I haven't gotten laid in a month." Fran raises a brow in challenge.

"I can take care of that for you," one of the guys at the table says, and Fran flips them off.

"Fine." I straddle the bench so I can reach her better. Scooting towards her, I cup my hands along her jaw and pull her towards me. Running my thumb over her bottom lip, I close my eyes and kiss her lightly before pulling her bottom lip between my teeth. With a soft bite to her lip, she opens her mouth on a moan and grants my tongue entrance. I kiss her slowly for several seconds before pulling away.

"God, if that did it for me, I would be the luckiest girl in the world," Fran says.

"I'm going to need a few minutes before getting up," Blake injects.

"We can't all be gay," Theo says with a shrug of his shoulders.

"Damn you can kiss." Fran fans her face.

I roll my eyes again and on the downward roll, I catch Reid's eyes still on me. He raises a single brow at me. Fuck is he sexy. We continue to make our way around the table. Rainbow Warrior and Screw the NFL Kicker blocks have been drawn ensuring everyone is well on their way to being drunk. The lightweights are there already.

Reid pulls his first block. "Swap Meet," he says and turns the block over. "Exchange an article of clothing with the person directly across from you."

He looks up at me. I wait to see if he is going to do it or take five drinks. He grabs the back of his sweatshirt and pulls it over his head. Fran's hand squeezes my thigh when he stands to hand me his t-shirt. His jeans hang low on his hips highlighting his chiseled stomach and a sculpted V. I'm grateful for Fran's nails digging into my leg or I would have been too distracted by this vision to hear what he was saying to me.

"I believe you owe me an article of clothing," he says when I take his t-shirt. Unfortunately, he puts his sweatshirt back on.

I pull the vintage handkerchief off my head and hand it to him. "My top won't fit you."

He shrugs and, with a goofy smile, wraps it around his forehead and ties it in the back. I can't help but laugh as I remove my cardigan to pull on his t-shirt. I have been so busy trying to ignore him that I just now see what his shirt says. It's a maroon t-shirt with "Save a Broom, Ride a Quidditch Player" in gold lettering across the chest. I pull my cardigan back on and take my seat. Gabby pulls the "change up" block and makes changes to where everyone is sitting. I am now on her left with Reid to my left. I pull the next cube.

"Hands Across America." I turn it over. "You must keep physical contact with the person to your left for the remainder of the game." I hiccup. "I think I'll take the five drinks."

Reid stops my drink in midair.

"I don't think you can handle five more drinks in a row. Just… hold my hand." He holds his hand out, and I place mine in his before he brings them to a rest on his thigh. He pulls his block.

"Bipolar. Compliment the person on your left and insult the one on your right." He turns to his left. And I'm wondering how buzzed he is when he jokes to Ryan. "I'm sorry this wasn't the kissing block because I am sure you would be good at it." He seems pleased when everyone cracks up. Some harder than others depending on their drink level. Then he turns to me, and I think he is going to do what appears to come naturally to him and insult me for a second time tonight, but he chooses to take five drinks instead. When he's done, Ryan takes his turn. I can't help but notice that Reid has threaded his fingers through mine and his thumb is skating metrically over mine. I watch him. He truly seems to be enjoying himself, and I'm surprised how comfortable I am with him. He's laughing at a story Blake is telling when he becomes aware that I am watching him. Turning to face me, his eyes hold mine and there's an unmistaken warmth in them.

Theo pulls a block and the tower sways but somehow manages to stay upright.

"10% lie." He flips the block over. "Every player who masturbates drink one." Everyone at the table drinks one, but I drink five with a blush thinking about earlier.

"Elise." Theo says my name, not buying it and knowing better.

"I'm not saying I don't, I'm not saying I do. I'm just not saying."

"I told you," Blake says. "Vanilla."

I finish the last of my drink five and am grateful when the tower falls on the next pull.

Having anticipated our Drunk Jenga night, Owen has chauffeured golf carts waiting out front to take everyone back to their cabins. After we have said our goodnights, the team loads up and heads out.

Theo and I return to our room. When I come out of the bathroom, I find that he has a full glass of cold water and four Advil waiting for me on my bedside table. I hastily drink the entire glass, and then I shed my clothes leaving on only my tank and cotton boy-shorts underwear.

"I think I'll get one more glass to have when I wake up with cotton mouth. Do you need anything?" I ask him. He's already under the covers.

"No, babe. Want me to get it for you?"

"No, go to sleep. I'll get it." I rub his head and turn off his bedside light.

The water has helped sober me somewhat. I check the doors off the balcony in the darkened living area to make sure they are locked before making my way to the front door, then the kitchen. The moon or outside lights, I'm not sure which, light the room enough to see to pouring another glass of water. I catch Reid in my peripheral as he enters the kitchen. He's in pajama bottoms sitting low on his hips and even in the muted light, I can see the dark trail of hair that makes me want to follow it down. He stops beside me and reaches for a glass.

"Water?" I offer softly without turning to look at him.

"Please." He sets his glass on the counter and I begin to pour when I feel his fingers brush along the inside of my thigh. He aligns his body behind mine, and I feel his erection against my backside. Leaning down, he scatters kisses across my shoulders. Moving up my neck he finds the sweet spot behind my ear and I know he can feel my accelerated pulse. I don't know if it's the alcohol, being called vanilla when I'm not, or the argument we had earlier, but my inhibitions are lowered, and before I can talk myself out of it, I turn and mount him. Wrapping my legs around his waist, my hands curl around his neck pulling him to me, deepening an already volatile kiss.

He releases a string of expletives when I grind against him, rubbing my sex along his. He shoves us against a wall, and if it weren't for the cotton barriers between us, he would be balls-deep inside me right now.

With my body supported, his hands are free to roam, encircling my waist before moving under my tank to squeeze my swollen breasts, heavy with need. A need to be fucked.

He applies pressure to my clit with his thumb, and his lips encase mine, absorbing the orgasm that slams through me with only a single touch. It's enough to send us both into an urgency of needing more. There isn't time to take his pants off. Sliding my underwear to the side, he frees his cock and buries himself in me in one forceful motion. My sex pulses around him, feeling like it has found what it has always been missing.

"Please. Oh my god, Reid." I breathe at the fullness of him inside me.

The sound of my voice brings him to an immediate halt. His head coming to a rest in the curve of my neck.

"Fuck!" he curses. "I'm sorry. I shouldn't have."

"What?"

"We can't do this," he growls as we gasp for air. He lowers me to the ground, making sure I have my balance before pulling out of me.

"I'm sorry, Elise."

chapter four

Reid

I hit the back of my head against the closed door to my bedroom. *Jesus, Beckett. Get a grip.* That should have never happened. Here I am giving Theo shit about separation of work and relationships, and I can't go five fucking minutes without thinking about her. Without wanting to smell her. Feel her. Taste her. Touch her. Bury myself in her. I knew as soon as I saw her shadowed figure in the kitchen that it was a mistake to go near her. But since meeting her, I appear to only make decisions with my dick.

Tonight had been an education on how she and Theo interact with the team. I was surprised to learn Theo is more detached than I originally thought. I don't remember who said it, but it's true: Theo is the dad, and Elise is the mom. They revere Theo, but they love Elise. This is a problem. I don't need a fucking prom queen who wants to be loved by all running the show.

Stripping out of my clothes, I opt for a shower to once again reign in a dick that's so hard it could pound nails. Elise plays on repeat in my mind, and my hand does little to dull the need I feel. I let out a yell and come, hard, shooting my load across the shower. *Fuck.* Even in its intensity that did nothing to ease my discomfort.

I towel off and climb into bed without any clothes on. I just need five minutes. Five minutes of not thinking about Elise Donovan, so I can get some rest. Five minutes of not seeing the hurt and confusion on her beautiful face when I left her in the kitchen. Turned my back on her. I count the seconds turning into minutes. With no relief in sight, I toss back the covers and make my way to the closet to throw something on. I can't sleep if I don't make this right.

Padding softly across the living room, I enter their wing, knocking softly when I come to the closed bedroom door. There is no light or noise to indicate anyone is still awake. Turning the knob, I softly open the door to find Theo and Elise in bed, both asleep. A moonbeam shoots across the bed, lighting a path, and I can see the features on her beautiful face. And sure enough, in a space barely suitable for a small child, Elise is glued to Theo, just as he had attested, her back pressed against his. On the other side of her is an entire king size bed that could comfortably fit two more people. On the other side of Theo is a drop-off to the floor.

I contemplate waking her, but don't want to alarm Theo, and she has mentioned more than once that she is exhausted. With a shake of my head, I close the door and go back to a bed that feels emptier than before. Even if Theo only gets a small sliver of bed, at least he has Elise's warm body pressed against his. Never did I dream I would be envious of who my gay friend sleeps with. Punching my pillows, I turn fitfully on my side wishing I could dismiss what happened as easily as Elise did and sleep.

Nova wakes me early the next morning with two paws planted firmly in my chest, ready to go out.

"Really bro? You couldn't let me sleep another 30 minutes?" I rub his head as he lays across me. "I did after all drink a fifth of vodka last night." I rub my pounding head. I can't remember the last time I had that much to drink. Nova gives me what I am quite certain is a look of disapproval peppered with some judgement. "Okay. Let's go."

It's early and there is no sign that anyone else is up yet. It's a beautiful morning and Nova is enjoying being in the great outdoors. I toss a stick for him to fetch, letting him get a little exercise before I head inside to pour a cup of the coffee.

"You're up early." Theo's deep morning voice startles me. I turn to see my friend who looks like he was run over by a car that decided to circle back around and do the job again.

"Nova wanted some fresh air. Coffee?" I offer with a smirk.

"Asshole." He nods, adding a "thanks" when I hand him a steaming mug of redemption. "I am getting to old to drink like this."

"You're 27. Not 50."

He takes a seat at the kitchen bar. "Not all of us can drink like a fish and then look ruggedly handsome the next day."

"True. It's a gift. So, how is Ross?" I ask at an attempt at conversation, but I don't hear a word of the answer because at that moment Elise walks into the kitchen. I've never known a woman who looks fucking edible in leggings and a t-shirt. My t-shirt. She's wearing my t-shirt from last night.

I move to position my hips behind the kitchen island to hide the hard on forming in my sweats. These are not the pants to provide me any cover.

"Good morning." She greets us both, but her eyes don't meet mine and I feel lost without them. Elise's eyes are like snapshots of what she is really feeling. Watching her last night, I realized her line of work has taught her to have control over her facial expressions. But her eyes. If you know what to look for, they give everything away.

She hugs Theo from behind and places a light kiss where her head meets his back before walking around to the refrigerator.

"I made some coffee," I tell her. I'm rewarded with the eye contact I was seeking.

"Thank you, but I don't drink coffee." She turns to get juice out of refrigerator. "Breakfast will be ready in twenty minutes."

"Are you making enough for the army or just us?" Theo asks her.

"Just us. I imagine they're still asleep." She sets ingredients on the counter. "Why don't you boys plan your day and I'll have it ready in about fifteen minutes."

"Sounds like a plan. Reid?" I look up to Theo saying my name. "We can meet for a while after breakfast and then go for a run. Sound good?"

"Yep. Sounds like a plan," I echo and make the first move to leave the kitchen, ensuring my reaction to Elise remains under wraps.

The balcony doors are open and Benny and the Jets is playing over the sound system. The front door opens at the same time I enter into the living room, and Theo brings in a bunch of wildflowers. I want to beat the shit out of him when Elise rewards him with a fucking fantastic smile and soft kiss to his cheek.

"Breakfast is ready." She greets me with the smile of two people who share a secret before placing a large stack of pancakes on the table. My breathing skips when her arm brushes mine as she picks up the remaining platter of bacon and eggs. She's pulled her hair up into a large bundle on top of her head. She looks adorable, and a small moan escapes me when I see her wrap her lips around a fork full of pancakes.

"These are delicious." I motion to my pancakes in an effort to divert attention from what I was really moaning about.

"Els can cook, that's for sure," Theo praises.

We discuss some of the accounts they have on-going over breakfast. As it stands now I plan to proceed with the merger, but Theo and I are going to meet later to go over the details. We all pitch in and the kitchen is cleaned in a matter of minutes. Theo takes a call as I place the last platter in the dishwasher.

"When's the last time you loaded a dishwasher?" Elise asks.

"I'll have you know I am perfectly capable of loading a dishwasher."

She raises a brow.

"So it may have been never, but I'm pretty sure I aced it." I beam at my accomplishment and get an eye-roll in return.

Folding the dish towel over the sink she turns to leave. I can see Theo on the balcony, still engrossed in his phone call, so I decide it's now or never.

"Elise, about last night." *Shit!* I should have given some thought to what I wanted to say. Motioning between the two of us, "This would really complicate things. Plus, you seem

like the kind of girl who…it's just that I don't have time for…"
Running my hands through my hair, I try to land on something intelligent to say. She nods but makes no attempt to
make this easier for me as she moves past. I stop her with my
hand to her elbow. "I don't do relationships and you seem like
a hearts and flowers kind of girl."

Her eyes on mine, she places a hand to my chest. "Reid. I
don't want to be romanced. I want to be fucked." And like the
goddess she is, she leaves me standing there resisting an urge
to drag her by her hair to my room and give her that wish.
Never have I wanted to possess someone like I want to her.

"Fuck me," I exhale.

Theo enters with a questioning look.

"What?" I ask, feigning ignorance.

"Why are you smiling like you are auditioning for a
toothpaste commercial."

"Just enjoying the break from the city. Let me change and
we'll go for a run."

Theo is a beast when it comes to anything athletic, so I'm
more than happy when we make it back to the chalet. We are
meeting the group for lunch before some team-building exercise that I'm sure will bore me. Theo has some calls to make,
giving me some time to seek out Elise. The balcony doors
are still open and Coldplay is playing, so she has to be here
somewhere.

"There you are." I catch a glimpse of her when I walk out
to the balcony. When I step through the doorway, I see Owen
sitting closer than he should be and making fucking googly
eyes at her. The only thing to mollify me is Nova laying between them watching Owen's every move. I know that stance.
Owen would likely lose a hand if he tried anything.

"He's been sitting with me," Elise says mistaking my

comment to be about Nova and not her.

"Owen." I acknowledge him and he greets me in kind.

"Your dog isn't very friendly," he says.

"What are you talking about? Nova is a sweetheart." Elise bends to kiss his nose, and I swear on all that is holy, Nova gives Owen a "fuck you" stare.

"He snapped at me when you went for a drink," Owen tells her. Pit Bulls are highly misunderstood. They are also highly protective. Nova knew exactly what he was doing.

"Where's Theo? How was the run?" She's wearing sunglasses, so I can't see her eyes.

"It was fine. He's in his room." I pat Nova on the head before leaving. He doesn't move from his spot. "Good Boy."

Another shower, another jerk-off that gets me nowhere. Maybe she is what she says she is. I recall thinking she seems like a girl who can separate herself from emotional decisions. The thought that we might make this work as a one-time hook-up is appealing. I want her enough that I would break my own rule of not fucking the staff. I turn off the shower and prepare for a day of planning. There's a little lightness in my step at the potential that lies ahead.

I'm disappointed when I see Elise is not at lunch with the team. She and Ryan have been pulled into a call about some crisis. It does, however, give me a few minutes to observe just Theo with his team. They obviously look up to him, but Elise's statement about his managing style is accurate and confirms what I have known all along. Theo is the face of the company and brings in the accounts while Elise is the brains and the glue. She has a keen sense for how to fix things. Both are needed, but I wonder how they will work apart?

"Why don't we head to the site?" Owen corrals everyone into the waiting transportation. It takes about thirty minutes to get to our location where there is—surprise—an obstacle course set up. God help me.

"We really are doing this kind of shit?" I ask Theo, who merely laughs at my contempt.

"Yes. Blame Elise. She thinks it shows who people really are. I have to admit, when I take a step back, I find she's usually right. It really has taught me some things about my team and how to better utilize them. I walk away understanding how their minds work. It seems lame, but I am always shocked how useful the insight is."

Everyone piles out of the SUVs, and we are joined by Elise and Ryan who are deep in conversation about a CEO's son gone astray. She updates the team on the new client and fires off some directives before pulling everyone's focus back to the present.

"Welcome to 'O' day, as I affectionately call it," she begins. Several of the team members sing the letter O in various notes, and everyone laughs and begins stretching. I assume it's a joke from past obstacle torture days.

"I know you all are as excited as I am. Owen has created a little something different for us this year." She turns their attention to Owen, but I'm still watching her. This girl is not like any girl I usually find attractive. For starters, she is all curves and I usually fuck twig girls, size 0 models with fake breasts. I swear my IQ points dropped just admitting that.

She laughs at something someone says. She has a great laugh. A goofy laugh. She's replaced my t-shirt with a fitted exercise tank to match the leggings she is wearing. Her long hair is braided down each side of her head into pigtails. She has on no makeup. I have never been with a girl like this. I am thankful my dick appears to be napping, and I am able to control my body's response as I watch her.

"So, normally our focus is to have you solve problems as one team," Owen explains. "This year you will be working on your own. Theo, Reid, and I will be observing. The course is timed but there is no prize for finishing first. Just do your best."

Owen sounds a horn and everyone takes off. The first obstacle is to walk on a rope over a muddy pond of water. The girls prove more efficient at this task and finish ahead of the guys. The next obstacle is an upper body strength challenge where the guys catch up and overtake the girls.

Theo is right. This is telling. Without anyone making this a competition, they have turned it into one. There are two things going on: the women are competing against the men and everyone is competing to be better than someone else. They are about halfway through the course with Elise and Blake leading the charge. Damn, this girl is competitive. And vocal. She's encouraging her team while she plows ahead trying to beat them. Even though Blake appears to totally be in his element and will easily leave everyone behind, I would put my money on Elise before I would him.

There's a ten-foot wall climb in the middle of the course with two ropes knotted in different increments. Elise makes a quick move that trips Blake up. It would be hard to catch if you weren't looking for it. Almost like tipping the elbow of your opponent about to shoot a basket. Unfortunately, Blake grabs her to balance himself, which is against the rules, and takes them both down. Hard. Elise lets out a whimper when she hits the ground, and Blake lands on top of her knocking the air out of her lungs. I reach out to stop Theo from going to check on her. Surprisingly, he stays put. Blake hops up and keeps going leaving Elise lying on the ground.

It takes a minute for Elise to get her bearings. Damn, that

was a hard fall. This has created an opening for Fran to pass them both. I watch as they regain their positions and overtake Fran at the wall, easily moving on to the next obstacle. Once over the wall, Elise heads towards the next course that requires more mental maneuvering than brawn, and instinctively I know this is where she will overtake Blake.

This is where things get interesting. Elise, seeing that Fran is having some problems getting over the wall, stops and calls to Blake, who is so focused he doesn't hear her. Or he ignores her and keeps going, I'm not sure which. Climbing back up the wall, Elise leans over to offer a hand down to Fran. It's no use, they are too far apart. By now, several others have mastered the wall and are well on their way through the rest of the course.

"Let's go, Fran." Elise picks up the rope and shows her how to walk the wall. Fran tries but is not able to accomplish the task. Her frustration has gotten the better of her, and she is now begging Elise to let her just go around.

"You got this, Fran. Turn off everything else and climb the wall. Focus."

"Just go, Elise." Fran's exhaustion and frustration is visible.

"No. We all finish." They make another attempt. She has Fran move up the rope ahead of her, and then Elise follows on her trail in hopes it will force Fran to keep going. Fran makes it about seven feet off the ground before losing her footing. She tumbles into Elise who has to choose to hang onto the rope and let Fran fall on her own, or to let go of the rope and fall together. Elise lets go of the rope and cushions the fall of the smaller Fran. It's Theo who holds me back this time. For reasons no man will probably understand, the girls are laughing. It takes them a minute to gather themselves and then Elise yells for Ryan who is now several obstacles ahead. He stops and backtracks to Elise. It's telling. She didn't yell for Blake. She knew who on her team she needed and figured out a new way to get Fran over the wall. I gotta say, she's not giving up. What's just as informative is that without hesitation, Ryan came to Elise when she called.

Elise explains to Ryan that she is going to lift Fran to him so he can pull her up the remainder of the way. Owen steps in and reminds Elise that Fran has to actually climb the wall for it to count. They engage in a heated exchange, but then a light bulb goes off for Elise and she leaves Owen mid-sentence.

"What the hell is she trying now?" Theo says with a smile full of respect for his friend. Elise takes one rope and has Fran take the other. Calling out when to step, Elise walks Fran up the rope with Ryan directly behind her. When Fran hits her proverbial wall at the seven-foot mark, Elise has Ryan support Fran's body against his, and Fran climbs the wall with her back plastered to Ryan's front. His arms have to be screaming. Elise beams with a look of pure elation when her friend makes it to the top. You would have thought someone handed her a million dollars. Elise finishes the course, pushing Fran over the line just before she crosses. Both women embrace and celebrate like they've just won the Olympics.

The team talks animatedly about the differences in this year's obstacles. Elise laughs, but is holding her side. She looks exhausted.

"Would Gabby have gone back for Fran?" I ask Owen and Theo.

"My guess is no. Not because she wouldn't have, but because she knew there was nothing she could offer. Gabby is even. Steady. She wasn't competing against anyone. She was just in her lane. It wouldn't have occurred to her that she *could* go back. She wouldn't have felt there was a reason to," Owen says.

"So, if Elise wasn't out there, who would have gone back for Fran?"

"I think it would have been Ryan. He may not have noticed until the end that Fran wasn't there, but he would still have gone back. Blake is strong and he's going to get it done, but he's got blinders on. He can't see what's going on around him. He's been trained to lead the way, finish the job and then come back to make sure no man is left behind."

"I agree," Theo says before dismissing Owen and turning to me. "Elise sees it differently. She understands Blake on a different level than I do. We had an incident a couple of months ago where Blake had to do a couple of questionable things to handle a problem for our client. I wasn't happy with the means he chose and felt like it endangered Elise. He just plows ahead with a fuck-all mind-set."

"Add it to our list of things to discuss," I tell him.

When we join the group, Elise is showing them her side. She is going to have a nasty bruise from one or both of the falls she took.

Owen talks to the team about some of the things he observed and what he wants each person to think about then gives them homework for tomorrow. Dinner is being served at the camp hall tonight. Until then, we are on our own.

Nova and I lay on a chaise on the balcony. I don't know what is going on with me this week, but I find that I don't want to work. I haven't not worked since I started my company. Working has always been my balance.

I've been attempting to read, but after reading the same paragraph several times over, I give up and settle for something else completely foreign to me—a nap. Tipping the brim of my ball cap low over my sunglass-covered eyes, I enjoy a rare moment of silence. It last about two minutes.

"Is he asleep?" Gabby asks, walking up to the four-top table near me.

Fran flaps her arms in front of my face like a crazy bird, and it takes true talent on my part to not laugh or change my facial expression.

She leans in and I close my eyes.

"He's asleep," she surmises and sets a deck of cards on the table. Blake joins them. This should be interesting.

"Will we bother him if we play cards out here?" Blake asks.

"Not if we don't get too loud. It's too pretty to sit inside," Gabby says and pulls out a pad of paper. From my angle, I have a visual on everyone except Fran. She has her back partially to me.

"Okay. I'm ready." Elise sets a drink on the table and takes a seat. "Oops. Is he asleep?" she asks in the worst whisper voice ever. Thankfully, no one notices my lip twitching. I roll my eyes when Nova leaves the spot next to me and goes to lay at Elise's feet, happy when she rewards him with a pat to his head.

"He's asleep. If I were reading," Fran leans over to look at the book lying open over my crotch, "a book on the state of our economy, I'd be asleep too."

"You look different, Frannie. What's going on with you?" Gabby asks.

"I know. I noticed it too Gabs," Blake interjects.

"She's poppin'," Elise grins.

"I don't know what you are talking about?" Fran says, shuffling the cards.

"You are bomb baby, and you know it." Elise pops some peanuts into her mouth. "What's the score?"

"Fran and I have 1038," Gabby replies. "You and Blake have 1122."

"We need to step it up," Elise tells Blake. They make their bids.

"Really? On the first hand, you're going Nil." Gabby shakes her head in disbelief.

"How long have you guys been playing this game of spades?" Ryan straddles a seat between Gabby and Elise. "We started it our first retreat. We play to 5000."

"I've decided who we need to go as for Halloween this year," Gabby announces. "The Spice Girls."

"There were five of them," Elise says, laughing when Blake thwarts Gabby's attempt to make Elise take a trick.

"So, we'll snag two more girls." Gabby shrugs her shoulders like the problem is solved.

I wonder when Elise plans to tell them she will be in New York for Halloween, I think.

"I have a couple of friends who would do it with you," Blake offers. "They just had babies, so they should be ready to show off their post-pregnancy bods by October."

"What is it about Halloween that makes all the moms want to turn it out? It's like they all have a secret desire to be sluts and Halloween is the only time they can show off."

"You know what tomorrow night is," Ryan says with his head propped up by his arms resting on the back of his chair.

"I'm not doing it this time," Elise says, throwing a card.

"You have to," Blake says. "You spit rhymes better than anyone."

Elise doesn't respond and they move on. The song changes to Celine Dion.

"I cannot stand this song. The reason she is all by herself is because she is singing that song." Elise laughs at her own joke. It's endearing.

"How's it going with Susie?" Gabby asks Blake.

"I had to break it off with her."

"'Cause her name is Susie?" Elise deadpans. I swear I almost give myself away.

"'Cause she makes porn star noises," he says.

Everyone stops for a beat and looks at him. Then, as if choreographed, they all move again at the same time.

"What about Joel," Blake asks Gabby.

"I had to break it off with him."

"Why?"

"He made ugly sex faces." She lays her card down, never missing a step.

Elise lets her hand fall to the table. "You broke up with him because of ugly sex faces?"

"Yes. It's a deal breaker."

"I don't understand," Elise says.

"Well, Elise." Gabby thrums her fingers over her lips. "How can I make you understand?" She pauses. "When he comes, he makes this face." Gabby makes the most awful face, and I bite the inside of my lip to keep from blowing my cover.

"I once fucked a girl who called me 'Daddy' when she came." Blake lays the last card. He and Elise high-five that she was able to take zero tricks.

"I have issues with any girl who wants to call me 'Daddy,'" Ryan says. "I don't like the visual or implication."

"Agreed," Elise says and leans down to pet Nova while Blake shuffles and deals. They make their next predictions and start another game.

"What about Aaron?" they ask Fran.

"I broke it off."

"How long was I gone for?" Elise asks indignantly. "I leave for six weeks and you all lose your significant others."

"We don't make sense without you, Yoda." Gabby says.

"So why no Aaron?" Elise asks.

"He didn't want to invest in me."

"So, you broke up with him because he wouldn't spend money on you?" Blake asks. Elise throws a peanut at him. Hard. She lands it right between his eyes.

"It's all fun and games until someone loses an eye," Blake says, narrowing his at Elise.

"I don't need him to spend money on me. I wouldn't care if he took me to McDonald's if that was the best he could do. It was like he didn't want to be seen with me in public."

"You know what they say," Gabby chimes in. "The most expensive meal you'll eat is my pussy." She lays down the queen of spades. This disgruntles Fran.

"What do you mean he didn't want to be seen with you in public?"

"I mean…oh no you don't, Elise. I ended it. It's fine."

"I was just asking."

"No, you were fixing. I don't need you to avenge a bad date for me."

"He wasn't just a bad date. You liked him. If he treated you badly, I want to know."

"I swear, Donovan. If I find out you did something."

Elise shrugs and continues with her cards.

"So, no run-in with Robert?" Fran asks as if she has just deployed her secret weapon.

"Nope."

"Good. I hated that guy," Ryan says.

"Ditto," all the others say at once.

"It wasn't his fault," Elise says.

"Whose was it?" Ryan asks. "And I swear to God, I will lose my shit, Elise, if you say it was yours."

"It was mine." She places a hand on Ryan's to stop him before he starts. "It's my fault for not demanding he be worthy."

"What the hell does that even mean?" Blake asks.

"It means the person I end up with will know they are the most amazing man on this planet, for he has my heart." Fuck, did I find myself wanting more and more to be that man.

"You're not the only one who can make phone calls." Blake tilts his beer to Elise.

"Trust me," she soothes him. "I handled it."

They play cards for about 45 minutes before Theo comes out and shoves my shoulder. I pretend to wake.

"I need to talk to you." He starts into the house. "Elise," he calls out. Instead of holding the game for her, they decide to call it and head back to their cabins, leaving just the three of us.

"Jackson Hollingsworth just called. He needs me in New York tomorrow."

"Need me to come with you?" Elise asks.

"Any other time I would say yes, but I'm not really sure why they need me. Emme Taylor has handled this beautifully. I see why people say she's so good."

"It must be going negative for Blaine Moore for Jackson to call you in," says Elise, who has transitioned into work mode in the blink of an eye. Maybe she never truly turns it off. "Why don't you take Ryan?"

"I'll be fine. I should be back the day after tomorrow, in time for the wrap-up and to make the announcement to the team. I had planned on taking you to dinner tonight since the team is going into town. Either join them or Reid can take you."

"I think I can manage a dinner on my own," Elise retorts. "Need me to help you pack?"

"No, I have my go bag with me," he says, giving her a kiss on her temple. He shakes my hand before leaving. Elise follows him out.

I watch from the window as she waves when he drives away. I'm as patient as I can be, but as soon as she turns to close the door behind her, I reach out and lock it before turning her to me and laying claim to her mouth.

chapter five

Elise

Reid devours my mouth the minute I walk into the chalet. His lips bruise mine as he pours himself into me.
This. Man. Can. Kiss.

He roughly turns me toward the door with my back
to him, pulls my shirt over my head, and unhooks my bra,
pushing the straps down my shoulders but not all the way off.
His hand fists my hair, turning my face to him, capturing my
mouth again.

"Do you want me to fuck you?" I can feel his hot breath
against my ear.

"Please."

"Tell me." He bites roguishly along my jawline.

"I want you to fuck me, Reid."

In another rough move, he turns me back towards him,
and his eyes heat with a darkness. My arms are trapped in my
clothing behind me causing my shoulders to pull back, lifting

and showcasing my breasts.

"Fuck, you're beautiful."

It surprises me that he says this while watching my face and not just my breasts. With a groan full of need, he lowers his head and bites my nipple. His hands move to cup my breasts from underneath. The course pads of his thumbs roll back and forth over my now tender points. He squeezes my breast, and his mouth traces a path through every peak and valley on the landscape of my upper body. The dip in my clavicle, across the slope of my shoulder, down my side. He tongue-fucks my belly button while his hands continue to knead my breasts. My sex vibrates making me want him to the point that I know I will shamelessly fuck myself against him if he tries to stop like he did before.

"Reid," I moan.

He stands to meet my eyes, both hands cupping my jaw.

"I know," he promises before closing my mouth with his.

His promise staves off my arousal with the knowledge that he understands. He feels it, needs it like I do.

"I have to taste you. Now." He easily slides me up onto the marble island, my ass resting on top of my hands that are still behind my back, providing an elevated angle. He runs his thumb over the crotch of my cotton panties, teasing me but not providing any of the pressure I crave. He grabs the hem of my panties and easily rips them from me before he removes his own t-shirt.

Planting his hands firmly on my knees, he opens me, exposing myself to him in a way that feels vulnerable, necessary, needed. He pushes my knees forward, rolling my hips slightly off the counter, and then he lowers his head. From the bottom of my sex, he runs the tip of his tongue to trace just inside the folds, making a full circle.

"Reid," I say again, only this time I'm begging and he knows it.

"I've got you, Dove," he says before his mouth suctions around my clit. The unexpected term of endearment shatters me. He proceeds at his own pace, relishing in the process. When I think I can't take anymore, he flattens his tongue, coaxing me into a deep, mindless orgasm that shudders through my body long after the initial spasms slow.

He lifts me from the island, kissing me with the taste of my arousal still on his lips, and carries me to his room where he deposits me in the middle of his bed. He undresses, and I am awarded with my first full vision of his magnificent body.

"You're exquisite," I breathe as he climbs over me.

"I don't compare to you, Dove." He lifts my back and pulls my arms loose of the clothing bonding them taking a minute to rub each shoulder. My fingers explore the front of his chest, charting the territory I intend to lay claim to.

"Are you sure this is what you want?" My hands rest on each side of his hips. "I don't want you to have any regrets."

"No way would I ever regret being inside you. I didn't stop last time because I regretted it. I stopped because I'm going to be your boss, and I don't want to muddy the waters. But waters be damned, because I can't think of anything other than getting back inside of you." He pushes my knees back to my chest, his cock resting at the entrance of my sex. "I should have said this before now, but I'm clean. I have the papers to prove it. That was the first time I've ever entered anyone without a condom. I just—" he shakes his head like he's looking for words, "I just lose my ability to think around you, but, God, do I want to be bare inside of you again."

"I'm clean, too. And I'm on the pill. I trust you, Reid."

His body falls on top of me, and his mouth sieges mine

as I wrap my legs around his waist. He pushes my knees back into position before he slams into me in one swift motion.

"Fuck me," he groans. When I move my hips to do just that, he stops me. "No, no, no. Just…" He makes a face and holds himself still. "I just need a minute. You feel fucking fantastic."

I giggle and he narrows his eyes on me. "I swear to God I'm going to fuck that giggle out of you." He rolls his hips before he pulls out and slams back in. The sensation is amazing, and I continue to meet his every thrust.

In an attempt to gain some control, he rolls me onto my shoulders, lifting my pelvis further off the bed. I can't move my hips in this position, so I am at his mercy as he fucks me long and hard.

"Oh my God," I whimper as he continues his delicious assault on my body, my senses, my everything.

"He can't help you now," he growls and abruptly pulls out of me before flipping me over and smacking my ass. Lifting me onto my knees, he fists my hair and grabs a shoulder to keep me from jolting forward when he slams into me again.

"Please," I beg. My body has never been owned like this and it's out of this world. "What the fuck!" I snarl when he pulls out again, this time replacing his cock with a finger.

"I'm in charge, Elise." He smacks my ass again, sending off ripples of need through me before he slams into me again, giving me the force I need. I feel his wet finger over my puckered backside and he slides it just inside. My head lowers onto the bed, changing the angle. His other hand snakes around and pushes once on my clit. The sensation diverts me as he slides his finger all the way in.

"Bet you're re-thinking that giggle now." He smacks my ass again and I push back on him, giving as good as I'm getting. I'm frantic with the need of him. My breathing fluctuates. I can't describe it. It's like he's hitting a reset button in me, and with each move in and out, I need and want him more.

"Get there, Elise."

My name on his lips is all it takes, and my muscles clench around him as I fall into the precipice in front of me. Reid thrusts into me a couple more times before howling an expulsion so strong I can feel it inside of me. Pulling my hips tight to him as his body convulses, he shudders through his release before collapsing on top of me. I love his weight on me.

His fingers entwine with mine, and he raises our arms above us on the bed, his head resting against mine. Neither of us speak as our breathing retreats back to a normal pace.

"You were amazing." He squeezes my hand and places a gentle kiss between my shoulder blades.

"Thank you," I answer softly.

"We're expected at dinner in fifteen minutes." He kisses me once more before climbing off of me. I immediately regret the loss of his weight on me.

"Okay. I need a shower."

He pulls me to him and kisses me deeply. "You don't have time. Plus, I like knowing you'll be wearing me tonight."

"Because you're a caveman?" I respond sarcastically, earning me a hard slap to my ass. It might have been meant as a reprimand, but to me it feels like a starter pistol.

"Elise, I run this." He motions between us. "Understood?" When I respond with only a look he pushes me against the wall, lifts me up, and impales me all in one motion. He raises our arms over our heads, and his hands move to what is already my favorite spot, entwined with mine.

"You're restart time is admirable," I tease.

"Elise." It's a warning. I lean forward and kiss him hard. He releases my hands, and I wrap them around his neck pulling him closer to me. His thumb circles my clit, and I'm on the brink when he stops again.

"What the…" I pull on him.

With his lips against mine he says, "Tell me what I want to hear."

"Kiss me." I try to deepen my tongue in his mouth.

"Elise." He circles his hips again.

I lean back, opening a little space between us and start rubbing my breast, pulling on my nipples. "Reid," I moan. I lick my lips and start bouncing up and down on his cock.

"Dammit!" I watch his control snap and he increases his movements. With another press of his thumb, I come as he drives into me until he finds his release again only a moment later.

"What the hell am I going to do with you?" he asks with his forehead rested against mine.

"Fuck me again?" I sprinkle kisses all over his face, and he moans when my sex clamps around him.

"Keep this up and you won't be able to walk tomorrow."

"Keep this up and you can rent me a wheelchair tomorrow, for all I care."

He throws his head back in unexpected laughter, and I lean in and kiss his Adam's apple.

"No laughing during sex," I remind him.

Gently he lowers me to the floor. "Get dressed." He kisses me before he heads into his bathroom.

I head to my room to throw on an easy jersey maxi dress. I'm ready in five minutes, waiting for him when he walks out. He's looking at his phone, but stops when he sees me.

"I can't believe you're ready already and you look gorgeous."

"Easy when all you have to do is throw on a dress." I open the front door.

"Seriously." He turns me to him. "You're stunning and you don't even try."

I don't know what to say to something so sincere, so I simply lean up on my toes and kiss him softly.

We're heaved forward when Gabby pushes her way into the chalet. Reid freezes. She looks from me to him, and he drops his hands off me like I'm on fire.

"Whatever," Gabby shrugs. "I've got bigger problems. I'll keep your secret if you keep mine."

"Deal." We hold our pinkies up at the same time and swear. She turns to a confused Reid, who realizes the same is expected of him and cautiously raises his pinky to her. She shakes it.

"Gabby never gabs," I assure Reid with a nod and a smile, but he's frowning at her. I turn to see why and see she's crying.

"What's wrong?" I immediately wrap my arms around her and close the door. Reid follows us into the living room. It's obvious that he's caught between his comfort zone of not getting involved and wanting to make sure Gabby is alright. I motion for her to sit, but when she does, she cries out in pain. The only words I can make out is "Owen" and "hurt." Reid stands with a clenched fist.

"Where the fuck is he?" he demands.

Gabby places her hand on his arm to calm him, and I realize she is crying and laughing all at once.

"Gabby, you just about had Reid beating the shit out of Owen. What is wrong with you?"

"I'm in pain and I need help. I can't fix it myself."

"What happened?" Reid asks, still slightly unsettled.

Gabby tries to calm herself. "Remember, boss man. I hold your secret…"

"I'll hold yours," he reassures icily.

"Owen and I have an obligatory hook-up each year."

"And? Tell me something I don't know."

"I thought he wanted you," Reid says to me.

"Oh, he totally has a boner for Elise. But she'll never go there. He's stellar in the sack, so I couldn't give a shit who he pines for. It's just a once a year fuck."

"You should write for Hallmark," Reid deadpans.

"Well," she half cries and half laughs, still standing precariously. "I took the walking trail when we left here today to stretch my legs a bit, and I ran into him." She blushes slightly. "On the trail."

"You did the nasty in the great outdoors," Reid assesses, crossing his arms. Gabby answers with a nod.

"Remember. Right now, we're equals. I have something on you, too," she says to Reid before turning to me. "It's like his dick is made for me. It has a curve to it that hits my spot dead center." She demonstrates with her finger, and Reid audibly groans.

Running his hand over his face, he looks at me. "I run a multi-billion-dollar company. People fear me."

His rhetoric tickles me. I know he is wondering how the hell he got pulled into this.

"Go on," I tell Gabby.

"So, we started making out, and we couldn't wait till we got back to the cabin, so he took me against the tree."

"Did someone see you guys?" Reid asks.

Gabby shakes her head no.

"Did you get bit by something?" I ask.

She shakes her head no again.

"Speak, Gabby. What is it?" I'm losing my patience.

Slowly, she turns her backside to me and lifts the back of her flowery skirt. I cover my mouth. Her backside looks like someone took a meat grinder to it.

"What the hell happened?" I burst out into my own tears of laughter.

"Stop laughing, Bitchtits."

"How?" It's all I can manage.

"He really got going, and when he was grinding me I didn't notice the pain."

I turn her back around and lift her skirt. "There must be a hundred splinters in your

ass."

"You have to get them out. Please." She's crying a little more now.

"Let me call Fran."

"No way. You know Fran. There's no way we can tell her."

"Then I'm going to need Reid's help."

"I don't care. Whatever you have to do," she whimpers.

"I'm not sure I'm qualified." Reid raises his hands in surrender and starts to back up, but not before Gabby grabs his arms.

"Please?" she begs him, giving him the puppy dog eyes that no one has ever been able to resist.

"Fine," he sighs. "Elise. Get some safety pins and the tweezers."

He leads Gabby into the kitchen. When I come back with the supplies, I see that he has closed the curtains and is locking the front door. Gabby is lying face down on the expansive island. Reid has located a flashlight and has kitchen towels strategically placed over Gabby to preserve as much dignity as possible.

"Here." He hands Gabby a full glass of Scotch. She grimaces and coughs but finally gets it all down. Reid slides a pillow under her head to make her more comfortable.

"This never happened," he states before we begin.

"What?" Gabby and I plead ignorance at the same time.

"Exactly."

He works on one side while I work on the other.

"Yes?" I stop to answer my phone. "I sent Gabby into town for a few things. Reid and I are working on a problem for Theo. You all do dinner without us tonight. Have everyone here at nine tomorrow morning. We'll get a late start. I'll cook breakfast." I hang up.

"Ryan," I explain to Reid.

An hour and a half later, Reid and I stop to stretch and get something to drink. Reid had Gabby drink another glass of scotch, and she is blissfully out of pain, having fallen asleep about thirty minutes ago.

"I'm sorry," I offer, for what it's worth. "I promise Gabby won't tell anyone."

"I believe her," he says. "I just don't want her to think…"

"She doesn't and she would never," I cut him off. Pointing to her ass, I add, "clearly she understands a work-trip hook-up."

He chuckles and we get started again. "I can't imagine."

"Me neither," I giggle. "This is why you don't have sex in the woods or on the beach."

"Everywhere else is an option?" He raises a brow. "This from the girl who will take five drinks so she doesn't have to answer a question."

"Since you are being so sweet and pulling pieces of tree bark out of my friend's ass, I'll let you in on a secret."

"Do tell. Yes! 73," he adds, pulling out a splinter he has

been working on for a while. He puts it in the pile. I insisted we count and make a pile to show Gabby when she's awake. "Spill," he says before moving on to a new one.

"I don't answer those questions because I believe sex should be between me and the person I'm having it with. If Gabby hadn't come in, she would have never known. I don't fuck and tell."

"That's refreshing. Most girls I fuck do nothing but tell. It's all about status for them."

"Everyone talks about what they won't do. I don't understand putting parameters on something until you've tried it. And what you didn't like with one person you might love with another." I add another splinter to the pile. "74."

"So, you aren't dating anyone?" he asks.

"No. If I were, we wouldn't have done what we did today. I'm monogamous in my relationships. You?"

"I'm never with the same person long enough for that to be an issue, and the ones I have been with understand what's in it for both of us."

"That being?" I rub Gabby's back for a minute when she squirms. She quickly dozes back off.

"No hassles. Sex for me. Money and status for them."

"That works for you?" I stop what I'm doing and watch him.

His eyes meet mine. "It does."

I hold his gaze for a moment then go back to tweezing.

"What about this Robert guy?"

"What about him?" I ask.

"I get the sense that you aren't finished."

"Oh, we're finished," I state adamantly.

"Your friends seem to think…"

"Only know what I tell them." I give him a look that lets

him know that this topic of conversation is over. We work in silence for a while until I think we have them all. Reid runs the flashlight against Gabby's skin, and we both inspect our work to make sure we didn't miss any.

"Looks like we got them all," Reid proclaims. "89 total."

"I think we should rub baby oil on her to help with the soreness." I start to remove the towels covering her.

"I'll let you do that part. Let her keep some dignity intact." He smiles, and he's never looked more handsome to me than he does right now.

"Thank you."

"For what?"

"For helping my friend."

"You have definitely opened me up to new experiences."

"I do what I can." I smile and grab some cotton.

Running my fingers through her hair, I place a soft kiss to Gabby's temple. "We're done, baby. Bedtime. You sleep with me tonight." She stirs and makes a move to sit up wincing a little. Reid lifts her off the island so she doesn't have to slide off on her rear.

"Thank you." She yawns and stands on her tiptoes to offer a kiss to his cheek. He bends slightly accepting her gratitude. "You coming?" she asks.

"I'll be in shortly. I have to shower and I want to cut my hair."

"You wanted me to. I'm sorry I forgot." Gabby yawns.

"Bed." I send her on her way. Turning back to Reid, I say, "I'm starving. Want me to fix you something."

"You're cutting your hair?"

"Yep."

"Why?"

"It's too long. Once it reaches my waist and I begin to look

Pentecostal, I cut and donate it. Then start over again. This year I'm donating in honor of Emily, Ryan's little sister."

He frowns but doesn't say anything.

The chalet has a fully-stocked fridge, so I have everything I need to make a pasta with shrimp I grill on the stove. I toss it together and grab the garlic bread from the oven. Reid has a bottle of wine open for us.

"This is delicious. You, my Dove, can cook."

My heart flutters at his commendation and again at his term of endearment. "My Momma made sure all of us could cook. Even my brother."

"Dove?" I question but he doesn't respond.

"How many siblings do you have?" He slurps a noodle.

"I have an older brother, Knox. He's thirty. And we have a younger sister, Bren, who's twenty-two. Do you have any siblings?"

"I have an older brother. Dean."

"Are you close?"

"We have our disagreements, like any bothers, but there isn't anything we wouldn't do for the other."

"What about your parents? Do you see them often?"

"When I get to Boston, I do. That's where they live now."

My phone rings and I answer on speaker. "Hey, babe."

"Hi, sweetheart. Did I catch you at a bad time?" Theo asks sounding tired.

"No. We didn't make it to dinner so we're just eating."

"Who's we?"

"Reid and I. Gabby just went to bed. She's staying the night."

"Okay. I won't be back until the day after tomorrow."

"Why? What's going on? Is the press that bad for Blaine Moore?"

"No. Like I said, Emme Taylor took care of that already. If you get a chance, go online. She found proof that it was the record producer who took the money. It's all over."

"Wow. She is good."

"I tried to hire her, but she turned me down. She's working with her best friend and only got back into the game to help Blaine. I'm calling because I got a call from Steve Bowens. He has a problem and wants to meet tomorrow. Their headquarters is in Denver. I've been pulled into an issue with Senator Haynes' son, so I will need you in Denver. They are sending a helicopter for you in the morning. I'll send you the details. Reid?"

"Yep," Reid answers.

"If you want to watch Elise at work, you should go with her."

"I might do that."

"I think you would enjoy it. She's really good at being on top…"

We hear a little static. Reid chokes on a shrimp and takes a long sip of wine. "What did you say, man?"

"I said Elise is really good at being on top of things. You should go. I'll see you day after tomorrow. We can finish up with everyone there. By the way, while you are in Denver I'll teleconference with the team. I'm going to need them to help on this one."

"Need me?" I ask.

"No. This isn't a case you want."

"Got it. I'm scheduled to speak tomorrow. I'll work it in after the meeting with Bowens. I'll talk to you tomorrow."

"Will do. I love you," Theo says.

"Ah, I love you too, man," Reid croons.

"Shut it, knob-head. I was talking to Els."

"I love you, too," I tell him and disconnect the call.

"I'll help you clean. Then I guess I need to read some emails." Reid stands and clears our plates. "My mom will be really happy to hear how many times I cleaned up after a meal this week."

I laugh and prop my hip against the counter. "Would you mind doing me a favor before you start on your work?"

"What?" he asks tentatively.

"Would you cut my hair for me?"

Without hesitation he answers, "No."

"Please. It's hard to make the first cut yourself and not jeopardize the straight cut you need for the donation. I can do the rest myself."

"Sorry."

"Fine," I pout like a teenager.

"Where are you going?"

"I have to get my scissors out of my bag. I cut it dry then wash it."

I sneak into my bathroom and feel around in the dark for scissors, a brush, and a ponytail holder. Entering the living area, I pull a stool in front of the large mirror and grab my glass of wine. I give my hair a good brushing and pull it into a ponytail at the front of my forehead, the way you should if you are cutting your own hair, but it takes too much length away from the part I'm donating. Brushing it back again, I pull it into a ponytail at the length I want it and take a large sip of wine. With Kendrick Lamar playing in the background, I proceed to cut my hair.

"Stop." Reid pulls the scissors out of my hands. "You're going to hurt yourself. These things are sharp."

"They have to be to cut hair."

"Tell me what to do," he mutters.

I show him where and how to make the cut.

"I can't believe I'm doing this." His eyes meet mine in the mirror. "I love your hair."

"And you'll love it short, too. Besides, I'm not doing a pixie like Fran's. It will still have plenty for you to grab should you choose to before the week is over."

His eyes darken and he nods. Without a spoken word he begins to cut, taking his time and concentrating on the task at hand. I feel it when he makes the last cut, and hands me my ponytail. I run my finger though it. I'd guess it to be about twelve to fourteen inches.

"What's next?" he asks, his hands resting on my shoulders.

"Make sure the length is even then rough it up a little. When it's shorter I like it to be a little edgier." I twist a strand of hair and show him how to run the scissors down it to create an even, layering effect. "You can't mess up my hair. I've been cutting it for years."

"It's so thick. You have so much of it," he says idly. I hand him my glass of wine, and he finishes it off before he gets started.

Slowly and methodically he starts to cut my hair, razor cutting the layers like I showed him and making sure it's even. He doesn't speak. He concentrates on his task. He steps back and flexes his fingers through my hair at the top of my scalp, watching the movement. He stops and cuts a little more. He repeats this process until he's satisfied.

"Now my bangs." I pull them forward so he knows what to cut. "I like to tuck them behind my ears so try not to cut them shorter than here." I use the middle of my ear as a guide.

He bites his lip as he makes the final cuts. I cast my eyes down for a moment and notice that he's hard. He shifts to stand behind me again, measuring to ensure sure my bangs are even in the mirror. When he's satisfied, he looks up and finds that I am watching his reflection. His chest moves rapidly. I stand, but before I can make a step, he lifts my dress, shoves my underwear down my legs, and buries himself inside of me.

chapter six

Reid

Fuck, if that wasn't one of the most erotic things I've ever done to a woman. I wanted to stop after I made the first cut and fuck Elise into tomorrow, but I couldn't tear myself away from the experience. I crave control. Need it. And she just handed it to me on a platter. Never has a woman given me that level of govern over her body. Jesus, this girl is surprising.

"Hand on the stool, Elise." Elise obeys and braces both hands against the stool. I move her dress up her back to make sure she can see me taking her, claiming her. "Watch," I order.

Elise turns her head and watches in the mirror beside us. I pull out to my tip and slam back in, repeating the move over and over. Her beautiful face never turns from the mirror, and I can feel her arousal climbing. My girl gets off on watching. The thought is enough to push me to the edge, and with a push to her clit, we come together in a mind blowing release.

Out of breath and heart pounding, I wrap my arms around her and rest against her back. Another advantage to her having a healthy body is I can lay on her. I don't feel like she'll break if I fuck her hard.

When she says my name in a breathless whisper, my cock twitches inside her.

"Shower." I stand and pull out of her. "You said you wash after the cut." I pull her to my bathroom and strip her of her clothing before removing my own. I want to finish what I started and wash Elise's hair.

"Is that too hot?" I ask, moving her under the water.

"No," she answers softly. Lathering my hands, I work the shampoo through her shortened hair. Her beautiful eyes are fixed to mine, and her hands rest on my hips. My half-erect cock is resting against her stomach. I lean down and kiss her nose when I reach behind to work the shampoo to the tips of her hair. I tip her chin and rinse the suds before repeating the step with conditioner. Only this time when I rinse her hair, her hands move to my chest and she lazily rubs her thumbs over my flattened nipples. It sends a sensation directly to my balls. Squeezing the last of the water from her hair, she reaches down and pulls me to her by my erection. Rising onto her tiptoes she slides onto my cock torturously slow, releasing the most sensual sound I've ever heard.

Elise pulls my chest to her and playfully bites and sucks my nipples. Her tongue darts out to lick the trails droplets of water have left behind. Positioning me balls deep in her warm, swollen channel, she pleasures herself on my dick. I hold her face in my hands. She looks young and innocent as the water rains over her. I run my thumb over her swollen lips. It pleases me that she takes what she wants from me, but I can't stop myself from taking control of the movement and the pace.

"Eyes open, Dove."

I push her against the wall to leverage myself deeper within her. Her climax builds, but I can feel her holding it back. Her eyes close and I know it is because of the intensity she is feeling. I am feeling it, too. "Open," I demand softly. As soon as her eyes open and focus on mine, she quakes into an orgasm so incredible to watch I pour into her.

"Just a work-trip hook-up," she says. I think it's a quiet attempt to keep us focused on what we started. But I know as quickly as this began, that I have already crossed a line. A line so far gone I can't even see it anymore.

We wash each other's bodies and dry off.

"Is this tender?" I ask, running my hand over the bruise on her side from her earlier fall.

"Not really. It's a good thing, huh?" she teases with a wink.

"Sorry." I respond sheepishly. Guess that question would have been better served before I handled her the way I did.

"I'll see you in the morning." She kisses my cheek.

"Stay." I can hear the pleading in my voice, but I don't care. I want to wake up with this girl in my arms.

"I told Gabby I would be in to sleep with her." With regret in her eyes and a gentle kiss to my lips, she leaves me wanting more than any woman before her.

I try to sleep, but I just keep tossing and turning. I finally get up and make my way to the kitchen. Maybe if I have a bite to eat I'll feel like sleeping. I stare into in the fridge for several minutes, but I know what I want is not in here. It's in the bedroom.

Could I? Just one glance? Unable to stop myself, I shuffle to her room and open the door with the moves of a stealth ninja. I can't help but chuckle at the scene. Elise is spooning Gabby from head to toe and has her tucked inside her arms like a child holding a teddy bear. They are balanced on the edge of the bed with a vast space behind Elise. A space big enough for me, I muse. *Creepy, Reid. Creepy.*

Nova and I enter the chalet to a room full of people. The entire team is here.

After a restless night of sleep, I finally got up and took Nova for an early morning walk and let him chase the birds for a while. He makes a beeline for the kitchen and is given what he is in search of: bacon.

"Just in time," Ryan says, setting his plate on the table. Breakfast is being served buffet style. Everyone circles the island to prepare their plate.

"Coffee's ready," Gabby says to me. "Eat something. Elise makes a great breakfast. She just went to change." I can't tell if this is a casual announcement, or if she could see my eyes scanning the room for Elise. Either way, I pulled a two-by-four's worth of wood out of her ass last night, so I think we are on equal footing.

Nodding my thanks, I pour my coffee and wait for the line to die down. I hear her laughter before I see her. She rounds the corner, and I have to cover my audible gasp with my coffee mug. She looks fucking fantastic. I had no idea she had curly hair. It skims the top of her shoulders, and it's the sexiest style I've ever seen on a woman. She was right. I like her hair long but I love it short.

She smiles and gives me a wink as she bends over to offer a piece of bacon to Nova.

"You're getting played. That's his second piece," I warn her.

"He told me." She shrugs and hands me a plate. I move to her and she discretely grabs my ass. No one seems to notice besides Nova. And he's not saying a word.

I pretend to drop my fork and lean down to pick it up. Slowly, I skim my fingers along the inside of her leg and up her thigh, delighting in the feel of my fingertips skimming the underside of her ass cheek. She chews her lip and quickly fixes her plate to put some distance between us.

"So. The yearly cut." Blake motions to Elise's hair.

"Yep." She digs into her food.

"I'm sorry," Gabby says. "I would have cut it for you if you had waited. But you did a good job. It's the perfect length."

Elise doesn't say that I'm the one who cut it, and I find that I like knowing it's something else for just the two of us.

"Someone had a late night," Ryan instigates with an ill-behaved look, and for a minute, I think he's talking about me.

"I slept over here with Elise," Gabby answers with spunk. She and Ryan must be cabin mates.

"Then you have my apologies," Ryan says with a twirl of his finger.

"Seriously. Why did you sleep with her? The whole reason we saddled Theo with her is so we wouldn't have to sleep with Octoboss," Fran says.

"We watched a late movie, and I'll have you know, she never complained once," Elise defends herself.

All utensils halt in mid-air as the entire table looks to Gabby for confirmation. She suddenly becomes very interested in her food.

"Gabriella Jane," Elise snips. "You know it was not that bad."

Gabby musters her courage and looks Elise directly in

the eye. "At one point you tried to unzip me and crawl inside my body."

"Tall tales for someone who isn't even five feet," Elise digs with a gleam in her eye.

"I'm five-two," Gabby snaps back. This must be a sore spot for her. Like her ass, I imagine.

Elise grins and changes the topic. "I won't be joining you all today on your team building. Ryan will be taking the lead. There's a chance that Theo will be reaching out to some of you to help with a new client, his uncle, Senator Bowens."

"I'm already on it," Blake informs her without looking up from his plate.

"Already on what?" Elise asks in an uncharacteristically sharp tone.

Blake must hear the same tone. His eyes dart to Ryan and back to Elise. "I'm already working a few items for Theo."

"Since when?"

"Since last night." He sets his fork down and looks at her. "Elise," he says quietly, shaking his head. It's obvious he's at a loss as to what to say.

"And your role?" Elise's anger is obvious. She doesn't break eye contact with him.

"I'm doing what I always do. Find the dirt."

"Find the dirt or present the dirt?"

"Elise." Ryan says her name softly, but she has her claws in Blake and is not letting go.

"Blake? Find the dirt or present the dirt?" When he doesn't respond, she asks, "When was the decision made to go dirty?"

"It hit the obscure papers in D.C. this morning. Page ten, but it's only a matter of time before the top ledgers and the cameras pick it up."

"Why wasn't I told?"

"Elise." Ryan says her name again, this time with a little more force.

"I have a case in Denver. Then I have a speaking engagement at a local high school." It's silent for a minute before she shakes her head and quietly adds, "What a fucking hypocrite."

"He's just doing his job," Ryan says.

She finally turns to face Ryan. "I was talking about me," she says before standing and going to her room.

My eyes dart round the table and I can see their admiration and love for this woman. They do not like being on the opposite side of her.

"Dammit!" Blake yells, pushing back from the table.

"It's not your fault." Fran pats his arm.

"No. It's Theo's, and he better get his shit together," Gabby says, clearing the table.

"Alright. Everyone head out. I'll meet you there. Blake, Gabby, and Fran. Hang back," Ryan instructs. Watching the dynamic of these four leaders without Theo or Elise involved is interesting.

"Someone want to fill me in?" I ask.

"It's not our story to tell. But we've got a long day ahead of us. We all know what that look means. I've been here five years, and I can count on three fingers when I've seen it," Ryan says.

"When Elise is pissed. Look out," Fran adds.

The door opens and everyone watches Elise like she might explode. It's so at odds with the Elise I've seen the last few days, but this is the Elise that precedes her reputation. The look in her eyes resembles mine when I'm going into battle over a company.

"Elise," I say.

She stops and stares at me. "I'll be ready to go in twenty minutes. The helicopter will be here in thirty," she says in business mode. She pulls the keyboard to the TV out and after typing in a few things, pulls up a conference session.

"Hi, sweetheart," Theo croons to her through the screen.

"What's the name of the girl?" she asks calmly, giving nothing away.

"Laurie Townsend. Why?"

"She's my new client," Elise responds without batting an eyelash.

"Elise."

"I want everything, Theo, and if you hold back, I will bury you and your client."

"*Our* client Elise. You know we—"

"I know we had an agreement and you broke it. He could have called on a hundred other companies to handle this for him."

"We can't decide to have a conscience because—"

"Don't start, Theo. I don't have a problem getting our hands dirty. It's the nature of this job. But on this subject, we have integrity or we don't."

"It's not that simple." Theo runs his hand down his face. "He's my cousin. I know him. He didn't do it."

"Then you won't have a problem sharing what you have so far. If I find supporting information, it will exonerate him." She leans towards the screen and with a look of sheer force on her face she continues. "But if I find out he did it and you still choose to move forward in destroying this girl, you'll have my resignation before the ink is dry on the newspaper."

"Elise." Theo looks like he's going to be sick. She disconnects the call. Turning to her team, she begins handing out orders.

"Blake, you already have your tasks. Gabby, call Laurie Townsend. Explain the shit storm that is about to hit her doorstep. If you have to go to her, do it. I want to know what she eats, breathes, and sleeps. Ryan, I want you on the Senator's son. For every one we know about, there's a dozen we don't. If she's telling the truth, he's done this to others."

Everyone stops when she walks over to Blake. When she hugs him, the tension that has been building in him since their exchange visibly dissipates.

"Ten minutes," she says to me. This woman is fierce. Fuck, I want her.

The screen on my cell phone flashes. It's Theo.

"Beckett," I answer, moving to my room to dress at a record pace.

"Hey."

"Sounds like you fucked up," I tell him, putting him on speaker.

"I need a favor."

"What is it?" I slide into my suit pants.

"I need you to stay by Elise today."

"I'm not a fucking baby-sitter." I don't feel the need to tell him I have no plans to not be with her today.

"Just do it. She'll act like she's okay, but I know she won't be."

"What's the story on this Bowen kid?" I tuck in my shirttail.

"He's being accused of raping this girl."

"And if he did it? What are you going to do?"

Without hesitation, he answers, "Choose Elise."

I disconnect the call and grab my suit coat.

The team are working on their tasks. Elise enters a minute after me. She looks sexy as fuck. She's wearing a tight pencil skirt with a sheer silk blouse. I can see the curve of her breasts through her camisole. She uses the chair as support as she slides into high heels that lift her ass just so.

I pull my suit jacket around me, obstructing any view of my arousal. Owen knocks and enters. Even in the midst of craziness, Elise and I catch each other's eyes and smirk. Gabby is all business, unaware of our childish behavior.

"I have a car ready to take you to the clearing," Owen says. "I also have someone making sure Nova is looked after until you are back."

"Thank you." I pull on my shirt cuffs from under my suit. When I look up, Elise's eyes are a dark gray and by now, I have learned the look of desire on her face. She shakes it off and follows Owen out. I'm disappointed that we won't be alone in the car. It's only five minutes to the clearing, but it would have given me five minutes alone with her.

Owen makes small talk. All I really want is to tell him not to fuck girls against trees, but I don't.

The helicopter is waiting for us. Elise ducks and grabs my hand for balance as she walks on the balls of her feet across the soft grass. One of the men up front climbs out and opens the door for us. I help Elise in and am rewarded when her skirt pulls up mid-thigh as she slides across the bench. I climb in behind her, and the man makes sure the door is secured.

The pilot points to the cans in front of us, and we slide them over our ears.

"Mr. Beckett? Miss Donovan?" he asks, and we nod our heads in confirmation. "It'll be about an hour flight. There's water if you would like some." He points to the beverage holders by our feet before turning back to the controls. A few minutes later and we are flying over the mountains headed to Denver.

"Want to tell me what was going on this morning?" I ask Elise. She's reading a report that was emailed to us right as we were leaving.

"I'm not a girl scout. I have no problem fighting dirty if someone fights dirty with us, but I'm not okay with destroying this girl's life to save a senator's career."

"So, when you said you were a hypocrite?"

"I apologize, but you guys are on VOX. You might want to hold your conversation," the pilot informs us.

"Thank you," Elise says and finishes the email before putting her iPad away. She watches out the window, but I can tell she doesn't see anything. She's too lost in thought. I have been in unfamiliar waters since I met this woman. I want to comfort her, but I don't want to insult her. Grabbing my phone, I attempt to lighten her day.

"Wanna explore my chamber of secrets?" I press send and wait, watching the landscape fly by. I hear laughter but will myself not to look at her. My phone buzzes and I check her response.

"Would that make me be your Dumblewhore?"

"A man can dream, Dove."

Throwing caution to the wind, I tuck her hand in mine and am rewarded with an air kiss before she drifts back to her thoughts.

We land on the roof of the corporation we've been called on to help. There are two men waiting to greet us. I have to stop myself from breaking the fingers of one of the guys who places his hand on Elise's lower back to guide her into the waiting elevator. Their appreciation for my girl is evident. It's both interesting and irritating.

"Elise Donovan?" the taller one asks.

"Yes. And this is my associate Reid Beckett."

The tall guy doesn't hide his surprise. "Mr. Beckett, what an honor." He offers me his hand.

"I'm sure," I answer haughtily to maintain the upper hand. I don't have to turn to Elise to know she is rolling her eyes. The doors open and we enter into a large reception room. Hargrove Corporation owns the largest all-natural food chain in the states. They are a multi-billion-dollar corporation that has recently fallen into some bad press with overpricing issues.

The men see us into a conference room where the CEO Spencer Hargrove is waiting.

"Elise Donovan." She offers her hand and gives a firm handshake. I start introduce myself but he stops me.

"Reid Beckett, it's nice to meet you." He shakes my hand.

"Thank you."

"Please, have a seat." He motions for us to sit around a conference room table.

"What can we do for you, Mr. Hargrove?" Elise begins.

"Spencer. Please." He studies her for a moment. He's maybe 35. "Have we met before?" he asks with his head cocked to the side as if he's trying to conjure up a memory.

"Not that I'm aware of." She smiles politely and, fuck me, she's beautiful.

"It'll come to me," he says. "I heard Theo was in the area, and I wanted to get ahead of some bad press we have been experiencing for the last few months."

"Price gouging," Elise nods.

"I prefer to call it scale malfunctions."

"You can put whatever color of lipstick you want on it, it's still price gouging. You have a problem at multiple stores in multiple venues that all suffer from the same issue: charging for a product the customer is not receiving. Add to it the natural food market is already pricier than other leading chains."

"It's why our patrons come to us. They want quality. There's a price that comes with that," the tall guy states.

"Agreed. You already know they are willing to pay more because they are in the store. The difference is you aren't charging them for quality. You are charging them for a product they didn't receive. It's greed. We can't fix greed. That has to come from the top."

"And I assure you it is," Spencer counters with evident surprise at Elise's bluntness. "I have cleaned house the last three months, ensuring new management in the stores that were cited, and we have implemented checks and balances to make sure our staff doesn't feel like they have to cheat to make their quotas. The reason I have called you here is for direction on a new issue. It will be on the nightly news tonight that we have been utilizing prison labor to make some of our products."

"I don't think it will be an issue," the tall guy interjects. "My team has a statement prepared to announce we will phase out our prison labor. That should address it."

"Why?" Elise asks.

"It has to be addressed, Elise. Surely you would agree?" By his tone, it's obvious he doesn't like being questioned, much less by a female.

She turns her attention to Spencer. "Why?"

"Our patrons have stated they aren't comfortable with a product that was made in a prison."

"What is your goal here, Spencer?"

"To avert another black eye on the company's image. We can't have another hit this soon."

"You have bigger problems than your image. You don't

have a direction for your company. I assume your PR and Marketing are all in-house?"

"Yes." He points to the tall guy. "Jeff is our CMO."

"You're the CMO, and your solution is to stop the prison labor?"

"It is. The customers speak and we listen."

"That's a problem," she says to Spencer. "Your team should be ahead of the curve, telling the customers what they want. Yes, you listen to your customers and gather ideas from them, but if your customers are the ones driving the vision for this company, then that's a problem. Marketing is statistical. And anyone who tells you otherwise is doing you a disservice."

Spencer stops the man who is about to interrupt Elise, and she continues.

"If you were looking at statistical data, you would know only about four percent of your customers state they are not comfortable eating a product that was grown or created in a prison. This tells me that you are about to embark on a change for a small portion of your customer base."

"Squeaky wheel gets the grease. The ones who are unhappy are getting the press," the tall guy volleys.

"Change the narrative," she responds.

"You don't get anywhere by telling your customers they are wrong. Even if it is only four percent."

"You do if it solidifies you with the other ninety-six percent. Your customer base is comprised of middle and upper class. Because of price point, you have less than three percent of customers who fall outside of those classifications. What your team should be telling you is that ninety-three percent of Americans think our penal system is broken. Latest polls also show that people like being told they are good. They are seventy-five percent more likely to buy shoes from a company that donates a pair to the needy. Eyeglasses. Water. The list goes on and on. Handled correctly, you have the opportunity to tap into an untouched customer base.

"My prediction is you would see a growth once the announcement is made. Your stats also show that three out of five customers come back. This would give you about a seventeen percent increase for this year. Considering you have been averaging less than five the last four years, this would be a significant increase."

I have an excellent CMO, so I happen to know her numbers are accurate. What I'm surprised about is Elise's ability to call them out when she had no prep given to her for this meeting. This is the Elise Donovan I've heard about.

"So your suggestion would be?" Spenser asks her.

"Come out in support of your company and start a conversation around what needs changed. The system is broken. That is something everyone agrees on. Prison is big business. People don't want to fix the system, because people are making billions off the system. Including you. Prison labor is pennies on the dollar. Send them the message that you are teaching skills to people who will need to be productive members of the community. If we don't provide a way to rehab these inmates and give them a way to support themselves and their families, they will never have what they need to break the cycle."

"It's not our place to fix the world," the tall guy interrupts.

"You have an image problem. Your customer comes to you for wholesome, organic food. It represents wholesome, organic living. It's people dancing in a field of flowers where everyone loves each other. It's not a multi-billion-dollar company that is so greedy it has to alter prices and produce something for pennies at the perils of others."

"My suggestion is to determine what it would cost you to have these items made in a regular factory. Subtract from that what you are paying for the prison labor and use it to facilitate change. Half of it goes to an organization with a long standing reputation for addressing these issues, and half of it goes to building an education and skill set for incarcerated men and women. Possibly setting aside jobs for them. We're not talking about an amount of money that would cripple you. It'll probably have little impact on your pocket. But the payoff will be significant."

Elise stands and everyone follows.

"You've only been CEO here for six months. I am telling you your company has a problem: you're greedy. You've been overcharging your customers, and you use cheap labor to benefit yourself. Only you can make that right. Once you do, you will need a CMO who understands who your customer is. Right now, you just think you know. But you don't. It's why you haven't had growth the last few years. You're marketing to someone who's already shopping here. You need to bring in people who have never shopped here."

She offers her hand, but tall guy chooses not to accept it.

Yep. You just got bitchslapped. By my girl.

Spencer dismisses his team.

"I realize where I know you from. You spoke at Stanford, my sister's college, two years ago. I was in her city for a meeting and arrived early on campus to pick her up. You were speaking when I got there. You're a great speaker. Do you still speak?"

"I do, depending on my schedule, but I try to do a speaking engagement at least three to four times a quarter."

"It was educational. The students relate to you."

"Thank you," Elise says.

I want to ask questions, but I would feel like I was intruding. She's off today. It's not something Hargrove would notice, but I'm very aware of it.

"Thank you for your advisement today. I'll let you know where we land."

"We have a team in place ready to implement if you so choose," she says and shakes his hand, which he holds longer than necessary. Clearing his throat, he informs us there is a car waiting for us per Theo's request.

We share an elevator with several others. When the door closes Elise slides her hand in mine. It's a simple gesture, but I feel the weight it carries. She's telling me she needs to feel me, and I find myself wanting to wrap her so tightly into my arms that she knows without question that she is protected with a force field that I would not let anyone or anything penetrate.

The doors open and she attempts to release my hand, but I don't allow it, instead guiding us to the waiting SUV.

"You're welcome to go back by helicopter," she tells me as she punches an address into the GPS.

"I'd rather be with you, if that's alright."

"I'd like that." She smiles sweetly at me.

"Lunch first?" I turn onto the street.

"Sure," she answers, but I think I've lost her again. We are near the Denver Biscuit Company, and I pull in to park for us to eat.

"It's easy food, but thought you would like an experience unique to Denver," I tell her while opening my door. Her hand on my arm stops me and closing the door, I shift in my seat to face her. She does the same. She seems…anxious.

"Until you, I've never slept with anyone that I just met or had only known a couple of days. Work has been completely crazy, and as you know, I've been gone for several weeks. Then you were there and I just felt this electric pull to you, like an intensity that I've never felt for someone before. Especially in only a day or two of meeting. I'm just not someone who hooks up just to hook up, if that makes sense. And it's all happened so fast."

She's babbling and her eyes are downcast.

"Elise. What is it?" The look on her face troubles me, and I know I am not going to like where she is going with this. Is she not enjoying our time together?

She lifts her chin and her cool gray eyes envelope mine. "I just want to explain why I haven't said anything before now." Taking a breath, she pulls her shoulders back and proceeds, "During my senior year of college, I was raped. Multiple times in one night by the same guy." She releases a quick nervous breath.

I know I will look back on this moment and wish I would have said so many things. Wish I would have had the perfect words. Pulled her onto my lap and told her no person will ever harm her again, for fear that I would send down an army of retribution on them so intense just the mere thought would stop them. Told her that the only thing that matters is that I can't go a minute without thinking about her or wondering what she is doing. That I call her Dove because I grew up hearing my grandfather use it with my grandmother. She was strong but gentle, like Elise. That I feel emptier when she isn't with me. If only we had instant restarts.

"Why didn't you tell me?" My voice is cold, even to me.

"I'm not ashamed of it. It's just not something I tell people until they know me better or I am involved with them. I don't feel the need to always tell my story to someone."

"If that were true, we wouldn't have just left a meeting

where a man who's never met you, never been inside of you, never fucked you, knew. And if I'm not mistaken, we are headed to a classroom of kids who you are about to tell. Right? This is what you speak about? This is what caused the issues with Theo's cousin's case this morning." I run my hands through my hair. "How could you not tell me?"

She places her hands in her lap and waits. But when I fuck up, I do it big, so I just continue to ride the "I'm Fucking This Up" Pony Express.

"You didn't think I deserved to know before I immobilized your arms? Slapped you during sex? You didn't think I needed to know your history? That's not being very honest with me." My voice cracks a little and I sit. Elise watches me but says nothing.

I would have never done those things to her, been that rough with her.

After several long minutes of my mind racing, I finally speak. "I think I would like a do over." My voice is soft and filled with regret.

"Not necessary. One thing I have learned from my own experience and from others over the years is that rape is like throwing a rock in a pond. It only breaks the water where it lands, but it sends out ripples that affect the rest of the pond. There's no way you can have words ready when you hear something like this. Give it a little time and we can talk more on our way home. We'll have two hours to kill." She pats my hand. "But for now, I would like you to buy me lunch."

When I don't move, she turns back to me.

"I know it's a lot to take in all at once. So don't. Don't take it all in at once. Give yourself some time to process. Now, I'm hungry, and that sign says they have an amazing strawberry shortcake."

chapter seven

Elise

Lunch was quiet. I devoured my food, but Reid barely touched his.

I should have handled this differently. I just never thought a one-week hookup would become what this has become. It's so much more. At least to me. But there's so much at stake. This man is about to be my boss. How would this work? Could this work? Is it wise to add a relationship to an already stressful time with moving to a new city and launching the next phase of our company? It's a lot of changes for anyone to handle.

"We're here," says Reid.

I look up to see that we have arrived at the high school I am scheduled to speak at. He parks and comes around to open my door for me.

"Thank you. You're coming?" I am surprised when he follows me as I walk toward the door.

"If that is ok with you?"

"Of course, but you don't have to. You deserve to hear this one-on-one and not in a room full of high schoolers. If you prefer to wait in the car, I'll understand. I won't be long."

"No, I think I'd like to come."

I find I connect to the kids more if they see me as approachable, so I've changed into some worn jeans, a Kendrick Lamar t-shirt, and flip flops. I've pulled my short hair into two pig-tails that stick out.

"Tracey!" I say fondly to the teacher who has been waiting for me. We embrace and I introduce her to Reid. "Tracey's brother went to BC. He was on the rowing crew with me and Owen."

"So nice to meet you," she says. "Thanks for doing this Elise. When Owen told me you were going to be out here this week, I was hoping it would work with your schedule."

"I'm happy to do it."

"You'll be speaking to our Junior/Senior classes. It's about 300 kids. They all have signed permission slips from their parents, so you are free to do your regular talk."

"Perfect. I don't expect to be more than thirty minutes. Anything longer than that and they tend to gloss over," I laugh.

"This is an engaged group of students. I think you will be pleased at their attentiveness."

We enter and I'm tickled by the looks Reid receives. He's still in his suit looking sexy as fuck. Even to high schoolers. Tracey directs us to some empty seats off to the side while she introduces me to the room.

"Thank you, Tracey." I take the microphone from her and have a seat on the edge of the stage, my legs dangling over.

"My name is Elise. I was on the rowing crew with

Tracey's brother. Her older brother. Her very *hot* older brother," I tease, and the kids laugh. "Have her show you a picture some time ladies. Or gentlemen. Whatever flavor you favor." I'm rewarded with a laugh and a few shocked faces.

"I speak to groups of high school and college students about sexual assault. I have two speeches. One is informational and one is personal. With your parents' permission, I am going to share my personal story today starting with some statistics. Hang with me. I promise to be quick and not make your eyes gloss over." I smile and dig in.

"Sexual violence and rape have become a proliferating health issue in our country. The Centers for Disease Control—they're the ones you hear on the news talk about flu and virus outbreaks—the CDC has data that says that nearly 1 in 5 women and 1 in 71 men in the United States have been raped in their lifetime. Not will be. But have been.

"One in 2 women and 1 in 5 men have experienced some form of sexual violence. Eighty percent of those who are assaulted do not report their attack to authorities. Ninety percent of the people who commit these acts of violence get away with it. The odds that a rape was committed by a repeat offender are also approximately 90 percent. Reports show that most offenders don't rape once, but instead average 14 victims.

"The statistics alone are sobering. Enough to stop you in your tracks. While these statistics are shocking, they don't really impact us. They don't change our daily way of doing things or how we see things. We all have a false sense of security in thinking this wouldn't happen to me. This guy is my friend. This is my boyfriend. I trust him. Eighty-six percent of rapes are acquaintance rapes, meaning you know your attacker in some way. They are someone you hang out with, someone you date, someone you vaguely know through a friend. In my case, it was someone I had met once before. I was the coxswain—yes, let's get all the snickers out of the way." I gesture for everyone to let out a hearty laugh.

"As I was saying, I was the *coxswain* for our rowing crew, that's the person at the front who faces the rowers and tells them when to row. One of my crew was friends with Dexter. Dexter is not his real name. Ironic, isn't it? He rapes me, but I protect his name. To be honest I am not sure why I even do that. In some ways not acknowledging someone's name de-values them. Maybe that is what I am trying to accomplish?"

Tracey is right. These kids are engaged. They are listening and appear to want to hear what is next. I glance to Reid and wonder if he feels the same. What I am sure is a learned trait, he has completely masked his thoughts and emotions.

"I was introduced to Dexter at a party thrown for our crew when we won our division championship. We were cel-ebrating. We had beaten our rivals." I smile at Reid, knowing he rowed for Harvard.

"So, I was surrounded by my crew. Eight guys who were like brothers to me and protected me like I was their sister. There's no way anyone touches me with these guys around. There was nothing that had my guard standing at attention. No gut feeling that I wasn't listening to. I was stuck in the land of 'this would never happen to me.' So I didn't pay at-tention to the signs. I didn't look for red flags. I never knew it was coming.

"I started the night off with a drink that I got from the kitchen on my own. I was underage. Only twenty at the time. I wasn't a heavy drinker. My girls and I had heard all the cautionary tales. We had a rule that we always attended par-ties with a girlfriend, and we had a pact to make sure we left together. Since I was with my crew, I didn't think that was necessary, but I still had my roommate Gabby there. It was an unspoken standard that we had each other's back.

"Dexter took the seat next to me and we talked for a while about a professor we both were taking that semester. We laughed about the same movies, liked the same songs. We were having fun.

"He asked me to dance. He was cute. Preppy. Looked just like the kind of boy you would take home to meet your parents. He was polite. He didn't cuss. He disengaged Gabby from talking to a guy he didn't think was someone she need- ed to be hanging with. He was the perfect gentleman.

"So we danced, laughed, and then we moved on to talk to other people. Eventually he worked his way back to me and we danced some more. When we came off the dance floor, he grabbed me a bottled water and then he grabbed some of the punch they were serving. He handed me my water. Mind you, I had a rule not to accept drinks from anyone outside of my inner circle of trust. But, like I said, he had proved to be a gentleman thus far. So, when he handed me my water, but stopped and opened it for me first, I never thought anything about it. I mean, in my mind that was the equivalent of pull- ing my chair out for me or holding my door open.

"He asked me to dance again. He maneuvered me to the other side of the room where the front door was. I told him I didn't feel right and that I needed some air. He followed me outside. And before I was in control of what was happening, he was carrying me to his apartment.

"I woke up some time later with him on top of me. Raping me. I was awake but my body wouldn't respond. My arms wouldn't move. My feet wouldn't move. I passed out again. Some time later I awoke again. He was passed out. I turned on my side and attempted to crawl off the bed. I fell when I tried to stand, waking Dexter in the process, who returned me to his bed. When I woke the third time, he was raping me again, only this time I had full usage of my body and voice again and I attempted to fight. He bound me to his bed and raped me for two more hours. He never hit or punched me, but he kept calling me a slut. Told me how much I was enjoying it. Told me how much he was enjoying it.

"When the sun came up, he untied me and asked me to leave so he could get some rest. I was in shock. It was like my mind could not process anything after that. I don't remember how I got back to my room. I don't remember telling Gabby what happened. I don't remember asking to be taken to a hospital. I remember nothing until I arrived in the emergency room.

"There was a nurse who talked to me. I thought about how much she reminded me of my mother. A mother I was going to have to call to tell her her daughter had been raped. She held my hand and gave me the most precious gift anyone could have given me: she believed me. She didn't judge me. She encouraged me to be strong and to find my voice.

"Unfortunately, that advice only got me so far. See, the system is broken. Once I admitted that I was raped, I had to be transferred to another hospital that was equipped with personnel certified to perform a rape kit. This process takes multiple hours and is very invasive. Most victims have described it as the rape after the rape. My body was processed for DNA and evidence. I was photographed. I had bruising on the front and back of my thighs, as well as visible handprints on my pelvis, torso, neck, and face from where he covered my mouth."

The auditorium is completely silent. I look to Reid to

make sure he's okay. I have experience sharing this story, so I understand it is difficult to hear. His eyes are glued to mine. "Okay?" I ask him, and he nods for me to continue. His eyes are damp but fierce.

I turn back to the students. "The police were called and I was questioned by two detectives. Both male. I was never told I could have a victim's advocate present. I thought, who better to tell what happened to me than me. Right?

"I was questioned for more than four hours. At one point a detective asked me if I had a boyfriend. When I told him no, he said that sometimes girls cheat on their boyfriends and don't want to tell them, so they claim they were raped. He felt like it was worth clarifying.

"I was finally released and sent home. I was told later that week that they had interviewed Dexter, and he admitted to having sex with me but claimed it was consensual. They interviewed people at the party, including my crew, and no one saw me in distress at any time. Mind you, my crew believed me when they found out what had happened, but the truth was, they didn't see me in distress. There was nothing that drew their attention.

"It was weeks later that I was told the DA chose not to take my case to the grand jury. They didn't feel like there was enough evidence. There was too much he said/she said involved. It was the first time I realized that they are not there to represent and protect me. They are there to represent and protect the state. One of the ways they protect the state is by not wasting tax-payers' money taking cases to the grand jury that are not a slam dunk.

"I took my case to the University. They investigated, they had hearings, but in the end they felt that, even with the DNA evidence and pictures from the rape kit, there wasn't enough evidence to expel Dexter. Like the state, I find universities act in their best interest and not the interest of the person who was violated. They don't advise you to tell your parents. Their goal is to handle it internally and as quietly as possible.

"So, now that I have told you about my experience, let's talk about some takeaways." I stand.

"First and foremost, the message I need for you to hear is I was not raped because I was drinking underage. I was not raped because I was at a party. I was not raped because I was bumping and grinding with a guy on the dance floor. I was not raped because I was in an outfit that was too short, too tight, or too revealing. I was not raped because my friends weren't there to save me. I was not raped because of my social or economic status. I was not raped because I missed the signs. I was raped because Dexter chose to rape me. He participated in a sexual act with me without my consent.

"The second message is to set a plan in place before you need it. I had a plan and it still happened to me. A plan doesn't make you untouchable, but it can save you from many situations.

"And lastly, if this happens to you or has already happened to you, I would encourage you not to go it alone. Tell someone. I was fortunate that I have best friends who were with me every step of the way, who encouraged me to tell my family, to get counseling, and eventually to share my story. Some of you have already walked this path, some of you will walk this path. Some of you will be put in a position to go against your friend or loved one and call them out for harming you. One day, some of you might be in a position to influence change. Whatever your story is, I wish nothing but the best for you."

I turn to Tracey to let her know that I am done, and she

joins me on stage.

"Would you mind taking some questions?" she asks me.

"Sure. I don't mind."

"There are mics at the end of each aisle. Does anyone have a question?"

A girl from the back comes forward. "Do you regret reporting your rape?"

"No, I don't. But that's a good question. It is not uncommon for people to regret reporting it. Since the burden of proof is mostly on the victim, it can be very daunting and traumatic for people to report their rape. In fact, several rape advocates worry it's too damaging to the victim, and therefore they wouldn't encourage it.

A boy comes forward. "Did your friends and family ever want to do something to get even?"

"Honestly, yes. It is unbelievably difficult on everyone. Parents struggle because they are wired to protect us. Like I said, I was the only girl in a nine-person crew. I was surrounded by guys who wanted nothing more than to avenge what happened to me. I've had the same best friend since I was five. He's a guy. It was very difficult for him to watch what I was going through. My roommate Gabby struggled for a long time with feeling like she had let me down. The best I can tell you is time heals you. Therapy heals you. The people you love heal you. For me, my faith played a huge role in healing me. Also, I am hard-headed. There was no way I was giving Dexter control over my life. I wasn't going to be scared of him on campus. I wasn't going to not attend my graduation because of him. But, that worked for me. It doesn't everyone. Some victims aren't able to leave their house. There is no wrong or right way to handle it. Each victim does the best they can do. There are still times when I feel scared or anxious, but I've been given tools by people smarter than me to use, and they have worked."

"What happened to Dexter?" a kid in the back asks.

"Nothing. I filed a civil suit against him that is still pending. I don't expect anything to come of the suit, but it's on the books and anyone looking would see it. For me, it's more about doing what I can to make sure it's harder for him to do it the next time."

I answer a few more questions before the students stand and applaud. When I come off the stage, I go directly to Reid and wrap my arms around him. He places a chaste kiss to my lips then bends to whisper in my ear.

"I think you are amazing, Dove."

When the students are dismissed, Tracey sees us out and we walk through the parking lot to our SUV.

"Miss Donovan?" I turn to match the sweet voice with a young student.

"Yes. What can I do for you?"

"I was wondering if you would mind me emailing you sometime. I have class so I can't talk now."

I offer her my hand, and Reid discreetly takes a few steps back. "If you would like to talk to me right now I have time."

"Like I said, I have class and I'm not sure how ready I am to talk."

I grab a business card out of my wallet and hand it to her. "This has my email and my personal cell on it. Call me anytime. Day or night."

She starts to tell me her name, but I stop her. "How old are you?" I ask.

"Seventeen."

"Still a minor. Don't tell me your name. I can't promise you that I wouldn't report it. You can call the crisis hotline if you want to remain completely anonymous."

She nods but doesn't say anything. I place a hand on her arm and pull her gaze back to me. "I do hope you will reach out to me or someone you feel safe with."

"Thank you." She motions to the business card and walks back to the building.

Reid is waiting for me when I turn the corner of our SUV, and before I can do anything, he claims my mouth in a kiss so passionate and desperate it takes my breath away. When he finally stops long enough to catch his breath, my cheeks are wet.

"Thank you," I whisper.

"For what?" His thumbs wipe away my tears.

"For not letting him win. You haven't done anything to me that I haven't loved and wanted more of. I don't want to be treated like glass. I want sex with you to be about me and you. Not censored because of what happened to me seven years ago."

"That's easier said than done," he confesses. As desperate as I am for him not to change his ways with me, I understand I need to be patient and give him time to catch up. He's only known for a couple of hours. I've had seven years to get where I am today. Pulling his mouth to mine, I attempt to ignite a desire within him.

He pulls away. "Fuck. In the car."

He helps me up to my seat before climbing into the driver's side. Without a word he drives us back downtown and pulls up outside of The Four Seasons. Tossing the keys to the attendant he walks with my hand in his to the front desk and offers a black credit card to the girl behind the desk.

"Is your Presidential suite available?" he asks her.

"Yes, sir." She motions for the manager who comes over.

"Mr. Beckett. We appreciate you staying with us."

"Sorry. We're in a bit of a hurry. Can you give us the key and I'll sign everything later? You can hang on to my card," Reid tells the man, who colors slightly at his imperiousness.

"Of course. James here will show you to your room."

"We'll be fine on our own. Thank you." He dismisses the man, grabs the key, and practically drags me to the elevator. We ride in silence, then exit onto our floor. Our room is the only one on this level. In a sudden motion, he bends down and lifts me caveman-style over his shoulder.

"What the…" I start to say but am cut off by a sharp crack over my behind. Reid holds the card against the lock, glides through the door, and secures it behind us before he marches into the master suite and deposits me on the floor.

"Strip," he orders as he quickly removes his suit and underwear. His arousal is flagrantly on display. I lick then bite my lip.

"Christ, Elise. Do that again and this is going to be over before either of us wants it to be." He grabs me by the sides of my face and pulls me to him with a growl. He consumes me with a kiss, stopping only long enough to toss me onto the middle of the bed before picking up where he left off.

I reach between us and feel the wetness at the head of his cock. Spreading it with my thumb, he flexes his hips into my hold. Sinking two fingers in me he finds me ready and a second later he is inside me. It's only then does he calm down, like he has found his balance.

His eyes glued to mine, he begins the slow methodical movement that tortures me. Tortures me into thirsting for him. I wrap my legs around his waist. His body summons mine. With my hands grasping his forearms and his name on my lips, he thrusts me into an orgasm driven by intent, need, and desperation. Our connection is powerful, and I hold the gaze of his dark and smoky green eyes.

"Reid."

"Tell me what you need."

"I need this."

"Elise."

"I'm okay." I kiss him gently.

"I'm not," he admits, his forehead against mine. He's still inside of me, but he doesn't move. I pull him down on me and cocoon him in my arms and legs. I thread my fingers through his hair until I hear his even breathing. I know he has drifted off. Only then do I give in and rest my eyes.

Purple and orange light come dimly through the window, and there is electricity running through my body.

"Reid," I moan, grabbing a fistful of his hair. His head is between my legs making a meal of me. He's back, and the message he is sending by waking me from my sleep with sex connects exactly with what I need. With a flick of his tongue, I shoot into an orgasm so penetrating I spring into a sitting position. He looks mercilessly into my eyes, and I watch his tongue rolling my clit. A second orgasm pushes me back onto the mattress. He wrings every ounce of pleasure from me, and I beg him to stop. I can't take it. It's too much.

Stalking up my body his wet lips overtake mine. He stops to look at me, and with determination he says, "He doesn't win. He doesn't control us." His tone is fierce and protective.

I gently shake my head. "No. He doesn't."

"Trust me?" he asks.

"I do."

He leaves me on the bed and enters the bathroom. He comes back with a robe tie, a wet cloth and a spa mask. Sitting astride me, he says nothing but shows me the tie. I nod my

consent and he leans down, kissing me fervently before se-
curing it through the headboard above my head.

"I don't want to tie you up. He doesn't win, but I'm not
sure I'm there yet. What I want you to do is to hold on to each
end of this and don't let go unless I say you can. Understood?"
He waits for my confirmation and I wrap my hand around
each end a couple of times to ensure I don't let go. He slides
the face mask over my head. and before he pulls it over my
eyes, he gives me a naughty smirk and bends down to whisper in my ear, "Enjoy, baby. This is us. You and me."

chapter eight

Reid

I sit back and take in the sight of Elise, naked before me. Her arms are tied above her head, and her eyes are covered in a blue silk sleep mask. Her rose lips are full, slightly parted. Her hair is a wild, curled mess. Her breasts are raised and modeled perfectly from the position she is in. Even with my weight on her lap, I can feel her hips moving, asking for more.

Christ, this girl does it for me. How does this happen? A few days ago I was fine. Now I can't have a fucking moment without thinking about her. For someone who didn't know he was lost, I sure as fuck have been found.

"Reid?" she breathes. I lean down and kiss her, so she knows I'm still here, even though it should be evident with my weight straddling her thighs. She attempts to deepen the kiss, but I pull back and drink her in.

I don't know why I acted pissy about her revelation. I'm

not owed her confidence. It wasn't about me, but I was so blindsided by what she has experienced that I didn't handle it the way I wanted to. The way I should have. I was torn. I should have been just listening to this woman I am falling in love with talk about how she overcame a horrible experience. But I also wanted to avenge her. But listening to her tell her story, I made myself a vow that no one would ever harm her again. I see Elise without her even realizing it. Strong. Always giving to others. Taking a horrific story and telling it over and over again in hopes that one person won't have to experience what she went through. In hopes she can save just one.

I know if I don't put this in a box on a shelf somewhere inside of me, it will make me crazy. I don't know how Theo survived actually living through it with her. It wouldn't surprise me to find out this man died an unfortunate death that was made to look like an accident. I know my friend, and despite the fact that Elise would argue she knows him better, I know he's like every other man whose mate has been wronged. There's a side that could do unspeakable things if provoked.

I release a deep breath and move back to Elise, who is waiting for me. Leaning forward again, my body comes to rest along the length on hers. I love that she's strong. She isn't going to break. My lips nudge hers apart, and her tongue chases mine as my hands slide up her arms, my fingers intertwining with hers. She deepens the kiss and my hands tighten around hers, clinging to her like she is my lifeline. Her hips begin to undulate against mine. She whimpers, frustrated that she can't reach my dick. It brings a stupid smile to my face.

"So eager," I chastise.

"Fuck you and your smile," she growls knowingly, even though she can't see me.

Her legs wrap around me, and I can feel the wetness between her thighs running down her pussy as she continues to rub against my body. I find strength I didn't know I had and force myself to stay in this position, my dick just out of her reach. Propping myself up on my hands, my body tightens to hers. My mouth maps her body, nipping and sucking my way across her jawline, down her neck, over her shoulder and landing in the curve of her armpit before moving down to her side. I apply enough suction to leave my mark before moving to her rose-colored nipples. Her body writhes against mine. I watch her hips move, mesmerized by her pleasure. Moving back to her breasts, I bite her nipples pushing her over the edge. She convulses in an orgasm. I push back and my mouth suctions over her pussy, siphoning her juices from her. The feel of my mouth and tongue on her extends her orgasm, and I feel her body shudder when it's too much.

"Oh, Elise. You came." I tut my tongue against the roof of my mouth, feigning disapproval. In one quick motion, I turn her on her stomach and lift her ass into the air. My hand connecting with it, leaving a red outline of my print on her left cheek. She moans her appreciation.

I lean my body over hers and kiss my way down her spine, my fingers following my tongue's trail. I reach the small of her back. The place where my hand naturally guides her. Where it comes to rest when I slide just the tips of my fingers inside her waist band. Where my hand rests when we sleep. She fits my hand perfectly. I spend a few minutes here and pay my respects to this part of her body that allows me to tell others she is mine.

My lips soothe the still reddened handprint before kissing the top of her crack. Resting a hand on each globe of her ass, I part them slightly revealing a puckered rosette of skin.

Without hesitation, I run my tongue down the crevice circling my target. My hands move to Elise's hips to pull her onto my mouth as she tries to pull away slightly, like she isn't sure.

"Every part of you, Elise. I want it all," I assure her before I devour her, tongue fucking her ass. She moans my name and pushes back against me, wanting more. Ignoring my wet and hard-as-nails cock, I kiss my way down as I position myself on my back under her before lowering her hips above my mouth. She's dripping wet, and I can feel her body quake as my hands guide her back and forth over my face.

"Reid," she begs, blending need and desire. My cock twitches at her voice. "Fuck!" she cries out and takes control of her movements, riding my face when my fingers enter her from behind. My free hand slaps her ass again, causing an orgasm to ripple through her.

"Oh my God," she whimpers as her body slowly shudders to a stop. I lift her weight off of my face and position myself behind her. I drip a healthy amount of baby oil on my cock, catching my breath as my body adjusts. I release another deep breath, as I slick the oil over my length. Once I'm covered, I dribble oil on Elise's backside and run my fingers down her crack.

I lean over her, my dick resting against her ass, my hands on each side of her shoulders supporting my weight. I kiss the sweet spot behind her ear.

"I want all of you, Elise, but the power is yours and I will always respect what you want."

"I want all of you, Reid." She turns her chin towards my voice, her lips searching for mine. I give her what she wants, sliding two fingers into her tightness, preparing her. My tongue glides against hers and I add a third finger, kissing her harder when she whimpers slightly. Once I think she's ready,

I shift back onto my knees and run my dick up and down her crack, teasing the head against her entrance.

"Reid." The need in her voice is inviting.

She whimpers softly when I enter her just enough to be inside her, letting her acclimate.

"I'm going to ease in. Push out when I do." I run my hand over her backside, gradually working my way in and out until I'm seated against her delectable ass. She clinches around me.

"Fuck. You gotta stop that, Dove, or I'm going to blow. I want this to last." I slap her ass before pulling back to the tip and thrusting back into her.

"Fuck me, Reid," she moans and pushes back on me, wanting more. I give her exactly what she wants.

"I love taking you from behind," I grunt between clenched teeth. I run my hands over her hips. "The shape of you from your waist to your hips to your ass." I move in and out of her faster and faster. "There's no one sexier than you. The things I want to do to you. Every inch of you is mine." I leave another red handprint on her ass, and I feel her body begin to tremble. "You like that?" I move to the other cheek and rain three slaps in quick succession. It sends her over the edge. She yells my name and clamps down on my dick, setting off a rush of heat as I still and spill into her. I give her maybe a millisecond to adjust when I pull out of her and flip her onto her back. Despite my own orgasm, I am still hard. I run the wet cloth over myself and sink balls deep into her heat in one fluid motion.

I slow to a crawl, moving in and out of her. Her hands are still held above her head, and I know her body has to be sore from my less than delicate explorations. I lower myself to my elbows and delve my tongue into her mouth, pouring all of me into my kiss.

"I want to see you," I say, lifting the eye mask off of her. She blinks momentarily, adjusting to the soft light peeking through the windows as night sets in. Her eyes settle on mine.

"You're beautiful," she tells me.

"I swear whenever you look at me like that I feel like a fucking god who could conquer the world."

She pulls her head up silently asking for my kiss again.

"Reid." She says my name so simply, but with so much meaning. "Thank you."

"For?"

"Fucking me like you did before you found out."

"The pleasure was all mine." I kiss her before adding, "And watch your language."

"Are you going to spank me again?" she teases.

"No. I just want to make love to you." My voice is low and tentative. My eyes lock on hers to gauge her response to my words. She says nothing, but a lone tear falls down her temple to the bed below. I increase the pace and pressure as I make love to the woman I am certain I am in love with. Her eyes open when I command them to stay on me as her orgasm rips through her, pulling from me the most intense experience I've ever had.

I reach up and release her from the robe tie before rolling onto my back, pulling her on top of me. She moans in appreciation as I attempt to massage some feeling back into her arms. Her eyes droop heavily, and I feel her breathing evening out.

"Sleep, sweetheart." I kiss her forehead, concentrating on matching my breaths with hers.

When I wake on my stomach, I'm burning up. Elise is suction-cupped to my body, and I appear to own only a small territory of land on this mattress. My smile at the thought is cut short when I hear Elise whimper. I try to roll us to the center of the bed, causing Elise to tighten her hold. She burrows into me, and I hear a slight whimper again.

I kiss her forehead and lift her face to mine. She is asleep, but her eyelashes are damp. Shit, she's crying.

"Elise? Dove, are you ok?" When she doesn't wake, I try with a little more force to pull her from her sleep. She cries out softly, and her eyes fly open when I shake her shoulders for a second time. They are confused. Uncertain. Scared. "Dove?"

Her hand cups my jaw and she lightly kisses my lips. "Are you okay, baby? Do you need something?" she asks me.

"You were crying in your sleep."

"I'm okay. Usually when I tell my personal story, I dream bits and pieces of it that night. Sometimes for a few nights. I'm okay, Reid. Just my mind and body processing."

She's consoling me, and my heart cracks wide open for this girl.

"Elise." I roll on top of her, and she wraps her arms around my back. Her face is soft and sleepy. I run my thumb across her cheek. "Find your comfort in me, Dove."

There's a small, questioning dip to her brow. Her hands slide up my back and neck, coming to rest on my face.

"I am okay, Reid. I've worked really hard to be, and I don't want you to see me as a victim."

"No," I answer, my eyes locked on hers. "Never a victim. Survivor? Yes. You are. You are so strong."

She leans up and kisses me like I am loved.

"Will you tell me about it?" I ask.

She shakes her head. "No one needs that floating around in their head."

"Will you?" I ask again. She rolls us over and I prop myself up against the headboard. She runs her hand down my cock. I'm hard for her in an instant. She straddles me and lowers herself onto my dick inch by agonizing inch. When my hips reflexively push into her, she slows me down with a kiss.

"Not here. Not like this." She rotates her hips once. "This is you and me, Reid. No one else has a place here." She leans forward, bites my Adam's apple, and rides me like I've never been ridden before. I want to make this last, but the intensity of her eyes locked on mine as she takes her pleasure from me is too much.

"Dove," I gasp. Everything within me tightens. The electricity skates over my skin, and I know she will wear bruises on her hips from my unyielding grip as I explode into her. My orgasm tears through me and for a minute I think I'm going to be ripped in two.

"Fucking-fuck," I blurt out.

Elise laughs as she comes.

"Laughter. Really?" I give her a hard slap on the ass. She has the grace to look regretful when she leans forward and captures my lips with hers. While I'm still inside her and we are face-to-face, I figure now is as good of time as any to tell her.

"Elise, I want more. I don't want this to be a one-week hookup on a work trip. I know technically I will be your boss, but I'd really like to continue seeing you after this week."

"Technically? You *will* be my boss. There is no technically about it."

"So, this is a problem for you?"

She makes a move to get off of me, to gain some distance, but I don't allow it. No running.

"None of this has been very smart, Reid. Are you sure you want to take this to New York with us? What will happen when we're done? Where will that leave me? Out of a job?"

Her comments put me on edge, and I can feel myself bristling. I sit up straighter and taller so there is no confusion of the control I want, feel, and need.

"When we're done?" There's an edge in my voice.

"Have you ever had a relationship that didn't end?"

I want to say, *No, but I've never been in love before.* But I don't. It would send her running for the hills. So I settle for, "I want to explore more with you, Elise. I was hoping you would want the same."

"I want that, too. I do. But you have nothing to lose. The company will still be yours. I will be the one without a job if this doesn't work out. Do you know how scary that is in today's economy?"

"You have my word, Dove. I will make sure you always have a job." My thumbs run over her nipples, and reflexively she bows her back and pushes down onto me.

"Think about it." I end the conversation by rolling her onto her back.

We had a naked picnic of room service on the bed before I made love to her one last time. I let her sleep as long as I could, but I knew she wanted to be back before daybreak, so we had to get on the road. I thought we might talk some on the drive, but Elise fell asleep about fifteen minutes outside of the city and didn't wake when I stopped for gas. It's almost 3 a.m., and I am ready to be in bed, asleep next to OctoElise. I shake the goofy smile off my face and finally pull off onto our road. I park and come around to her door.

"Dove? We're here."

When she doesn't stir, I lift her into my arms and make my way inside. I shift her slightly to reach for the door handle when it opens. Theo is standing there. He looks pissed, but his countenance immediately softens when he looks at Elise. I carry her inside. His face darkens when I take Elise into my room and put her in my bed.

I remove her jeans and pull the covers over her before kissing her forehead. *Might as well get this over with.* I turn to head to the living room to have the talk with Theo, only to find him standing in the doorway watching me. His expression is threatening.

"Now," he says before turning and heading into the kitchen. I follow, steeling myself for my friend's discord.

We face each other for a couple of minutes, him trying to control his temper, me trying to decide if this will go easier if I let him start first.

Fuck it. I'll start.

"Theo."

"What the fuck are you playing at, man?"

Okay, he'll start.

"Elise is the real deal. The whole package. She isn't some girl you pick up in a titty bar and fuck for your amusement."

Yep. This is going to get ugly.

"You know, fuck off, Theo. I know you are upset, man. I understand. Really I do. But this isn't a hook-up for me. You are one of my closest friends and I respect you, but I'm not going to walk away from this because you don't like it. I want Elise. I'm not giving her up. I...I love her, Theo."

He straightens up, and I swear he's gotten three inches taller since we walked into the kitchen. "You sure as fuck better decide what love means to you. 'Cause if you make her cry..."

"She's a big girl who knows what she is getting into. We both have been very clear with each other."

"Yeah? Well, let me be clear about something." He takes a step closer to me. "You are one of my best friends and soon to be my business partner. Make sure you know what the hell you are doing, because if this goes south, I choose Elise."

I nod and release the breath I was holding. As far as confrontations with one of your nearest and dearest goes, it could have been worse. Theo steps to the side to move past me. His shoulder pushes into mine.

"Also, to be clear, Elise isn't yours to not give up," he says coolly. "She's mine and will be until I entrust her to someone. It's yet to be determined if that someone is you."

chapter nine

Elise

The room is dark, so it takes me a full minute to get my bearings. I remember we drove home late last night. Reid is asleep on his stomach next to me. I watch him, thinking about our day together yesterday. I've never dated someone who responded like this to what happened to me. His fierce reaction was matched only by those closest to me at the time. I had told Robert about it, and his reaction was to ask me if I was looking to be raped again when he saw me dressed to go out with some friends. Reid's response was much more understanding.

I rest my head on his bicep, drape a leg across the back of his, and take him in. His smell, the way his skin feels, the heat his body gives off. His dark curls. Everything about this man calls to me, and it is terrifying. I have never felt this for anyone. Exhaling deeply, I close my eyes and try not to freak out. I rub my hand across his back and it comes to rest on his shoulder. I feel the pull that automatically calms my spirit. He stirs and turns his head to face me, but he doesn't move.

"I love feeling you wrapped around me."

His voice is deep and gravelly with sleep. His green eyes are steady and don't hide from me. I run my fingers through his hair; he shifts slightly and kisses my nose.

"Theo knows."

The minute his comment sinks in, I sit straight up in the bed.

"What do you mean Theo knows? How do you know he knows?" My question is harsher than I intend, but I don't know if I am ready for Theo to know. I'm just now coming to terms that this is more than a crazy hookup. Reid sits up and looks at me. It's clear he is not pleased with the accusation he hears in my tone.

"He was here when we got home. You were asleep, so I carried you inside. I could have gone right to his room or left to mine. I went left."

"How could you do that?"

"How could I do what?"

I was right. He is not pleased.

"How could you make the decision about when we tell Theo."

"He's one of my closest friends, and I am about to buy controlling interest in his company."

I shift onto my knees.

"But he's *my* Theo. You didn't have the right to tell him. You should have asked me first."

"You wanted me to *hide* what is happening between us?" The disbelief in his voice is almost my undoing.

"For a little while, yes."

He starts to say something, but he just shakes his head

and stands to pull on some shorts. My body immediately feels the pull to his, and I feel a dampness between my legs.

"Don't fucking look at me like that, Elise."

"Reid."

"I can't get women to keep their mouths closed, and the one woman I want to lay claim to doesn't want it public. Fanfuckingtastic."

His movements are sharp. He's sitting with his back to me, and I can feel the tension in his shoulders. He ties his shoes with such force, I'm surprised the laces didn't snap.

"Reid, just take a minute to see this from my perspective. Theo is my heart. He deserved to hear this from me first. And no, I don't want it out there. You're a man. You don't understand. When a man sleeps with his boss, he's given a promotion. When a woman does it, she's sleeping her way to the top. She's a slut. There is more at risk here for me—"

"Just stop, Elise. I know you felt it yesterday. I just… I just thought you were braver than this. My mistake."

I know the words from someone I met less than five days ago shouldn't have the power to slice through me, but his words cut to a place I thought I had encased in steel. My breath escapes me, and his eyes reflect regret, but no other part of him backs down. Without another word, he leaves. I sit in the wake of his anger, not really knowing what to do with it or how to feel about it.

Time to face the music.

A walk from one side of the chalet to the other has never felt so long. Theo doesn't have the blinds closed, so this room is filled with light compared to the dark one I just left. Fitting, I muse as I slide under the covers. Without opening his eyes, he lifts his arm for me to come to a rest against his body like I have so many times in my life. When I've settled and my arm rests across his torso, he wraps his arms around me.

"I'm sorry you heard it from Reid before me."

"I'm sorry about the Bowens case. They're family and I didn't know how to say no. I didn't want to believe it was true."

"I'm sorry it was."

"The more I do this shit, the more I realize I am making the right decision selling to Reid."

"I know you are."

"I was mad at you last night." He pauses. "When Reid took you to his room and I realized what was going on between you two, I thought I would kill him."

"Theo."

"But then I called Ross," he says quickly. "He reminded me what a great guy Reid is and how he has never let me down or disappointed me before. He said maybe I could take a step back and see that he is someone I would trust with you. Someone I would be okay giving you to."

"It's been less than a week. I don't think we are talking about giving me to anyone."

"Did you tell him about your history?"

"Yes."

"And?"

"And, he was really great about it. I think it was a shock for him at first, but once he had a minute to absorb it, he was all in."

"That's good right?"

"It is. Better than Robert who basically said I deserve to get attacked when he didn't like what I was wearing." I cringe that I let that slip. Theo's body tenses up.

"Yes, well, that is better." He grinds out and I breathe a sigh of relief that he is going to skate pass that one.

I can remember being seven and sneaking out to Theo's house. We would talk and share secrets, or just listen to music. We would lay then like we are now. It was our ritual. My parents weren't crazy about me sleeping in the same bed with a guy, but they grew tired of grounding me. Eventually our parents stopped fighting it. I think they knew we were friends at heart and were never going to have romantic feelings for each other. Theo has always been my rock, and my parents grew to value him for that.

"I think I messed up with Reid."

"Not possible, babe. If anyone is going to mess up it would be Reid."

I sit up and look at him. "No, it was me. I got upset that he told you before I had the chance to, and then I basically said I didn't want anyone to know."

"Now or always?" He sits up.

"Now. It's just a lot, you know? And I know guys don't think this is true, but it's harder for girls in the business world. We are measured not only by how we perform, but how we function outside of work. And forget it if you want to embrace your sexuality *and* be good at what you do. It only takes one rumor to ruin my career. I just need a minute to think about that and make sure I am ready for that to be a consequence."

"Maybe this will be the best thing you ever did. Maybe this was all meant to be. Me selling. You meeting Reid."

"That's some pretty big maybes, and I live in the real world. The odds of this working are not great. Reid is an admitted player who doesn't commit and I am...well, I'm me and all that entails."

"I love all that entails." He reaches out and grazes just the right spot under my chin that tickles and makes me laugh.

"Theo," I warn him.

"Elise," he sings, watching me as if I'm prey. As soon as I make a move, he uncoils and wrestles himself on top of me, tickling me with no mercy. I try to turn the tables on him and get to his ticklish spots, but he's stronger than I am. It only takes one move for him to capture my wrists and hold them above my head in one hand while the other continues to torture me.

"I am going to pee all over you."

He bends to kiss my nose. "Wouldn't be the first time and won't be the last."

"Please don't pee in the bed. I would like to take a nap, and I don't want to do it in a puddle of urine." We hear a familiar voice.

Through my tears of laughter, I see a vision propped up against the door frame. I catch my breath long enough to say, "Ross! What are you doing here? Save me!"

"I wanted to be here when you guys tell the team today. Theo, let her go. Deep, dark, and broody over here is about to pummel your ass." Ross nods his head at Reid, who is standing in the doorway with him dripping in sweat. He must have gone for a run.

"I don't know how you put up with it," Reid says to Ross.

"I know my man's heart. He's a better man because of his love for Elise. And when I catch him on top of her," he looks to Reid, "I remind myself that my man loves dick."

"Not just any dick." Theo stands and pulls Ross into a hot kiss. "Only yours."

"Fuck yeah," Ross growls. He grabs Theo's face and kisses him like a man possessed.

"Elise." Reid gestures for us to leave the room.

"Are you serious? This is like gay porn. I could sell tickets to Fran and Gabby."

"Elise, get the fuck out," Ross growls again, pulling Theo's shirt over his head.

"Fine," I giggle. Reid grabs me under my arm and pulls me out of the room. We enter the living area and I stop. I meet his eyes.

"I'm sorry if I hurt you earlier."

Before he can answer, he's interrupted by a loud thump from the bedroom. It sounds like someone's trying to tear a wall down. We both look back in the direction of the bedroom when front door opens. Blake, Gabby, and Fran enter with Ryan following behind.

"We brought muffins and cards," Fran says.

There are several more loud thumps, and Reid's lip twitches.

"What the hell are they doing in there?"

"I *know* I don't have to explain it to you of all people."

We make our way to the kitchen, and Reid pours us each a glass of milk while I pick through the muffins.

"Thanks for bringing breakfast," Reid says to Fran.

"No problem," Gabby says, reaching for an orange. "I know how you love a good muffin." I have to hold in a laugh. Reid gives us both the side eye before putting the milk back in the fridge.

"What kind do you want?" I lift the box for him to choose.

"I'll just take a bite out of yours."

I look around to make sure we're alone.

"Mine has crème in the middle."

"Even better." He leans towards me and runs his tongue along my jaw line.

"Blueberry."

"What?" he asks, pulling himself away.

"You get blueberry." I put one on a plate and hand it to him before picking up my milk and heading to the outside deck. It's a beautiful morning.

"So, what's the plan for today boss?" Blake asks, shuffling a deck of cards. Reid comes out and takes a seat across from me.

"I'd like to have a low-key day. The rest of the team is with Owen. We've wrapped up the emergencies, and I'd like to go over a couple of things, do some brainstorming."

Ryan takes a seat next to Fran, and his eyes bug out with an 'I don't think so' look when she announces that she can take 6 sets. Fran, Gabby, Blake, and I are starting another game of spades.

"So, if you could have dinner with one person, who would it be?" Fran asks while rearranging her cards.

"Carol Burnett," I answer.

"Oh, good one," Gabby says. "I like that. I think that's the dinner I'll go to."

"You can't choose someone else's dinner," Blake tells her.

"Why not?"

"'Cause it's not yours."

Shrugging, I say, "I don't mind if she comes to my dinner. Gabby makes for good conversation. I imagine Carol Burnett would enjoy us as much as we enjoy her."

"That's not how this works," Blake continues.

"Oooo, think she would yodel for us?" Fran asks, laying her next card down.

"Now you're going?" Blake shakes his head in frustration.

"Can I borrow your pink sparkle heels for the dinner?" Gabby asks Fran. "I think they will go great with the dress I would wear."

"To where?" Ryan asks.

"To the dinner with Carol Burnett."

"You know it's pretend, right?"

"You have no vision, Ryan."

"What happened with the guy you met at the bar last night?" Blake asks Fran.

"Ugh. I'm flypaper for freaks." She shakes her head in frustration.

"Too many freaks, not enough circuses." Ross joins us on the deck with a chocolate muffin on a plate and a cup of coffee.

"What did I tell you about talking in t-shirt quotes?" Theo warns, taking the seat next to him looking more than pleased with himself. Reid and I both chuckle at the same time. Theo raises his eyebrow at us.

"Elise, I almost forgot. The girls dragged me into town yesterday, and I saw this and thought of you." Blake pulls a plastic phone case out his back pocket. I reach for it and turn it over. It has red, white, and blue bomb pops on the back of it.

"Blake."

"Why are you looking at me like that?" He has a shit-eating grin on his face.

"Yes, Elise," Ross says. "Why are you looking at him like that?"

"No reason."

"Spill," Ross says to Blake. I have to admit, Ross has one of the best profiles I've ever seen. The man is ruggedly handsome and always sports what looks like a three-day beard. His hair goes in a hundred directions, but it works for him.

"Blake," I warn before I throw my next card.

"Alright, now I'm intrigued," Ryan says. "What does

Blake know that I don't?"

"I'll be right back." Blake hands his cards to Ryan, who of course shows them to Fran. "I saw that," he says, returning to the deck. He takes his seat and sets something covered in white paper in front of me. I reach for it, and as soon as I feel the cold, I know what it is. Blake cannot contain his joy.

"How long have you been waiting for this?" Theo asks, shaking his head. He already knows where this is going.

"It's melting, Elise." Blake's eyes never leave mine. Mine cut over to Reid, who has silently been watching this entire interaction. "I never pictured you to be a scaredy cat."

"I'm not easily baited by ridiculous taunts," I reply.

"No, but you're not one to back down from a challenge either, are you?"

"It's not going to work, Blake."

"What are you hiding, Elise? What is she hiding?" Ross asks. Theo only shrugs.

"No secrets. Ever. You swore it on our wedding day."

"That's not gonna work on me, Jacobs," Theo grins.

"It's not anything to be embarrassed about," Blake says.

"Oh, for crying out loud. I'm not embarrassed."

"Then why don't—"

"Fine," I snap.

Blake shuffles the deck and begins, "Elise and I were at Navy Pier this summer. And it was what? 100 degrees?" He looks to me and shuffles again. "Anyway, there was a vendor selling popsicles, so we each got one and did some people watching while we ate. But it was hot, so what do you think happened?"

"It melted," Gabby interjects.

"It did. So, I'm people watching and the next thing I know I hear three guys sitting across from us all groan so loud that

I have to look over and see them looking at my boss," he looks at me and winks, "who is deep throating a bomb pop."

"Blake." Theo rolls his eyes.

"I kid you not. The *entire* thing was in her mouth."

"I don't believe you," Gabby says. "There's no way I didn't know Elise has this talent."

"More than 37% of the population don't have a gag reflex," Ross offers.

"Thank you, Dr. Jacobs," Theo says.

"I won't believe it unless you show me," Fran says to me.

"Not gonna happen."

"Sophomore year. Billy Buckman."

This is the only thing she could have said to get me to do it, and Gabby knows it. It's a story only the two of us share, and I have given her the right to say it five times in our life. When she does, I have to give her what she wants.

"You want to use a Billy Buckman on this?"

"Yep," she says with a pop of her lips.

"Who's Billy Buckman?" Ross looks at Theo, and I see Reid doing the same.

"I honestly have no idea."

"This I gotta hear then. If my husband doesn't even know, it must be a story."

"Tell it or lick it Donovan," Gabby says.

"I hate you." I pick up the popsicle and peel back the paper. It's already sticky from sitting in the warm sun. I suck the juice just from the tip before rolling my eyes and shaking my head. I cannot believe I am about to do this. Sober. And for some reason the only thing I can think about is taking Reid down the back of my throat. I'm actually shocked I haven't yet.

"You know this is only, what, six inches? I'd hardly call

that amazing," I tell Blake before I push the bomb pop to the back of my throat and close my lips around the popsicle stick. I lift up both of my hands and wiggle my fingers for show.

"Jesus," Blake says, when I swallow the juice that has melted and Theo slaps the back of his head.

"Don't make me fire your ass."

"You don't have anything to worry about, Boss Daddy. I about killed three men myself that day."

I look at Reid, and the heat in his eyes sends a charge to the bottom of my stomach.

"While we have you here," Theo drags my attention to him, and I know he's about to change the subject. Ross slides his hand in Theo's. "I wanted to tell the four of you before we tell the rest of the team. Jacobs Inc. will be expanding."

"You finally made Elise a partner!" Fran squeals.

"No," Theo replies.

The silence that follows is a bit awkward, and I feel the need to bail Theo out.

"I've told you guys more than once I have never wanted to be partner. Theo is only abiding by my wishes. You were saying?" I throw it back to Theo.

"I am taking the business to a global level, and we will be expanding into new markets. But it will be with me as President of the company and Reid as CEO."

"What does that mean?" Fran asks.

"I have sold Reid control of Jacobs Inc."

No one says anything for a few minutes. Theo and I give them the time to let it sink in.

"So what does this mean for us?" Blake asks.

"It will mean very little for most of you," Reid answers. "You will still work directly with Theo and Elise like you do now. For the most part, I will be a silent owner, only entering into the picture when it's what's best for all. We will be expanding the business of taking over failing corporations. Similar to what Elise has been working on the last six weeks."

"Alright." Ryan steps up to the plate first. I always know he will be the one to bring the team along and try to put a positive spin on things. "So, this is good. This is a good thing. It gives us more exposure. It's going to open us up to a different group of people and players we would have never had access to before."

"I'd like to think that is true," Reid confirms. "I don't plan on making any staffing changes. In fact, I would like to think that each of your personal teams will see growth as your areas expand."

"So, you'll run the office from New York, or are you moving to Chicago?" Gabby asks.

"I will be staying with the office in Chicago," Theo says. He pauses and looks at me. "Elise will be moving to New York to start the office there."

"What? When? You were gone six weeks and that seemed like forever," Gabby says.

I square my shoulders and just say it. "I move next week."

"You're moving next week and you are just now telling me?" Tears spring to Gabby's eyes.

"I barely had three hours of sleep a night as it was," I explain. "This last job had to have my full attention. I didn't have even a minute to think about what the next steps were going to be, and Theo and I wanted to be together when we told you."

She's shaking her head. She's hurt. I can see it on her face. "I get you not telling the rest of the team, but I can't believe you didn't tell *me*."

"It was my decision," Reid steps in.

"Reid." I'm not about to let him take the heat for this. He needs to build a relationship with these people.

"The sale wasn't finalized until this morning. She would have been in breach of contract if she had told you anything, and I made my legal actions clear if that breach were to occur."

"Talk about trust. Our team is built on trust. Without it, it doesn't work," Blake says.

"Enough." My voice is louder and firmer than I intend. "Enough," I say more softly. "Reid is attempting to take the heat off me. There was no threat of legal action and my contract is with Theo not him. Theo is at a place where he wants to put Ross first. They want to have a family. He shouldn't have to apologize for that."

"He doesn't. I'm not upset with Theo," Gabby responds.

"The decision was mine. My family is in New York…"

"I thought we were your family."

"You know you are Gabriella Jane. It makes sense for me to start the New York office. It's what's best for everyone, and you know it. I wish I could have given you more warning, but it just wasn't in the cards. I will be traveling back and forth, as will Theo. There's no way we can be apart for that long." I smile at him. "I will be meeting with each of you later today to go over what I see as your role moving forward. I expect each of you to step up into a more active leadership role. We will need a replacement for me in Chicago, and I will need strong people to get New York moving along. As you know, when a corporation gets ripe for the picking, we have a finite amount of time to secure it. I will need each of you to be at your very best. Is that understood?"

Crickets.

"Is. That. Understood?"

"Then we better make the best of the time we have left

this week," Ryan says to everyone. "Why don't we take some time to process and all meet back here for a late lunch?" He stands and waits for the others to stand with them. He catches my eye and winks at me.

I watch as they leave and, with the exception of Ryan, none of them make eye contact.

"Well. That could have gone better." I struggle to keep the emotion out of my voice.

"Elise." Theo and Reid say my name at the same time.

"Theo, I'd like to see you in our room please." Ross stands and waits for him.

"I'll be there in—"

"Now, Theo." Ross gives Theo a look.

I know what Ross is doing, and I know Theo is not happy about it. Just like I told the others, though, we might as well start adjusting now. Theo and I are going to live in different cities for the first time in our lives. No longer can he be there to kiss every boo-boo. I have to start figuring out these things for myself. Theo reluctantly stands, and I see him nod to Reid before leaving the two of us on the deck.

"Elise," Reid says with enough force to pull my attention to him.

"Don't contradict me in a meeting again."

"What?"

"I said, don't contradict me in front of the staff."

"I didn't."

"You did. I had already explained the situation, and you countered what I told them."

"I told them the truth because it was the truth. Why would you want to start your relationship with them on a sour note?"

"First off, I don't have a relationship with them. I am

their boss. Second, I don't care if they think I am an asshole. It usually ends up in my favor when people think I am. I took responsibility because that is how I wanted it to go. It's a lesson you need to understand. I am not Theo and I will not baby you like he does."

"Theo doesn't baby me, asshole, nor do I allow him to talk to me the way you are right now. I'm not going to apologize to you or anyone else for the way I run my team. If you want something different, then say the word. I'll give you my notice, and you can bring in someone you feel is better suited for your needs. Just like I've told Theo, *this* is my team. You are owner in name only. So step the fuck off." I stand and head inside, ready to punch something.

"Watch your tone," Reid snarls, grabbing my arm and spinning me to face him. Pushing my back against the wall, he moves within inches of my face. "I told you in the beginning, I run this." He motions between us.

"Fuck you, Reid."

"Trust me, Elise. You're about to." His lips clash hard over mine in a battle for control. When I won't give him access, he bites my lip in a way that causes the pain to shoot directly to my sex. I open for him, and his tongue glides over mine.

"I can smell your sweet little pussy, Elise. Wet and ready for me. Fuck."

His fingers slide into my sweats and through my slickness before drilling them in and out of me. After the shitty morning I've had, there is nothing more that I want than to give up control for a while. To not have to be anything to anyone other than Reid. And at this very minute, he wants what I want.

"On your knees, Elise, and I won't say it twice."

chapter ten

Reid

Fuck me standing. Elise actually does as she's told and lowers to her knees. Before I have a chance to make a move, Elise pulls my shorts just low enough to free my swelling cock. She is the most infuriating woman I have ever met. I saw the pain in her eyes when she realized she had hurt her team. I just couldn't let her shoulder that burden. Not when I could carry it for her. I know exactly what she needs.

"Put your hands on your thighs."

She obeys immediately.

"You just couldn't stop yourself from protecting me, could you? You had to take responsibility for not telling them, even though I had already addressed it." I edge the tip of my cock over her lips. Her tongue skates out and pushes into the wet slit. "You and your big mouth. You just couldn't keep it shut could you? Well, I think it's time you showed me how deep your mouth really is."

When she looks up at me, my heart melts at the trust and desire she is giving me. As rough as I want to be with her right now, I can't stop myself from touching her and running my thumb across her cheek in a moment of gentleness.

"Open for me, Dove. I'm going to fuck your sweet little mouth."

When she does, I begin to move my hips forward in little strokes. Enticing her. Letting her get used to me. She starts to bob her head, taking me deeper with each movement.

"Don't even think about it. Hands on thighs, Elise," I command.

She growls in frustration, and I feel it in the bottom of my balls. Christ, this girl is so many things: unexpected, challenging, smart, sexy, kind, protective. When has anyone ever been protective of me other than my family?

I grab her hair, using my other hand to brace myself against the wall. In this position, I'm able to thrust at an angle and, fuck me, it's amazing.

"I told you, Elise. I run this."

My hips lunge forward and I feel it, the minute this woman I've fallen head over heels for shows up and shows me whose boss. Before my hand can even guide her, she takes me to the back of her throat, and I can feel her lips against my pelvis. Slowly and with more control than anyone I've ever known, she eases, millimeter by millimeter, to the edge of my cock before she lets it pop out of her mouth. Her tongue glides just over the tip before she takes just the head in between her lips and applies a suction that has my knees buckling. My hand leaves the back of her head and finds a place on the wall with the other one. With her hands still on her knees, her eyes never leave mine as she takes me to the root again, this time twisting her mouth in circles as she moves. Sliding her tongue along the underside of my dick, she slips me out of her mouth. Bending down, she dusts her tongue across my balls before she sucks one into her mouth. Moving my hips closer, she has to lean back slightly to adjust to the new closeness. My cock jumps as she kisses her way up my shaft before taking me between her full lips. The sound of her desire vibrates down my cock, and I feel the electricity map across the nerves in my body as the currents move through me and I come down her throat.

I pull out slightly to finish coming on her tongue, letting her swallow. She runs her mouth over me, cleaning me before her full lips slide off the tip of my cock. She leans forward, placing a light kiss to the middle of my thigh. The gesture is so sweet and unexpected. I am so screwed.

I run a thumb over her lips before helping her off her knees.

"Holy shit." That's all I can get out. I can taste myself when my tongue sweeps across hers.

"I need to go see my team," she says before sliding out of my hold.

It unsettles me that she can easily move on to the next thought after what we just shared. "Give them time to take it in, Elise. Coddling them isn't going to change anything."

"I care about them, Reid. I care how they are feeling. I care when they are upset. You see that as a weakness in my management skills. It's not. It's one of my greatest strengths."

And just like that, she leaves me standing there, wanting more. By the time I arrange myself and walk back into the chalet, I see one of the black SUV's pulling off.

"Ross wants to go into town for some things. Why don't you go with us?" Theo says from behind me.

"Nah. I'll let you two hang out."

"He'll be shopping the whole time. You and I can grab some lunch and talk business." He pushes me towards the door.

"I've got a ton of work—"

"You're going," Ross insists, grabbing the keys off the counter.

I slide into the backseat of the other SUV, and the three of us ride in a comfortable silence into town.

It's really beautiful here. I can see the appeal to having a second home in this area. The town square is quaint and appears to have been updated. There are a few restaurants, a hotel, several boutique stores. We pass a used bookstore that I would like to get lost in for a while. I follow Theo to a grassy section in the middle of the square that has games etched into the tables. He takes a seat at a chess board, pulls open a drawer attached to the bottom of the concrete table, and pulls out the pieces.

We each set up our game pieces. Theo makes the first move and hits his button on the chess clock. We're several moves into our game before either of us says a word.

"Did you tell Elise?" Theo breaks our silence.

"Did I tell her?"

"That you love her."

"No."

"Because?"

I hit my button and look up. His attention is on me and not the game.

"I'm not sure she's ready to hear it. I don't know if she would believe it."

"Have you given her a reason not to believe you?" he asks coolly, but the twitch in his eye lets me know he's anything but.

"No, I haven't. And even though I know her very well—"

He clears his throat and gives me a look of warning.

"—We are still getting to know each other. You know her better than I do. Has she given you any idea what she is thinking?"

Theo makes another move and sends the clock back my way. "Elise is straight forward. What you see is what you get. She doesn't play games. She truly doesn't care what others think, unless it's someone she loves. She trusts her gut and goes with it. Give her some time. It's been less than a week."

"When did you know Ross was it for you?"

"The minute I laid eyes on him, I knew. It was instantaneous for me."

"And Ross?"

"That fucker made me work for it. It was six months after I told him I loved him before he finally said it back."

"Jesus. That sounds painful."

"Consistency."

"Consistency?"

"Yes. Consistency. I was consistent with him. I wanted him to say it back, but I didn't need him to say it back. I knew. I knew he was my love and I was his. I just had to give him the time to catch up with me. I was even. I was his soft place to land. I made sure he knew I would always be there. Consistent."

"And it worked, baby." Ross kisses his temple before pulling up a chair to watch the game. He turns the chair so that he is straddling the seat and props his arms up on the back. He looks at the board for a minute before floating a suggestion my way. Glancing down, I realize he's right and make the move before hitting the button. "But I wouldn't recommend it," he says taking a bite of an oversized pretzel.

"Wouldn't recommend what?" Theo frowns at his husband.

"I wouldn't recommend him telling Elise he loves her this soon."

"I thought you said it worked for you?"

"I said your consistency worked for me. The first time you told me you loved me, it freaked me the hell out."

"Only because you were afraid of commitment."

"It was our first date, Theo."

"Well, forgive me. I couldn't keep it in."

"And now I can appreciate it. Then it just made you Creepy Theo. I mean who tells someone they love them when they haven't even been together 12 hours?"

"I do," Theo retorts, giving Ross the side-eye. Ross laughs and winks at him.

"Are you pushing Reid to tell Elise so it will blow up in his face and you don't have to worry about him?"

That's an angle I never considered. I give Theo my full attention.

"No, if I have to give Elise to someone, I would prefer for it to be Reid. He's honorable, for the most part." He gives me a pointed look. "He just has a problem keeping his dick in his pants."

"I've never stepped out on anyone, and you know it." I bristle.

"No. All your pussies knew the drill. Except Amber."

"I never stepped out on Amber."

"No, but that crazy cat is a piece of work."

"But it wasn't because I wasn't honest with her."

"Amber?" Ross asks, and I wave him off.

"You're using the word 'give' again." I hit the game clock. "Check."

"I'm not going to have another dick measuring contest with you, Reid."

"I for one would love to be present at that contest," Ross interjects.

"Good, 'cause you'll lose," I say.

"I don't know about that. Have you seen what my man is—"

"Look, man." Theo stops Ross from finishing that sentence. "I'm on board, alright? Ross already had the talk with me. Give me a 'Team Beckett' t-shirt. I'll wear it and do a fucking cheer. I believe you love her. I also believe you're becoming intimate with her on a certain level, but it's not on the same level as me. Not yet. You are going to have to put in the work to get to my level. I'm not going to just give it to you."

"I'm Team Beckett, too," says Ross. "But if you hurt Elise, I'll surgically remove your balls and hang them on our Christmas tree this year."

"Checkmate." Theo hits the button.

Ross finished his shopping while Theo and I went over the final contracts for the buyout. I never thought Theo would give up control of his business, but he hasn't even batted an eye.

"Do you think the team will come around?" I ask Theo as we climb into the SUV.

"They love Elise too much not to. It was just a shock. They'll adjust. You can't step in between her and her team. Elise runs the show."

"I wasn't. But I also wasn't going to have her take the hit for something she has no control over."

"Elise does have the control. She decided she wanted to

move to New York. We could have made it work with her staying in Chicago. They know that. They are smart people. You trying to take the blame doesn't change that. Her team dynamic is why the company is a success. You can't interfere. Trust me. Learn a lesson from the road I've already paved," Theo says over his shoulder. He brings his hand to rest on Ross' thigh, who promptly lowers his from the steering wheel to interweave their fingers.

I know Theo is right, but I'm too stubborn to do this any way but my own. Maybe this is too fast. I mean, what the hell do I know about love? I've never been in love before. Am I really ready for that kind of commitment? Why do I feel the need to be stubborn about the team and find myself digging my heels in? Elise has me thrown off balance, and it's not a feeling I am used to.

"Reid?"

"Sorry, what?" I look up and catch Ross' eye in the rearview.

"We're here. Theo and I are going to run one more errand."

Looking around, I realize we are in front of our chalet. I had no idea we were even on the campgrounds. Elise's SUV is parked out front. She must be back.

"Thanks," I nod and exit the car, stealing a deep breath before I tell Elise what I think. What that is at this very moment, I have no idea. What she will walk away with is an understanding of how I expect this company to run.

I set the items Ross got today on the island before making my way to find Elise. The sounds of her soft crying has me quickening my pace, and when I round the corner, I find her on the couch. Tears are streaming down her face, and Nova is furiously working to lick each and every one of them away.

Her arms are wrapped tightly around his neck.

"Sweetheart." I pull her into my arms. This just makes her cry harder, and I'm at a loss for what to do. It's not that I'm a total dick, but I don't know if I've ever consoled someone before. I rock her gently and whisper words of comfort in her ear. Eventually her crying stops, and she hiccups softly as she tries to bring her breathing back to normal. All I can think about is how I want to make sure she never cries like this again.

"What happened?" I ask.

She starts to cry again, and I run my fingers through her hair. "Shh, baby. Just take your time." I am seriously about to lose my shit. I am already making a mental list of whose balls I am going to hang on Ross' Christmas tree when she tries again.

"He died. Champ died."

"Oh, Dove. I am so sorry. Who's Champ? Was he sick?"

"No. *Champ*," she says like I should know. "Champ. He loses his sight and then he dies and little Ricky Schroeder…" She starts to cry again, harder this time. It's then I realize there are credits rolling on the TV. I can't help but laugh, but this makes her cry even more.

Lifting her head off my shoulder, I wipe her fresh tears with my thumb. She's beautiful. Her lips are soft and full from crying, and I can't stop myself from kissing her. She opens for me without hesitation.

"Better?" I ask. She nods.

"I'm sorry. I'm just exhausted. Physically and emotionally and that movie…have you ever seen that movie?"

"No. I don't even know what it's called."

"Champ!" she cries out in frustration. "They should not show that on regular TV without some kind of warning system. I thought I was watching an old movie. I got sucked in and had no idea it would end like that."

She wraps her arms around my neck. I stand and carry her to the bedroom kicking off my shoes before laying her in the bed. I remove my jeans and climb in behind her pulling her to my chest. Her ass wiggles against my forming erection. Pulling her tighter to me, I whisper in her ear to go to sleep. After a few minutes, when I hear her breathing even out, I add, "I love you, Dove."

I realize she's holding her breath. She must have heard what I said.

"Breathe, Elise. I don't expect you to say it back. I just wanted you to know."

She turns to face me but doesn't say anything. Her large eyes watch mine for several minutes before she finally speaks. "How do you know?"

"I've never felt this way before."

"That could just be gas."

Wait. What? "Did you just compare my declaration of love to gas?"

"I'm just saying weird feelings often turn out to be gas."

"This isn't a weird feeling, Elise. I am in love with you. I am certain of it. I feel like a part of me is missing when you aren't around. I want to know what you think—about everything. From whether or not I should put blueberries on my pancakes to how you think I should integrate Theo's business. I want to be deep inside you every second of the day. Not because I want sex, but because I want to claim you. Make you mine. I want to be a part of you. I need you to be a part of me."

"It just seems sudden. I mean you didn't even know me a week ago. With 'I love you' comes decisions, nexts. I don't know what's next. I still have to carve out a place in the new company. I'm leaving my team. There are so many unknowns for me right now."

I roll on top of her. My eyes never leave hers. My body does what it knows to do when it is this close to Elise. It begins to move into hers, rubbing her, even through our clothing.

"I know you think you are going to scare me off, Dove. But you aren't. I can be very patient when I need to be. I can wait for this to catch up to you."

"Reid…"

I lower my mouth to hers before she can lessen this with an apology. I don't need an apology from her. I just need her to be open to the idea of us. It only takes a few moves before she responds. Two more moves and we've both discarded our clothing. One more and I'm deep in the woman I love.

I smell something delicious when I wake. Alone. No Elise. She must be completely freaked out. I roll my eyes at the thought, then climb out of bed, and pull on some clothes. When I enter the living room, the doors off the deck are open and the sun is just setting behind the trees. Rhianna's "Love on the Brain" is playing, and Elise's ass sashays back and forth to the music while she cooks. Leaning against a wooden post, I watch her cook and drink her wine. She sings out of tune and doesn't hold back. Her hair is pulled into a big messy bun on top of her head, and even with her back to me, I know she is wearing my t-shirt again.

There's commotion at the door and part of the team comes in carrying booze. Only then does Elise realize I was watching her.

Gabby pats my arm and gives me a wink when she passes by. Ryan stops in front of me and offers me a handshake before making his way to the counter.

"Dinner is ready," Elise announces, pulling dishes from the oven.

"How long was I asleep?" I ask quietly when she hands me a dish to carry to the table.

"I made most of it this afternoon while you and Theo were gone. All I had to do was heat it."

She looks so young and fresh with no makeup on that I want to make a meal out of her.

"I'll take that," Fran says, pulling the dish from my hands. "Go let Theo and Ross know dinner is ready."

I do as I'm told. I knock on their bedroom door and enter, relieved to find them reading and not up to something I can't un-see.

The usual group—Elise's core team—is seated around a table covered in Mexican food and dishing food onto their plates.

"There are enchiladas, tacos, flautas, tamales, and, of course, beans and rice." Elise gestures at each dish. "The shells and the tamales are made from our favorite Mexican restaurant in town." She sits in her normal spot, and Blake starts passing around shot glasses.

"Boss," Blake says.

I look up, surprised to see that he's addressing me.

"We didn't handle the news that great today, and we want you to know it won't happen again. Elise is one-of-a-kind, though, and we know we will never have another leader who has our backs as fiercely as she does."

He fills some of the glasses with tequila and then passes the bottle to Ryan, who fills the glasses on his end of the table.

Fran passes around a bowl of limes.

Blake lifts his glass into the air. "Elise, we love you as much as your family in New York does, and we will always be here for you. We couldn't ask for a better person to work for. Arriba, abajo, al centro, pa' dentro!"

"Salud!" the rest of the table responds. They all move their drinks up, down, and then to the middle of the table before throwing back their shots. Before I can ask what the gesture means, they are already filling their next round of shots. The food is delicious and by the time most of us are on our second helping, we are more than a little buzzed.

"So are you guys going to finally end the card game tonight?" Ryan asks.

"There will still be card games," Elise answers. "I'm still going to be your boss. I'm still going to be spending time with you, and some of you will be coming to the New York office with me."

This is news to me, and I must not hide it well because Fran makes a comment.

"Uh, you might want to talk to the new Boss Daddy about that, because he looks shocked."

"It's not his say," Elise says, passing a platter to Ross.

"It's my company," I remind her.

"It's my team."

"Who work for my company."

"Which doesn't survive without my team."

"Elise," I say harsher than I intend. I don't usually have someone challenge me in front of my staff. Well, not if they plan to stay employed. She gives no response, so I turn my attention to the end of the table. "Theo?"

Theo doesn't say a word.

"Why don't we all do another round? Break up some of

the angst in the room," Blake suggests, trying to make light of the situation. "We need to keep going if I'm going to get Elise drunk enough to rap with me."

"Not gonna happen."

"Come on, Elise. We didn't get our usual karaoke night in town this trip."

"Then—" Elise is cut off by a knock at the door.

Blake answers the door to two men who are dressed in black from head to toe like something out of an action movie.

"Elise Donovan," one of the men say, holding out a phone to her as she meets them at the door.

"Elise Donovan," she says into the phone. After a pause, she walks quickly out onto the deck. "Mr. Speaker..." we hear her say as she walks out of earshot.

Immediately, the team picks up their cell phones.

"Got anything?" Ryan asks Fran.

"Nope. Whatever it is, it's still under the radar."

Elise enters and hands the phone back to the men. "Blake," motioning him with a nod to follow her. Elise walks to the stereo and turns up the music loud enough that the people several cabins over can probably hear it. Blake bends down toward her, his hands resting on her hips. She wraps her arms around his neck, and he listens as she whispers in his ear. I'm surprised by the jealousy I feel even though I know it is strictly business. Jealousy is not a feeling I am accustomed to. She lets go of his neck, and Blake leaves without saying a word. Elise turns the music back down.

I appear to be the only one at the table who is confused by what just happened. Everyone else is moving on like it's business as usual. I feel only slightly comforted by the fact that Theo doesn't feel the need to ask questions.

Elise asks everyone what they did this afternoon, but I

can tell she isn't listening. Ten minutes later Blake is back, changed, with a duffle bag in hand. He sets his bag in the chair he vacated and picks up in the conversation like he never missed a beat. He's obviously comfortable with whatever his role is. It's now that I notice he's wearing a Glock on his hip. As he casually answers Gabby's question about something they did today, he pulls out a second smaller handgun and hands it to Elise.

"No," she shakes her head and continues to eat.

"Elise," Theo says in a tone that is not to be brokered with. I start to say something, but Theo gives me a look that I understand from many years of friendship.

"Theo. I don't like—"

He cuts her off. "It's that or Ryan stays with you 24/7."

"You don't even know what the case is about," she argues.

"Don't need to. It's Blake's call and you know it."

"Theo."

"If it were Fran or Gabby…" he says.

She sighs and, after a beat, reluctantly holds out her hand.

"Stand," Blake says, and when she does, he fastens a holster to her thigh then checks the weapon one more time. "Safety's on," he says and holsters her weapon for her. "Draw and click, one motion, just like I taught you. You covered?" he asks Ryan, who nods and pulls a weapon out of the back of his waistband. It's the fucking Wild West in here, and I don't have a clue what the fuck is going on.

Blake removes a phone from his bag and hands it to Elise. He zips his bag, and I can hear a helicopter passing overhead.

"Be careful," Elise tells Blake as she stands for a hug. She kisses him on his cheek and says, "I love you."

As irrational as it is, hearing her say it to him when she didn't say it to me earlier has my blood boiling. On top of that, I have no clue how to manage this team when I don't know what the hell is going on. I know this isn't the time or place to bring it up, so I have to check myself. Inside I know two things: one, I am not okay with Elise being in a situation where she needs to have a gun on her person, and two, as soon as Theo and I sign these papers, she's fired.

chapter eleven

Elise

"Reid, you haven't signed the papers. You aren't protected. If push came to shove, you wouldn't be covered in court."

"You're not a lawyer, Elise. It's not like you have client-attorney protection."

"I know that, Reid. I've been doing this a few years. I understand more than anyone what is at stake. I'm not going to put you at risk."

"That isn't how this works, Elise. You don't protect me. I protect you. We seem to keep having the same argument. I don't understand why that is." He aggressively runs his hand through his hair, which really only serves to make all my girlie bits spring to life.

"Theo." I catch him out of the corner of my eye, and I know he has been listening to the conversation. He gives me a look but reluctantly steps up to the plate. Or so I think.

"Reid, Elise is right. We don't have a signed contract. It's likely going through, but you know how mergers are. There are those items that stay secret until after everything is signed. There are certain things that you aren't going to know. Hell, there are things you won't know even after the papers are signed. I won't even know what this is about unless Elise or Blake need to pull me in. It's just part of it. Elise is known in circles that none of us realize. This is what she does. This is how we have made the bulk of our money. If a politician or institution with a lot of money needs something fixed, quietly and quickly, everyone in the business knows that means Elise."

"Actually, I rarely say yes to being pulled into political messes anymore," I add. "It's a full-time job on its own, and I don't like putting my team in the situations we have found ourselves in in the past." I load the last plate into the dishwasher. "Okay, that's the last of it. I'm going to run a book over to Fran and I'll be back."

"I'll take it," Theo says.

"Nah, I want to stretch my legs. This is our last night here."

"Elise, you know the rules."

"What are the rules?" Reid asks.

I roll my eyes as Theo answers, "Blake is the lead on security for the team. He's ex-Army, Special Ops. What he says goes. He can be a little unorthodox sometimes, and I have felt the need to reign him in before, but he's the best in his line of work."

"You only felt the need to reign him in," I point out, "because his comfort level with my role is different than yours. You're overprotective. He knows that he has all his bases covered, but he doesn't baby me. That doesn't make him reckless.

There's a difference."

"Please, can we have this conversation again for the hundredth time?" Theo asks.

"Separate corners," Ross says, entering the kitchen. He grabs a bottle of water from the fridge.

"I need to take a book to Fran. Want to walk with me?" Theo asks Ross. I exhale all the air in my lungs in total frustration. I pull the book from my bag and hand it to Theo, who kisses me on the forehead before leaving.

I plop myself down on the couch and Reid takes the chair across from me. He watches me for a minute but doesn't say anything. He rests his elbow on the arm of the chair and runs his finger back and forth over his chin like he is trying to choose his words before he speaks. His ankle is propped over his knee, looking sexy as sin.

"Why don't you just say what's on your mind, Reid."

"Elise, I understand that you and Theo have a process that works for you when it comes to working together, but you need to wrap your head around the fact that I will be your new boss. Yes, Theo will be running things and will stay on from Chicago, but you will be in the New York office."

"Reid—"

"Let me clarify so there is zero confusion. If you and I are discussing a difference of opinions, you don't call Theo in to save the day for you. You are in a relationship with me, not Theo."

"Am I?"

"Are you what?"

"In a relationship with you?"

"What does that mean, Elise?"

"It means, it's been a week. Are you ready to say you're in a relationship?" As soon as I ask the question, I see the difference, the sudden shift in his eyes.

"I told you, I love you. I've never said that to a woman before, Elise. For me, with 'I love you' comes a relationship. I have no doubts about what I am ready for. You're the only one who has to decide. And you have to make this decision. Just you. Not you and Theo."

I choose to ignore his last comment, because I hate the uncertainty I see in his eyes. I stand and walk to his chair. He lowers both feet to the floor as I straddle him. Our eyes never leave the other's, but neither of us says anything.

Finally, he lowers his hands to my knees and slowly slides them upward. His eyes darken when his hand reaches the pistol still affixed to my thigh. His thumbs skim my sex before his hands move under my t-shirt—his t-shirt. He moves his hands up my torso, his thumbs brushing against the underside of my breast.

Lifting my hands to his face, I trace the lines of unease. I wrap my fingers around his neck and pull him to me for a kiss that I hope will calm him. I go straight for the soul-wrenching, feel-it-in-your-toes, I'm-claiming-every-part-of-you kiss. I want him to know what I'm just not ready to say out loud yet. He doesn't take control. He doesn't move us to the next step. He just let's my kiss stand on its own, telling him the next part of our story.

"I do want this relationship with you, Reid. I just don't know what that looks like for us yet. We have a lot of unknowns in the next few weeks."

"So, let's define it."

"Define it how?"

"Give it some definitions so you can know what it looks like. So that you can have what you need to feel good about this."

"I already feel good about this, Reid. A definition is not going to change that. There is just a lot going on. I have an entire house to pack and move in five days. What I need defined is the parameters of how we are going to make this work in an office setting. You are going to be my boss. Already you have fought me on how I manage my team, and my relationship with Theo. You don't understand what I do in this company and that worries me. I can't do the things I do with limitations placed on me."

"I do not want you taking jobs that will put you in harm's way."

"Would you feel like that if I wasn't the victim of rape?"

He doesn't answer. He seems to be sitting with this question.

"That's a problem for me, Reid. I don't want to be seen as a victim. Especially by my partner, and even more so by my boss. If you only see me as a victim, you can never fully see me at my greatest potential, which is to see me for what I am. A survivor."

"I have never treated you as a victim, nor have I held back my passion for you. I wish I could explain it to you, Elise, but I can't. I've never felt this protectiveness for someone before. I don't want you in a situation where you have a gun strapped to your thigh. I don't want you in a situation that you can't tell me about. I don't want you in a situation that could jeopardize everything you have worked for."

"Reid, I've told you from the beginning, my team fixes shit. Most of it is average, everyday corporate issues, but some of it is fixing what no one else seems to be able to fix."

"It has to stop."

"Or else?"

"Elise." He pins me with a look so intense, I admit I'm a

little intimidated. "It has to stop. You are not a 'you' anymore. You are a 'we' now. You say you're a fixer. Fix this."

It's late. Theo and Ross came in right after Reid and I finished our conversation. I use the word "conversation" loosely. "Stalemate" is probably more accurate. Somehow we were both able to pull it together enough to share some wine and talk about things other than the merger.

It's our last night together for at least a week, and instead of spending it pretzeled around each other having amazing sex, we are at a standoff on opposite sides of the bed.

"Fuck it," I say and roll over on top of Reid.

"Elise," he warns, clearly still not in the mood to make nice.

"Fuck. It," I repeat, grabbing the fly of his plaid boxers and pulling until I hear a ripping sound.

"What the fu—"

I cut him off when I envelop his dick with my mouth. His scent turns me the fuck on. I apply suction as I pull out to his tip before slamming back to his pelvis. I gently skim my teeth the length of his now-hardened shaft, giving him a light nip at the head.

"Jesus Christ, are you trying to kill me?" he says in the middle of a full body tremor.

I wrap my hand around him and give hard, pulling strokes while caressing the soft section of skin under his testicles. His chest rises and falls in a rhythmic pattern. His eyes are closed and he's letting his hips move freely of their own accord. I love the way his face flushes when he's feeling pleasure. My thumb dances across the tip of his cock, spreading pre-come in its wake, while I wet the middle finger on my free hand. Lowering my mouth to take him again, I peruse the area of puckered skin before slowly inserting my middle finger into his ass. He moans and shifts his hips back, giving me permission and wanting more. Fully inside him, I run my tongue along the underside of his cock, giving him time to acclimate. I know the minute I move my finger that I have found what I am looking for. Petting the bundle of nerves with the pad of my finger, I watch his body respond to me, and it's an aphrodisiac to my soul.

"More?" I ask him.

"Fuck me running, yes."

His encouragement is all I need, and between my mouth, my hand, and my fingers, I guide him through an orgasm so intense his fingers and toes are gripping the mattress around me. I use his come to lube his still rock-hard cock before running some over me. Straddling him, I slowly push out as I guide him into my ass. When he realizes what I am doing, his hands cup my bottom and help support me until my cheeks reach his pelvis. Tonight is all about giving Reid pleasure.

"Elise." He closes his eyes, and I can see he is trying to control himself. I sit still as long as I can, but my body has a mind of its own and it begins to move in small thrusts. Each time my hips gyrate in a circular motion another expletive leaves his lips.

He moves to sit up and I push him back down with my hands to his chest. I move my ass up and down on his cock. He's losing himself in me, and I relish the control I feel from it. Leaning down, I take his bottom lip between my teeth and bite. It pulls him out of his haze, and before I realize it, his eyes lock on mine. Whatever he sees there has his blazing.

Faster than I can see it coming, he has me on my stomach, ass in the air, a stinging handprint on my right cheek, and his dick is resting against the crack of my ass.

"Open, Elise."

He leaves a matching handprint on my left cheek when I don't comply.

"Elise."

Slowly, I run my hands over my cheeks and spread myself open for him. His dick twitches when it grazes my entrance. Inch by hard inch, he enters me again, and it's even deeper this way with my shoulders to the mattress. The expletives are leaving my lips now, and he sets a cadence of strokes and slaps that have me begging him for more. His hand wraps around my hair and he pulls me into a kneeled position, my back to his front. His hand wraps around my neck. My hands palm the side of his thighs as his pace intensifies.

"Reid."

"I run this," he reminds me. He slaps my pussy, adding a hard bite to my earlobe, and I shatter around him, my arousal running down my thighs.

A few more hard strokes and Reid's hand tightens around my neck as he comes again, inside me.

Connected, we fall forward, Reid on top of me, trying to catch our breath, coming to terms with the explosiveness of the feelings we both just experienced. His hands find mine.

"I love you," he says.

"I'm scared."

"Of what?"

"Of saying it back. Of what it means."

"What does it mean?"

"That you have the power to destroy me."

He places a soft kiss to my temple.

"I love you, Elise."

"I love you, Reid."

chapter twelve

Reid

Elise: My flight arrives at 4 Xoxo

Me: I'll pick you up

Elise: I can take a cab or the train

Me: Forget the train – just hop on my platform 9 and 3 quarters

Elise: You know you make my Huffle puff when you speak Harry Potter to me. If I opened my Gryffindor would you Slytherin?

Me: Speak Parseltongue to me and I'll let my snake out

Elise: Reid *feign shock*

Me: Girls call me Aguamenti- Every time they hear my name they get wet

Elise: smh

Me: You're staying with me tonight. My house is called the Shrieking Shack for a reason. I'll show you tonight.

Elise: Reid! I have to turn off my phone. I'll take a cab. Text me the address.

Me: Are you sure you're a muggle cause that ass is magical – I'll pick you up.

It's been almost three weeks since I left Elise in Colorado. It took longer than anticipated for her to get packed and close out the accounts she was working on. I want her to focus solely on building the New York office and laying some groundwork for how I want my company to function moving forward.

Ryan, Fran, and Gabby arrived last week. Blake arrived this morning after finishing whatever was going on with the Speaker. Elise never brought me in on the case. I tried to put feelers out to see what she was mixed up in, but I came up with nothing. I do know Theo had to increase the value of Jacobs, Inc. by $5 million last week when we were finalizing the papers. I still haven't told her that if she doesn't figure out a way to distance herself from the dangerous messes then she will find herself out of a job. I'm hoping she will come to it on her own and realize that she can manage fixers without having to be one. In truth, I'm not comfortable with anyone on the team being placed in harm's way.

"Got a second, Boss?" Blake knocks before entering the office I am using during the transition. I have redesigned a floor in the building I own just for this team. My main office is on the top floor, but I put a small side office here on the 23rd so I could have a place to watch and learn for a few weeks.

"What can I do for you?" I ask without looking up from my laptop. He eventually earns my full attention when he closes the door. The office is small, but it's state-of-the-art, and when he closes the door, the windows shade over and give us privacy.

"I'd like to talk to you off the record."

"What's on your mind, Blake."

"I know you have people in the field asking about the case Elise and I are working on."

"I don't know what you are talking about."

"Bullshit and you know it. You don't want to be mixed up in this. You keep poking around and it's going to draw unnecessary attention. Elise knows."

"What does Elise know?"

"I could fill The Garden with the shit Elise knows. Specifically, for this conversation, she knows you're poking around."

"Blake, I'm not Theo. I'm not here to be a Scout Leader. Things will be changing over the next few weeks."

"Look. Whatever, man. I'm flex and can work with just about anything." He leans forward. "Until you cut her off, you've got to let her do her job. You are putting her at greater risk by getting involved. Security is my job and I can't, scratch that, *I won't* have you fucking that up because you think Elise needs you to swoop in and protect her. She knows better than anyone when she needs to reach out for help."

"I don't need to be schooled on Elise. For damn sure that

is not your role here."

He lifts his hand in concession and sits back in a slightly less combative pose.

"I'm simply suggesting that you try trusting Elise. If Elise were mine…" He lifts his hands again in response to the surly look on my face and tries again. "If Elise were mine, I couldn't say I'd want her mixed up in this shit either." He studies me for a minute. "It's my job to know things."

"She told you?" I ask.

"No. I'm not blind."

"Does that mean the others know?"

"No. Except Gabby, but you knew that after her night in the woods with Owen."

"You know about that?"

"I told you, I know everything."

"Does Elise know you know?"

"We haven't discussed it, but yes. She knows I know. It's also her job to know what we all know."

"So what? Ryan and Fran, they're just slow on the uptake?"

"No. They don't have the instincts or backgrounds that Elise and I have. They typically handle the vanilla issues, the corporate accounts. They assist under our guidance on the cases better left in the dark."

I stare at him without adding anything more to the conversation. He eventually gets the hint and stands to leave.

"You can trust Elise. She knows when to call for backup and she knows when to say no to a case. See you tonight."

He leaves before I can ask him what tonight is.

Trust Elise. I swirl in my chair and look out my window at the city I love. The midtown buildings that overlap one after the other. Taller buildings standing in protection of the smaller ones. Trust Elise. I'm lost in thought when my cell buzzes.

"Beckett."

"My girl gets in at four. Make sure your sorry ass is there to greet her." As usual Theo forgoes any preambles.

"No. *My* girl gets in at four, and don't tell me what the fuck to do."

"While she is in New York and I am in Chicago, she will be your girl so don't fuck it up."

"Is that the only reason you called me?"

"Mostly. Ross and I will be there next Monday for the gala that night."

"Great. I signed the papers yesterday. The lawyers have them."

"Yep. I'm on the way to sign mine now."

"In about an hour, you'll have an insane amount of money to do with as you please," I remind him.

"And in about an hour, you'll own a company that is a complete mystery to you," he goads. But it's not the best day for it. The men in Elise's life are already overreaching boundaries.

"Go pick up our girl. We'll talk later." He hangs up before I can tell him, yet again, that Elise is mine.

When I exit the building, Coop is waiting to drive me to the airport. It's rare that I don't take the time to work and multitask, but for the first time in a long time, I'm nervous. Out of the close to four weeks we've known each other, we've only been together for one. One amazing, crazy, melt-in-your-mouth week. Fuck. I get a hard-on just thinking about her. The last weeks have been difficult not having her with me. It's odd how quickly you can acclimate to someone. I can't wait to have her next to me again. And not just for sex but for the everyday things, too. My phone vibrates and I resist the temptation to let it go to voicemail.

"Beckett."

"Hey, little brother. How's it hangin'?"

"What do you want, Dean?"

"I was just checking in. Wanted to see what time we were getting together tonight."

"We're not. I told you I have plans tonight."

"I know. The girl," he says like she's an inconsequential person.

"She's not a girl," I growl.

"Since when are you into dudes?" he asks in a manner so serious, it's hard to be frustrated with him.

"I mean, dicknuts, that she's not just some girl. Her name is Elise, and I'm in love with her."

"I'm just yanking your chain. Although, you can see why I would be confused, seeing as how you've never stayed with any one person long enough for me to learn their names. Except Amber. Please tell me you learned your lesson the first time around."

"Dean." I shake my head and run my hand over my face.

"What? That girl had fatal attraction written all over her."

"Was there a point to your call?"

"Tonight. What time?"

"I told you, I'm not going out tonight. I'm spending it with Elise."

"Which means you'll be going out tonight. I talked to that hot little spitfire Gabby today, and she said they are meeting Elise for drinks tonight."

"I'll call you back." I disconnect the call before losing my cool.

I watch the tiles in the tunnel scroll by like the stock

ticker in Times Square. I must have closed my eyes, because before I know it, Coop is alerting me that we've arrived at the airport.

I lean against the car as the plane taxis to a stop. Shawn opens the door once the stairs are in place then he and Elise exchange a hug before she starts her descent to meet me. I repress a growl at the thought of that fucker getting my hug the first time Elise and I flew together.

Elise bounces down the stairs in jeans and a white fitted tee. Her hair is loose and untamed and has on a sharp pair of shades. She looks absolutely stunning, and I mentally kick myself for not bringing the limo, so I could fuck her half a dozen ways on the drive back to the city.

She hits the last step and, without warning, propels herself to me, her legs wrapping around my waist without actually having ever touched the ground.

"Hey, baby." She greets me with a smile and a kiss that lets my cock know that rest time is over and Elise Time has begun.

"Hey yourself." I kiss her back, trying to play it cool. I don't want everyone to know how much I have missed this girl over the last few weeks. She slides her sunglasses to the top of her head, her eyes locking on mine.

"I want you to fuck me six ways sideways, backwards and front ways." She goads me by bouncing on my now very alert cock.

"Car, Elise. Now." I slap her on her ass before she puts one last kiss on my lips that has me wanting to beg for more.

She slides over the seat, and I have her under me in one swift move before they even finish loading her bags in the car.

"I missed you," I tell her when I finally break for air.

"I love you," she says. Once Elise finally said it, she hasn't stopped. A day doesn't go by without her saying it several times. I never thought I would have an insatiable need to hear someone tell me they love me, but with Elise, I find that I crave it. She says it just right. There's a certain inflection in my "I love you" versus the one she gives anyone else. It means something to me that this girl who draws people to her and freely gives them love, has a special love only for me. My dick plumps at the thought.

"You're in trouble."

"Me? What did I do?" She attempts to sit up, but I have her pinned underneath me, right where I want her.

"Did you make plans to see everyone tonight?"

"Possibly." She bites back a smile.

My fingers have deftly maneuvered the button and zipper of her jeans. I realize now she is wearing a body suit and not a fitted t-shirt. I slip the bottom to the side and my fingers easily slide into her wet pussy. I pull out and circle her clit before sliding back in. It turns me on that this girl, my girl, is always ready for me. She moans as I make another swipe to her clit.

"It's fortunate for you, Dove, that I am in a good mood today and will wait until after dinner to remind you what you appear to have forgotten since the last time we were together. I run this."

Her teeth mark her bottom lip as my fingers continue to work her towards an orgasm.

Her face flushes and her moans are like a mating call to my dick. When I hear Coop close the trunk, I hit the button to raise the divider between us and the front seat.

"Quiet, Dove. He can't see you, but keep that up and he will be able to hear you." I kiss her lips, a smile in my eyes. One thing my girl does not do well is being quiet. The driver's door closes and we feel the car begin to move. My free hand comes up to pinch her nipple, and I'm rewarded with this delicious little movement her body does right before she climaxes. We've only been together physically for a week, but already I know every one of her cues. The thought of anyone ever knowing Elise this way sends a wave of possession through me that I have never felt for another. Just the thought is enough to piss me the fuck off, and I increase the pressure on her clit. Her orgasm pours over my fingers. She held back as much as she could, but she certainly wasn't quiet.

She closes her eyes, stealing breaths. My fingers are soaked and I can't resist tasting her. In one move, I have her jeans pooled around her ankles. Her bodysuit has these handy little snaps that I am grateful for, and before she can protest, I have her bent in half, my mouth enveloping her sweet pussy. My tongue demands entrance inside her.

"Fuck," she moans as one hand grasps at the door for anchor. Her other hand grips my hair to the point of pain. This only has my dick dripping for her. My hands hold her thighs to her body, and I rock her back and forth as I continue my quest.

"Again, Elise," I demand.

As the car accelerates, so does my tongue. My hand covers her mouth as I lick her from bottom to top, suctioning her clit before biting it, a move that once again sends her over the edge. Elise pulls me into her, her pussy riding my face. Her mouth wraps around my hand and she bites. I pull away and leave one bright-red handprint on her ass as retribution. I pull myself up her body, and she closes her legs, trying to apply pressure to ride out the effects of another orgasm. I pop her ass again, moving her legs back to her chest, and shove so deep inside of her I'm not sure where I end and she begins. It was all I could do not to come in my pants when she clamped down on my hand, but now, with her sex fastened hard around my cock, I have to sit immobile for a minute to gain my composure. *This* is fucking. Raw and insatiable. There will be a time for lovemaking later. Right now, I need to leave myself inside Elise. Remind her after these weeks apart who she belongs to and who is in charge.

"Reid." Her eyes are closed. I know she is battling to give me one more, but I know it's in her. I know because I've written a manual to her body. I know what it can and can't do. What it can and can't give.

"Give it to me, Elise." My hand moves to stimulate her clit while I slam into her over and over. She cries out my name one last time as my body convulses and empties into her.

"I'm not a silly straw," she mumbles, calling attention to the fact that I still have her bent in half.

"Sorry," I chuckle and release her legs before snapping her bodysuit back together. She slides her jeans up. She is going to be walking around with my come dripping down her legs, and that is enough to remind my dick that there will be more later.

Once she's situated, she curls into my side and wraps her arms around my waist, her head resting on my shoulder. I'm struck at how this settles me as much as the sex did. Another reminder that I am in love.

The city is moving by and we are only a few blocks from my place.

"Whenever I'm in the city it always feels like home," she reflects. "No matter how much I loved Chicago. New York will always be my home."

Exactly, I find myself thinking. I want this to be her home.

"You live on Gramercy Park?" She sits up.

"Yes. I bought and renovated a townhouse about five years ago."

Coop pulls us into the hidden garage in the back of the building. It's disguised to look like two large carriage doors. As far as I know this is the only property on the park that has private parking.

Coop opens Elise's door and makes a display of removing his ear buds when she greets him. She blushes, and I appreciate Coop's ability to be discreet.

"I'll bring your bags in, ma'am."

"Elise," she corrects him. "And if it's alright can we leave them here until tomorrow?" She motions to the trunk of the car. "I'm only staying one night here, then I will be going to my sister's." She reaches in to grab a leather duffle that Coop easily beats her to.

"Of course," he says and gives me a questioning look before opening the entrance to the lift that takes us to the top floor. I guide her into my bedroom, setting her duffle on the bench at the end of the bed.

It's a beautiful day and Gloria, my housekeeper, has the doors to the terrace open. The master suite is the only area on this level. The view overlooks the park below, which is accessible only by the residents of the building. There are exactly 368 keys to the park, all numbered and accounted for. I have three of them.

"Reid, this place is beautiful." She turns and gives me her best smile. This girl. She elicits so many unexpected feelings within me. Pride that she is so taken with her surroundings. That I was able to work for something that put that smile on her face feels like an accomplishment. I try to hold back my emotions a little so that she doesn't see that I'm absolutely shit for giggles over her.

"I'm so proud of you and your success to be able to make this kind of home for yourself." She wraps her arms around me and kisses my lips.

"I love you, Dove." I say running my nose down hers. "Let me show you around."

We walk the length of the terrace before I show her the inside. The bed is in an alcove with skylights, making for a cozy and intimate space. Around the corner is a sitting room with a relaxed seating area with a TV and a fireplace and a floor-to-ceiling bookcase full of my favorite books. There are also iron-framed doors that provide access to the terrace. In the corner there is a hidden bar.

We take the interior stairs and walk the remaining three floors. The bottom floor has stone stairs leading to the street. Cooper has the street level apartment.

"So, what time are we meeting everyone?" I raise an eyebrow of discontent.

"We're meeting at 8:00." She looks at her watch. "It's 6:30 now. I think we are meeting at Bar 11 on 9th? That means we have what, almost an hour? Care to join me? She starts undressing on the way to the shower.

We walk up to the rooftop area reserved for our party, and everyone descends on her. They act like they haven't seen her for years. Hypocritical of me I know, given my reaction to her at the airport earlier today. I greet them before pulling Elise off to introduce her to some of my acquaintances.

"Reid Beckett late?" Dean smirks with a raised eyebrow. My brother has been on the receiving end of my tirades regarding his tardiness more times than he can count. I couldn't tell him about the escapades in the shower that left us running behind.

Before Dean can get out his next jab at me, Elise has enveloped him in one of her signature hugs. The fucker has the nerve to act like he's enjoying it.

"Fuck the fuck off," I tell Dean, pulling Elise back.

"I have to say, I'm glad you exist. I was beginning to think my little brother had made you up. You sounded too good to be true." He winks at her and she laughs.

"Thank you," she says to Gabby who's just put a cocktail in her hands. She turns back to Dean. "Oh, I exist. From what I hear, you definitely do, too."

He actually blushes. Gabby coughs into her hand, but Elise never breaks eye contact with my brother.

"Would you excuse us for a moment, ladies." I pull Dean out of earshot of anyone.

"You're fucking Gabby? You know she is my employee now."

"You're fucking your employee. I fail to see the difference." He tilts back slightly on his heels.

"We aren't fucking. I'm in love with that girl, and she's it for me. There won't be a mess to clean up. When you're done with Gabby, there will be a mess."

"And how would you know that little brother?" He leans forward, it's obvious I've hit a nerve.

"When hasn't it ever been a mess?"

We're cut off by a group of guys we've grown up with. Dean and I exchange greetings. I can see Elise out of the corner of my eye talking to her team, and I notice they are all looking my direction. I excuse myself and walk their way. I overhear Elise telling them that we are seeing each other. Gabby and Blake look indifferent, as they already knew. Fran looks curious. Ryan is the only one who looks displeased, confirming what I have suspected all along— he's got a thing for Elise. I'm not thrilled she felt the need to tell them without me.

"Our table should be set in a few minutes," I announce, having no idea if that is true or not but not really knowing what to say next. Elise smiles at me over her shoulder, wrapping her arm around my waist. I have grown to like this team, but this isn't open for discussion. This is not a group relationship. This is me and Elise. It's awkward for a beat until Blake breaks the silence with something work related, and the group moves on to talking about other things. I decide to see when our table really will be ready then make my way back over to Dean and some of our friends.

"Speaking of messes, little brother…" Dean says forebodingly. The bar area has begun to get crowded, and I already wish I was in our private area away from the crowd.

"Reid," Amber says seductively, and before I can anticipate her moves, she's plastered her body and her lips to me. I quickly move away, leaving a shocked Amber in my wake. I haven't seen her for weeks, but it's not uncommon for us to hookup.

"Our table is ready," Elise announces from Dean's side. She raises an eyebrow in my direction, and I know she witnessed Amber's tongue down my throat. Before I can stop her, she turns and walks to the area where her team is taking their seats.

"Go ahead. I'll deal with this." Dean motions his head, and I take a seat next to Elise.

"Elise—"

"Look, Reid," she interrupts me. "I don't do bullshit. And I try not to do drama. Until you give me a reason otherwise,

I trust you. I'm not oblivious to the fact you had a life before me."

I know her well enough to know she means what she says, even if she didn't like what she saw.

"She and I have always been casual. Usually just picking up where we left off. Sex only. I'll make sure she knows."

"Thank you. I appreciate it."

I wait for more to come, and when it doesn't, I'm not sure how I feel about it. On one hand, I find it refreshing Elise is not into all the drama that comes with so many of the women in our circle. On the other hand, I know the reason she is so easily able to detach herself from it comes from a lifetime of sucking it up and fixing whatever bothers her. I don't want to see her do that with me. I want all of Elise, no matter what's going on in her crazy head or how she processes something.

We're at a large table with booths on all four sides that each seat two. Ryan and Gabby are sharing. Fran and Dean are across from us, and Blake is in the booth to our right. When I glance up, they all look like they want to kick my ass. Elise notices and with a nod of her head, they all go back to their menus. Dean orders wine and some appetizers for the table. Elise takes my hand and relaxes against me, resting her head on my shoulder as everyone discusses what they are going to order.

"Do you want me to order for you?" I ask, since she hasn't picked up her menu.

She sits up. "Did you want to order for me?"

The seriousness of the question throws me off. "No. You just were resting your head and not looking at your menu, so I wanted to make sure." *Settle your feathers.* She sees a girl push her tongue down my throat, but she's not off balance until I offer to order for her?

"No, I've eaten here with my family before. I know what I want."

I hold back what I really want to say, glad to see an acquaintance walk up who is joining us for dinner. I stand to shake his hand and make the introductions.

"I'd like you guys to meet West Connors. We're going to be doing some work with him over the next few weeks."

"Southie?" Blake looks up from his menu a little stunned. "What the hell man." He pulls West into a one-armed hug. "You guys, this is one of my childhood best friends. We haven't see each other in what?"

"Ten years," West says coolly.

"Here. Have a seat." Blake shifts to the end of the booth next to Elise, making way for him.

"This is so surreal." Blake looks to Elise and their crew. He puts his hand on West's shoulder and points to him. "This guy is the only reason I made it out of my hellhole of a childhood. I used to stay with his family all the time."

"Why don't we order then you can tell us some stories about Blake," Elise suggests catching the waiter's eye.

West seems a little off balance. We listen in on what Blake was like growing up while I observe the team. They really are interested to know. They care about each other, but I'm still not certain what to make of it. Elise excuses herself to go to the restroom, as Dean picks up the conversation. Several minutes go by and there's a beep to Blake's pager and his phone buzzes.

"Where is she?" He's terse. Hanging up the phone, he leans over to me. "Elise is to the left of the bar. I need you to go over there and ask her if she would like another glass of wine."

"What does—"

"Now." The tone in his voice has the hairs on my neck standing up. Immediately I stand and spot Elise right where Blake said she would be. She's talking to Senator Blackwell. I button my suit coat as I weave between the standing tables. When I make my way to her, I slide my arm around Elise, planting a kiss to her temple.

"Would you like another glass of wine?" I ask her. My eyes lock on hers, but I can't read her. "My apologies. Reid Beckett." I introduce myself to the Senator.

"Mr. Beckett. I'm a fan of your work."

"Thank you."

"Maybe we could meet sometime?"

"Give my office a call. Sorry to interrupt. Elise, your guests are waiting."

"Senator Blackwell," she says before turning and heading back to our table. We take our seat, but before I can say anything, Blake gives a slight move to his head indicating this isn't the time or place. Elise never misses a beat and slides right into commenting on a story Fran is telling. Dean catches my eye, and I know my brother well enough to know what he's thinking. Yep, this isn't going to work.

chapter thirteen

Elise

I know Reid is still uncomfortable with my role. I caught the look he gave his brother when we sat down after he rescued me from the senator.

We all make plans to meet at Reid's tomorrow while they are putting the finishing touches on our offices at work. Plus, I want to take a step back and think about the roles I want everyone in. We will be doing more corporate work now that we are in New York with Reid, and I imagine we will be pulled into more political messes since we are closer to D.C. Somehow, I need to figure out a way to limit that happening without cutting off our ties and relationships with the people I need to get my job done.

We ride in silence on our way back to Reid's. The night didn't end as I had suspected.

"Where's Nova?" I ask, breaking the tension.

"What?" Reid asks.

"Nova. He wasn't at your house today when we were there."

"He was getting his yearly check up at the vet today."

I nod, and we ride the rest of the way home without another word spoken. Reid opens my door for me once we are in his garage, but instead of going into the main house, he directs me to the elevator to the master floor. I barely have one foot off the elevator when Reid pushes me against the wall. His eyes are filled with lust and frustration.

"Why do I have to keep reminding you that I run this?"

"You don't, Reid. You just need to understand that running this," I motion between us, "doesn't mean running me."

His frustration is palpable, and I feel it in his hands when he grabs the V-neck of my dress and tears it down the middle.

"You owe me $250 for this dress." I'm so wet for him, it's the only challenge I can think to give.

His eyes lock on mine, his face inches from my own. He watches me like he's trying to decide what he's going to do.

Finally, he growls, "I'm gonna make you come like no man ever has. I want to hear you scream."

"Make me."

It's the kind of day that reminds me why I love this city. The temperature is perfect and the sun is high over the skyline. Buildings surround Reid's courtyard, there's plenty of privacy, but you can still feel that you're in the city. He's having lunch catered today, so there is really nothing for me to do except work and gather my thoughts.

I'm doing some reading on my iPad when he comes out onto the patio. He leans me forward so he can crawl in behind me on the cushioned lounger then pulls me to him and puts an arm around my shoulder.

"What are you thinking about?" he asks.

"Just reading some reports for a case."

He leans down and kisses the top of my head. "Why are you reading a bill about a highway?"

"I'm not. I'm reading the amendments."

"Okay. Why are you reading the amendments?"

Propping my legs up, I lean back and attempt to explain it without giving too much away.

"Some bills are huge. Hundreds, even thousands of pages."

"Is this a Saturday morning special? I know how bills work, Elise."

"Sarcasm is the lowest form of wit, Reid. In a bill this huge, they attach crazy amendments that they know wouldn't pass on their own. This highway bill means a lot of money for a lot of states."

"So what did someone attach to it?"

"There is so much junk attached to this bill."

"But specifically what are you looking for?"

"A couple of things, actually."

I'm cut off by a ring on the iPad.

"Emily!" I wave into the iPad at Ryan's sister. She's lying back in her hospital bed, and I can see the tubing running along the mattress beside her. "How's my favorite little sister?"

"I'm good. Where are you?"

"I'm in New York. You're looking a little green today. What's going on kiddo?"

"They changed me to a new chemo, and it's not sitting to well with me. I can only talk for a few minutes; I've been getting sick every 30 minutes or so."

"What are they saying about your new regimen?"

"Elise, I call you to talk about girl stuff. If I wanted to talk about how I was feeling, I would call Ryan."

"I'm sorry. You're right. Did you read the book I sent you?"

"I finished it last night. He got the girl."

"He did," I smile.

"They always get the girl." She rolls her eyes, but secretly I know she wants to read books where the endings are always happy.

"Not always, but you'll have plenty of time to read those."

"How do you like being back in the city? Have you seen your family?"

"Not yet. My brother is traveling. My parents are out of the country until next week, and Bren is finishing a six-week escalated course at Harvard before finishing her semester at NYU."

"Are you still sleeping with your boss? Is that his arm I see possessively wrapped around you?"

"I'm gonna stop sending you those books."

"Mom found the one you tried to sneak in. She said she was going to have a talk with you. I asked her what she expected from someone who walks around naked in front of clergy."

"I wasn't walking around naked, and don't you dare rat me out to your mother."

"Fine. I'll tell her Gabby put it in there. She'll definitely believe that one."

We laugh, only hers is raspy and sounds like just the effort is exhausting.

"Can I say hello to the best sex you've ever had?"

"I'm the best sex you've ever had?" Reid asks over my head.

"Oh my God, Emily. Please don't give him a big head."

"Hi, Emily." Reid lifts his sunglasses and looks into the iPad.

"Holy shit."

Reid frowns at the use of her language. "You really have been hanging around the girls too much," he teases. This makes Emily smile.

"You said he was good-looking, but I didn't know he was that good-looking."

"Are you sure this is appropriate for someone her age."

"I'm thirteen. Not ten," Emily answers.

"Actually she's a twenty-year-old trapped in a thirteen-year-old body."

"Does your brother know you talk about this stuff?" Reid asks.

"No. And you aren't going to tell him. I won't get to experience this stuff on my own. Let me have fun while I can."

"One day you'll be sitting on a patio with your person in New York," I assure her. "She'll just be ahead of the game," I tell Reid.

"Elise." I can hear the change in Emily's voice. "You and I both know that isn't true."

"Emily, I'm not giving up, so you can't give up."

"I'm not giving up, Elise. I'm facing the facts. This treatment is the last option we have, and the scans aren't coming back any different."

"Emily, you never know what they will discover tomorrow."

"Elise, we talked about this. It's time. You promised me."

"Emily."

"Elise." She looks at me through the screen and her eyes haunt me. "Elise." Her voice has a command to it. "Don't let me down. Please. You promised. It's time."

I sit up and look into the iPad.

"I promised." I wipe the tears falling down my face. Emily grabs a bucket and starts vomiting before I see her fingers trying to find the disconnect button on the screen. She's gone.

"Elise?" Reid brings me back to the here and now, and when I turn to look at him, he's my undoing. Before he can prepare himself, I plaster myself to him, my legs wrapping around his waist. His arms encase me, and right then, I know there are times I need protecting. Protection from myself.

"Dove. What—"

"I love you, Reid."

He stares at me for a moment and then his hands wrap around my cheeks. "I love you, Elise."

"What does that mean to you exactly?" It's something I've been wanting to ask him for a while now.

"It means you own my heart."

"I mean what kind of love?"

"I don't understand?"

"What kind of love do you have for me, Reid? Do you love me unconditionally?"

"I. Love. You," he emphasizes before his mouth claims mine.

"We said we were okay with it. Not that we wanted to see it," Blake says as he enters, the others following behind.

"I want to see it," Gabby says.

"There really is something wrong with you." Fran rolls her eyes and sets her laptop on the table.

"I'll be right back." I make an escape without making any eye contact. Nova follows me into the bathroom, and I take deep breaths until I can contain myself. Releasing the last long breath, I make my way through the kitchen. Everyone is fixing a plate of the food Reid had brought in. Reid plants a kiss to my temple. I love the fact he isn't afraid to show affection in front of others. He really doesn't care what anyone thinks.

"Elise." Dean walks up behind me and kisses the top of my head.

"Dean?" I greet him with a furrowed brow.

"You are my sister-in-law. I think we are past the handshakes, don't you think?"

"I met you yesterday," I remind him, raising my left hand looking at my empty ring finger. "Would we really say I was your sister-in-law?"

"Potato, po-tah-to. My little brother has never said I love you to anyone. Or ever looked at anyone the way he looks at you."

"What are you doing here, Dean?" Reid walks back in to fix a plate. "Dean, leave Elise alone."

"No worries, bro. I'm here to get to know the team. After all, they're part of BE now. Gabby here?" He looks to me with so much hope that I can't help but laugh.

"I told you, no sleeping with associates."

"Really?" Dean and I say in unison at the shear hypocrisy of his declaration.

"Elise wasn't my associate when we first started sleeping together."

"Have you heard from Theo?" Dean asks me. "Has he signed the papers?"

"Yesterday."

"Fuck yes. Then I'm covered too, bro."

"What did you do?" Reid glares at his brother.

"We sealed the deal before she was our associate."

Reid looks from Dean to me, and I nod. "Two nights ago," I confirm.

"She told you?" Dean sidles up to me. "What did she say?"

"Has Reid explained my position in the company?"

"Yes."

"Then you know what I do for a living?"

"Yes," he says, not sure where this is going.

I pull out the gun I have tucked in my waist band and place it on the counter, never taking my eyes of him.

"I use dicks like yours for target practice. Don't give me an excuse to add yours to my collection. Understood?"

He doesn't hide his amused look.

"What are you smiling about?"

"You're not the only one with connections, Elise. I've looked into you. I have no doubt you mean it. I'm smiling because she must be willing to give me a chance if you are giving me the shoot-my-dick-off warning."

"Nice talking with you BIL." I pick up my gun and my plate and make my way onto the patio.

"At least you're carrying it," Blake says as I re-holster it into my waist band.

"Nice to see you, West."

"I wasn't sure if we would be covering the assignment we will be working on with him or not, so I thought I would invite him."

"It's fine. Has he signed a nondisclosure?" I look to Reid who nods a confirmation. "No problem then. Plus, any friend of Blake's is a friend of mine."

He seems a little uneasy, so I give him a welcoming smile.

"So is today all business?" Gabs asks, tearing into her bread.

"I brought cards," Blake announces, setting them on the table.

"Do any of you know what it's like to work in a real office environment?" Reid asks.

"Don't disturb the creative process, boss," Gabby says.

Blake answers his phone. "Thomas...When? Fuck a priest. Follow her. What about Fellinger? New York? Why New... did someone schedule a meeting with you?" He gestures for me to join the conversation.

I glance at my emails and see what Blake expects me to see. Turning the phone to him, I verbally confirm, "Senator Blackwell asked me to meet a client as a favor to him." I smile knowing we are closer to solving our case, but my smile is met with a frown from Blake. He disconnects his call.

"How long are you staying here?" he asks me.

"I'm going to Bren's tonight."

"She still have that place on 8th?"

"Yep."

"Can she let my guys in there?"

"She's out of town. I have the place to myself till she's back."

"Not anymore you don't. You have a new roommate. Can you let the doorman know I'm allowed in?" He dials a number on his phone.

"She doesn't have a doorman."

He looks frustrated. "Then give me the key."

"No."

"Elise."

"Blake."

"Hey, it's Thomas. Elise has been made. I want three men on her in thirty minutes. Coordinate with Reid's man, Cooper. I'm texting you his number now."

"Reid—" he starts, but I cut him off.

"No."

"Reid, I'm in charge of security for this team. I can no longer guarantee Elise's safety."

"You already have two guys on me. I saw them at the restaurant last night."

"I wasn't trying to hide them from you, Elise. If I was, you wouldn't know they were there. Why are you fighting me on this? You never argue with Theo when I make these decisions."

"Because, you aren't having a conversation with me about it. You keep running to Reid when I push back."

"Are you done?"

"Are you both done?" Reid asks. "Elise will be staying here with me. What are we looking at exactly?"

"Nothing that I can't handle, as long as I have her cooperation."

"Don't." Reid cuts me off.

"Ugh. Fuck a priest," I spit out in frustration. Blake is right. I wouldn't be pushing back if this was Theo still in charge. But it's not, and even though I respect Reid, I'm not convinced that he truly respects my role. He wants me in a protected box. I don't want to keep having the same argument. I need to win this one.

I stand and take the empty plates to the kitchen. West enters, bringing me a couple more.

"Frustrating to have people talk around you and not to you, isn't it?" he says.

"You sound like you have some experience in this area."

"I come from a very boisterous family with seven older siblings. My family wrote the book on this." He smiles and I realize what a truly beautiful man he is.

"You should model." I tell him. "You're stunning." He rewards me with a blush that makes me laugh.

"You've been around Blake too long. You have no filter."

"Maybe I'm the one who corrupted him."

"You forget, I've known him since he was a kid."

"True. I haven't had a chance to talk to Reid yet about the assignment, but I know he plans to have Blake take the lead. Is that going to be okay?" I study him.

"Of course. Why wouldn't it be?"

"Your reaction to seeing him last night just made me think you weren't exactly excited to run into him. Although he seems thrilled to have seen you?"

He looks around for a minute before leaning against the counter.

"We didn't part on the best of terms."

"Well, that was some time ago. He's changed a lot since I've known him, so I know he's changed even more since you guys parted ways. He's a good guy. You can trust him." I offer him a kind smile. He seems unsure.

"Trusting him was never a problem. We'll be fine. If you all think he is best for the case then I can work with that."

"Good. Now grab the bowls." I motion to the ones on the counter and grab the ice cream out of the freezer.

"So, how long has this been going on?" Dean asks. Blake is shuffling cards.

"Three years," Fran answers. Blake deals and I take the seat across from him. Reid is logging onto his laptop a couple of seats down. I motion for West to take a seat beside me.

"More," I tell Fran. She adds another scoop of ice cream to my bowl then takes her seat once everyone has a bowl and starts arranging her cards.

"When is Theo coming?" Gabs asks, shifting some cards around. Dean is watching over her shoulder.

"Next week. He'll be here for the benefit," Reid answers

from his perch.

"I can take 8," I tell Blake.

"You can take 8?"

"Yep."

"Are you sure? You always overtrick."

I feign shock and look at West.

"I think he just called you a whore," he says with a mischievous smile.

"Not helping, Southie," Blake grumbles, writing down our projections.

"Why do you call him Southie?" Fran asks around a mouthful of chocolate.

"My family moved to New York from Tennessee when I was five. Someone called me Southie and it stuck."

"I went out with a guy from Tennessee," Gabby says, laying down her card.

"Didn't work out?"

"He cried during sex."

"Ugh," Fran and I respond.

"Are you going to look up Frank while you are in town?" Ryan asks Fran. He's on the iPad I was using.

"No." The look on her face only invites more questions.

"What was wrong with him?" Ryan asks. "He was a nice guy."

"He's a no. He's a face-eater. Thought my lips went all the way to my forehead."

"How was he with your other lips?" Gabby asks. "I could forgive the messy kissing if it meant he knew how to kiss Roxy."

"You are the only girl I know who has named her vagina," Blake says, throwing the last card. We lost this round.

"How many times do I have to tell you Roxy is not my vagina?"

"Forgive me." Blake offers his hands up in a conciliatory manner. "Your love lady."

"You named your pus—"

"Dean," Reid says, not looking up from his laptop.

"Have you ever had a threesome?" Fran's question stops the conversation. Everyone turns to look at her.

"Why do you ask, Frannie?"

"I was just curious, Elise."

"Yep," Blake answers.

"Nope," some of the others answer. I raise an eyebrow at Dean, West, and Reid who choose not to answer.

"What about William?" I ask Fran. "He still lives in New York."

"No. He kept trying to slap my...Roxy...like it was a whack-a-mole."

West isn't used to this group and is unable to hold in his laughter.

"Newbie," Gabby says, nodding at West.

"Speaking of West," Reid interjects. "Graham Taylor has asked us to look into making the Rodman Community Center a viable center. It appears there has been some mismanagement of funds, and he needs us to see who's been working the books."

"Why doesn't the city handle it?" Ryan asks.

"The city closed it two years ago. The Foundation is rejuvenating community centers in urban neighborhoods. The initiative is to give jobs to the local adults while giving care to the youth of the area."

"The Foundation? Is that the one that all the billionaires created and gave like half or more of their money to?" Fran asks.

"Yes. No one knows what their resources are, but rumor

has it they are a 150-billion-dollar foundation. Graham's wife—"

"Emme," I correct Reid. "Her name is Emme. She is more than just Mrs. Graham Taylor."

"*Emme*, is passionate about reaching the youth of these areas and oversees all presentations that go before the board. Graham wants to make sure this project succeeds. We have to get a handle on where the money is going and minimize any negative publicity the mismanagement of funds could create."

"I take it since West is at the table he's been ruled out?" Ryan comments.

"Yes. He's a volunteer coach. He doesn't have any inter-action with the books. He is on the inside, though, and has a relationship with Emme. Graham says we can trust him, and he can help fill us in. Blake will be lead on the project and will update each of you when needed."

The conversation turns back to random things. I've been watching Dean who hasn't taken his eyes off Gabby. This doesn't deter Gabby one bit, and she remains as crass and rambunctious as ever. You have to love Gabby. She is who she is.

"If you could sleep with one celebrity who would it be?" Gabby asks, throwing an ace.

"Matt Bomer," I answer without hesitation.

"He's gay," Ryan says.

"And? What does that have to do with anything?"

"You can't choose a gay man, Elise," Fran says. "You've already slept with a gay man."

"Is there a gay-man quota I don't know about? And to be fair, when I slept with him, he wasn't out as a gay man."

"But was he—"

Cutting Blake off, I answer my ringing cell.

"Elise Donovan."

"Elise, this is Dr. Davis."

"Yes. Thank you for calling me back." I shuffle out from behind the table and head inside. "I wanted to talk to you about Emily," I say when I am out of earshot of the others.

"Yes, I saw her this morning. She told me I could expect a call from you."

"I gotta give it to her. She's thorough."

"She's an exceptional child."

"She is. The keyword is child. I assume she told you her wishes."

"Yes, her mom had gone back to the charity house to shower for the day. She discussed openly her desire to stop treatment. She asked me not to discuss it with her mom until she had a chance to talk to you. This is highly unusual, but I did see you are on the approved HIPPA list. Can I ask your relationship to the family?"

"I'm a close family friend. I call and check on Emily often, and I stayed with her for a couple of days so I could arrange for a few days away for her parents. I was added to her caregiver list then. I'm afraid I know a little more about you, doctor, than you know about me. Not to startle you, but I know you have three kids. One not much younger than Emily."

"You know this how?"

"It's an occupational hazard, I'm afraid. No one was going to touch Emily without a full background check. My apologies, but I need you to talk to me as a physician and not as a parent. Is this the right decision for Emily? I understand she is on a new experimental medication. What are the chances this one will work?"

"Well, we're getting smarter every day. More and more we are extending the life of the patients that have the kind of cancer that Emily has."

"Dr. Davis. please."

"This treatment I believe could give her a couple of months added to her life."

"Which gets us where?"

"As I told her mom last week, we are looking at three to six months."

"Is it three or six?"

"There is no crystal ball, I would err on the side of three."

"Three without treatment," I repeat, deep in thought.

"Three with treatment," he gently clarifies.

"Is there any experimental drug in the works that will be available in the next four to six months that would significantly change the timeframe?"

He pauses. "I'm sorry. No. There isn't."

"So, I ask you now as a parent. What would you do?"

"I would want to fight until the end. But that would be about me and not my child. As a doctor, I want my patients to have the best time they can have while they have it."

"So, let her have her wish and go home?"

"Yes."

"Thank you, doctor. I'll see you in the morning." I hang up the phone and stare out the picture window to the park across the street trying to catalog my thoughts.

"Elise?" Reid calls my name, and I turn to see everyone coming inside.

"What is it?" Gabby asks on full alert when she sees my face.

"Ryan." I look at him, and Blake wraps an arm around his shoulders, expecting the worse.

"It's not what you think. But it is about Emily. She called me today."

"What about?"

"Ryan, it's time."

He looks past me, out the window. "No, it's not Elise. This isn't your call."

"No, it's not my call. It's hers. And your parents. And yours. The four of you need to make this call together, because you are going to need each other to get through this."

"Stay out of it, Elise." Ryan's voice rises, and Fran moves to his side. He shrugs out of Blake's hold. "This isn't a case for you. She's not some assignment. She's my baby sister."

"Ryan, I gave her my word."

"When she was sick from chemo and high on pain meds. We would have said anything to make her feel better that week."

"Ryan, this will be easier for your parents if we go in there as a united front. It's the only way we have of convincing them.

"Elise…" His voice is filled with pain.

"Ryan, listen to her. She knows what she wants."

"She's thirteen, Elise. She's my sister, not yours. You don't know her like I do."

"You're right. But I gave her my word. No matter how hard this gets, I have to do what Emily wants. I'll be flying to Memphis in the morning. I will have a plane waiting for us. Once your parents see this is what Emily wants, they will fly privately home. I'll make sure there is a nurse on the flight, and I will have hospice set up for home visits before we arrive."

"She's not your client, Elise. You can't just ride in on your horse and take over."

"I made a promise to her. That makes her my client. I would prefer us to do this the easy way, but I am prepared to legally fight on her behalf. Don't make me. *Listen to your sister*," I plead with my friend.

"Fuck you, Elise. If you step one foot in Memphis, I'll have you removed. You're not the only one who knows how to play this game. I can do heartless. After all, I learned from the best."

"Ryan," Gabby says softly, knowing his words just ripped through me.

"Ryan." Blake puts his hand on his shoulder.

"Get off me." Ryan pulls away, taking steps towards me. I see Reid starting to move, but he wisely stops when Blake puts his hand up. With clenched fists and teeth, Ryan leans down, level with my face. The desperation in his eyes is more than enough to break my heart into two.

"Stay the fuck away from my family," he says and stomps out the door. Fran follows him.

"Elise," Gabby and Blake say in unison.

"I'm fine."

"Do you need help making the arrangements?" Gabby offers.

"No. Ryan is going to need you all to make it through this. I don't want anyone else involved. Blake, I'll call you with my details so you can arrange my security. Although, if someone was really going to try something, they might want to wait. I'm not in the mood for this shit."

"My guys will be ready when you are."

They all stand there frozen for another minute.

"Go." I wave them to the door. "Ryan needs you."

"Go ahead," Reid assures them, coming to stand beside me.

The door shuts, and Reid and I are left standing alone in his luxury townhouse.

"I'm going to be sick." I make it to the half bath just in time to empty the contents of my stomach into the toilet. Reid hands me a washcloth. I stand there for a minute, still holding my hair back, making sure I'm done before I move. I pull the ringing cell from my pocket. It's Theo.

chapter fourteen

Reid

E lise has been on the phone with Theo for more than an hour. I finally grabbed Nova and left for a run, taking my frustrations out on the pavement. Why did I ever think it was a good idea to buy Theo's business? I knew I would be positioning this team to do corporate takeovers and then to fix the companies I get for pennies on the dollar. I just didn't realize how involved they are in certain areas. I did my research and everyone agreed with Theo: Elise is the maestro. I underestimated not only her business connections, but her connections with the team. No matter what spin I put on this, I know the real unaccounted contingency is me. I didn't have a plan for falling in love with her.

Once again Elise found herself in a position to take the heat for something out of her control. I feel for what Ryan is going through, but it took all I had not to intervene when he said those things to her. One thing I have learned in business is to rely on those who know what they are doing to guide things. I had to trust Gabby and Blake to step in if needed.

Nova and I climb the steps leading into the townhouse. Elise is no longer in the living area. There's a note on the fridge saying she is across the street at the park. I grab an extra bottle of water before Nova and I walk across the street.

I love this park. Every time I insert the key into the gate I remember why I bought this place. In no other part of the city can you find an exclusive park right outside your door. Nova and I find Elise on a bench under an oak tree not far off the path.

When I sit down, she lays her head across my lap. "Should you be taking the day off? Aren't you behind?"

"I've been working. I'll work some more later. I'd rather talk about what happened in there today."

"There's nothing to talk about. You saw everything. By the way, I checked with your assistant and booked your plane for the next two days. I'm hoping his parents will see it Emily's way and let her go home. Since it will be a medical transport, you can write it off. I hope that's okay. I would have chartered one, but I'm not sure what the timeframe is going to be."

"I don't mind, and I could care less about the expense."

"I can ask to use one of the Taylor's planes if you are going to need yours."

"Elise, it's fine. I can fly commercial if something comes up. This is more important. I want to talk about how you are feeling. I know it hurt to hear Ryan say those things to you."

"I'm okay, Reid. Theo heard from Gabby as soon as they walked out. He's already talked to me about it."

My hand falls still in her hair, and I grow quiet.

"I love you, Reid. Theo and I have been together for a long time. He knows Ryan and this team. It's going to take some time for me to adjust to not talking with him about things."

"I don't mind you talking to him about work, Elise. What I mind is you talking to him about everything."

She sits up. "What are you saying? Reid, Theo and I have been friends my whole life. He's my best friend. We talk to each other. You and I are still learning about each other. Just because we are in love doesn't mean we don't have growing to do."

"I'm in a relationship with you, not Theo. How do you propose we grow when you tell him what you are thinking and not me? I already have to share you with the team."

"First off, I love the team, but they are not Theo. Secondly, what do you mean share me? I have relationships with people, Reid. I'm not going to be locked up and only pine for you. You fell in love with the wrong girl if that is what you are looking for."

"That's not what I want and you know it."

"Then what do you want?'

"I want your intimacy. I want to be your everything. And, no, I don't want to consume you, I want to complement you. I want to be to you what you are to me. I've never felt this way before, Elise. I swear to God I feel like I've stepped into the fucking Twilight Zone. I've never wanted to be a part of someone."

"I'm in this, Reid. Every step. You are my first thought when I wake up, and I dream of you at night. What else do I have to do to show you? I have given you a level of myself that I've never given to anyone. I don't have to be in a box for you to understand that. And I won't be. These are your issues, not mine. I suggest you fix them. I'm going back to the house."

I don't say another word, but I'm grateful when she lets

me wrap my arm around her. Nova climbs the stairs ahead of us once we are inside. When we reach the top floor, I can't contain it anymore. I pin her against the wall. Neither of us speaks a word. I slide off her leggings and her sweater to find she's not wearing any underwear. She's naked before me. Beautiful. Frustrating. I press my body against hers. Still fully dressed, I pull the front of my running pants down, freeing my cock. It falls rigid against her stomach. I bend my knees slightly and locks eyes with her beautiful grays before pushing into her in one solid stroke.

I pause—not out of a fear of losing control, but out of a need to be inside her. I eventually regain my composure and begin to rock in and out of her. The only audible sound is our breathing. I fuck her against the wall, working us to a point where we explode around each other. It's an encounter unlike any we've had. No frills. No unbridled passion. Just me inside of her. I'm struck by the intimacy of it.

I soften and slide out of her. Straightening myself, I leave her standing there naked, my come running down her thighs.

I make my way downstairs. I've only made it a few steps when Dean's voice announces over the intercom that he and Gabby are in the kitchen. Fuck me, why did I ever give him a key? I release a deep breath of frustration and take the remaining flights down.

"To what do I owe the pleasure?" Dean catches my sarcasm. Gabby doesn't. Or maybe she does and chooses to ignore it.

"How's Elise?" Gabby asks.

"She should be down in a minute."

"I asked how she is."

"You need to ask her that question."

"I'm asking you that question," she glares.

"I don't have an answer for you, Gabby."

She starts to say something, but either catches the look Dean gives her or decides to hold her tongue on her own. Either way, I'm grateful.

"We brought dinner," Dean says and starts unpacking Chinese cartons from my favorite place a few blocks over.

"It's not necessary."

"Just say thank you, Reid."

"Thank you, Dean." I roll my eyes.

"Chinese," Elise says, entering the kitchen. She's wearing flannel socks that stop at her thighs, two inches below my cardigan sweater. The V-neck dips low between her breasts. She has her hair pulled into a big bowl of curls on top of her head. Her gray eyes stand out against the blue of the sweater and her face is beautiful without a speck of makeup. This girl brings me to my knees without even trying.

"You're exquisite." The words leave my mouth before I even know they are coming. She's beside me now, and I can't help it. I have to kiss her. My lips brush hers with every ounce of love I have for this woman. Her eyes lower, but not before I catch their shimmer. Her arms wrap around me in a hug that seems to be more for my benefit than hers.

"I love you, Reid."

"I love you, Dove."

I grab a bottle of wine and point to a cabinet. Elise grabs four glasses and we take our seats at the table with Gabby and Dean.

I love this part of the house, the iron work on the large windows overlooking the courtyard, the city poking up through the trees. It feels like a place where people want to be. I hate that it gets used so rarely. I usually eat out or at the island.

"How's Ryan?" Elise asks Gabby.

"He's upset. He tried to lock Fran out, but she got the hotel to give her a key to his room. She is going to stay with him tonight. She doesn't want him to be alone."

"Good. I don't want him to be either."

"How are you?"

"I'm fine."

"Elise."

"Heartless, but fine."

"Elise," I growl. "I'm not impartial to what is going on. Ryan and I agree for different reasons. I don't want to see you hurting. I don't like you mixed up in this."

"I made a promise, Reid. Emily has fought for a long time. She's stronger than any of us could possibly be. She said she would say when she was ready. That was more than a year ago. She's done. She's not giving up, but she wants to be at home surrounded by her things. By her animals. Friends and family. She wants to be on the farm she loves. She wants her last months to be quality even if it changes the quantity."

"The thing is, Ryan knows this," Gabby adds. "This is what he wants for Emily. He just can't say it. He can't be the one who says it's time to stop fighting."

"That's why I have to do it for him," Elise says. "He's my friend. He may or may not choose to forgive me, but he would never forgive himself."

"Don't you think that's a heavy burden to carry?" Dean asks.

"Not for Elise," Gabby answers. "Elise is not heartless."

"I know that, babe. Anybody can see that," Dean responds, and I catch Elise's smile at his endearment for Gabby.

"That's just it. Not everyone sees it. When you do what Elise does, it's easy to think she is heartless. It's what gives her the edge over everyone else. They mistake her for being emotionless, but really she has a huge heart and reads people better than anyone I know. She can call a bull-shitter from a hundred yards. Her heart is directly connected to her ability to read people. That's what makes her formidable."

"But I don't always get it right." Elise bites into a spring roll. "I've made some doozies in my life time."

"Evil can slip in everyone's door before you realize it. It's sneaky. That happens to everyone, Elise. It's not a character flaw."

Dean and I watch these two women. We are merely spectators in this conversation. I have to admit, there's a history I don't have with Elise that these friends do—that Theo does.

"So, who won the card game?" Dean changes the subject.

I study him for a moment, wondering what has happened to him. This man who had not a serious bone in his body is now calling Gabby "babe" and is trying to direct the subject to lighter matters.

"Today it was me and Fran," Gabby answers. "We're still way behind Elise and Blake. We'd have to win the next three months to take the lead."

"Is it always like it was today?"

"How so?" Elise asks.

"So entertaining."

"Yes," I laugh.

Elise rolls her eyes. "It's just conversation. Whatever comes to mind." She gives up her chopsticks for the large spoon we used to serve. "What?" she asks when I can't hide a smile.

"Opting for the shovel?" I tease.

"I'm eating my feelings. Let me be. You knew what my thighs looked like before you fell in love with me. No judging."

I kiss her temple. "Eat it all sweetheart. I adore your thighs."

"Gag me," Dean says.

"I know, right?" Gabby rolls her eyes.

"This is good. Mindless conversation. Keep it coming," Elise motions with her hand.

"Fran," Dean and Gabby say at the same time, cracking up.

Elise leans forward. "What have I missed?"

Gabby shrugs her shoulders and raises her hands. "When you guys kissed at the retreat, she said she hadn't been laid in a month."

"Girl can kiss though. Wonder who she's thinking about having a threesome with?"

"You and Fran kissed? What kind of retreat was this?" Dean asks with a raised brow.

Gabby shushes him. "Does she kiss better than me?"

Elise releases a deep breath of air. "You know you are my favorite girl-kiss, Gabriella Jane." Elise breaks a fortune cookie open.

"You guys are going to make Dean's head explode with that visual," I quip.

"Don't be nasty." Gabby hits him on the side of the head.

"You were the one—"

"Anyways," Gabby interrupts. "I wonder who she was thinking about having a threesome with."

"Who knows," Elise says, pulling out a small piece of paper.

"Maybe she and Ryan will hook up tonight."

"Gabby," Elise warns.

"Now that he sees you are off the market, maybe he'll realize he is meant to be with Fran."

Elise makes a noise that sounds like two fighting kittens sneezing. "Clarinet," Elise says and shows Gabby her fortune.

Gabby opens hers and says something just as indecipherable. "Cook top," she explains, showing her piece of paper to Elise.

Elise responds to the looks on my and Dean's faces. "Chinese. The fortunes each have a word on it that you learn to say in Chinese."

"I'm one-hundred percent sure that's not how you pronounce those words," Dean says. Both girls shrugging in response.

"What does your fortune say?" Gabby asks Elise.

"All things are difficult before they are easy."

"Fitting. Mine says 'For rectal use only.'"

"Bullshit." Elise grabs the paper and cracks up, telling us all it really does say that. Wiping away her tears of laughter she says, "Thank you guys. I needed this."

"Glad we could help," Dean says like this was all his doing.

"So we really don't know who Fran was talking about? You'd tell me if you knew, right?" Elise asks.

"Maybe it was hypothetical," Dean offers. "Like you sleeping with a gay man."

"Gay movie star. She's slept with a gay man." Gabby loads the last of the boxes into the trash bag.

"He wasn't sure if he was bi or gay. He wasn't full-on gay until I introduced him to Ross."

"A week later."

"You've slept with Theo?" My intention was to ask this as casually as possible, but based on the looks I'm getting, I'm not nailing it.

"In college," Elise explains.

I try to maintain some self-control. I really do.

"I'm going out." I leave a stunned group at the table and snatch up my coat on the way out the front door. I'm not dressed for most places, but there's a bar I frequent a few blocks over that doesn't have a dress code.

The bartender greets me by name and pours me a double before I even warm the seat. My phone dings.

Elise: I can't fix this if you walk out.

I stew for a while. The bartender sets another double in front of me. Picking up my phone I text her back.

Me: I'm not a fucking case to fix Elise. Don't wait up.

It's less than a minute before it dings again. "

Elise: Read the text again, Dumbledick. I didn't say YOU needed to be fixed.

"Fuck it." I toss my phone on the bar and drink.

"Damn, you're a stupid shit," Dean says, taking the seat next to me.

"Go away, Dean. I'm not in the mood."

"You're throwing a tantrum, and you're about to sabotage the best thing that's ever happened to you."

I down the remainder of my drink, waving to the bartender for a third.

"How many?" Dean asks him.

"Three."

"Cut him off at five."

"Fuck you," I spit.

"Coop, he's all yours," Dean says over my shoulder. I turn to see Coop sitting at a table against the wall, nursing a beer. Wonder how long he's been there. I should have known.

Dean leaves, and I drink the last two I'm allowed over the next couple of hours. Coop never says a word. When I've finished my five, he walks me back to the house and makes sure

I am in and locked up before disappearing back to his place.

I stagger my way into the elevator. It seems like a safer mode of transportation to the top floor than the stairs.

Elise is already asleep, and instead of her normal, splayed sleeping style, she's curled in a ball around her pillow. She looks small. Lost.

I stumble out of my shoes and jacket and make my way to the closet to change into a pair of sleeping pants. I brush my teeth and down a bottle of water and some ibuprofen to ward off my impending hangover.

Something catches my eye, and I notice Elise is sleeping with her phone in her hand. I extract it as gently as I can, given I'm almost drunk enough to have to choose the one in the middle, and place it on the night stand.

I slide under the sheets, and it only takes a minute in her slumber for Elise to be drawn to me. She wraps her arm around me and snuggles in. I'm only so strong and in this proximity I can't hold out. I wrap my arms around her before drifting off to sleep.

I forgot to close the skylights last night and the light is pouring in, torturing me. I feel better than I should, but my head still feels like a mariachi band set up in it last night.

The bed is empty. I find Elise in the bathroom, sliding into a pair of old school Adidas. She looks so young in jeans and a striped shirt. She's fresh-faced again.

"I have to leave for the airport in thirty minutes. I was trying to let you sleep as long as I could before I woke you."

"So you were planning on waking me before you left?" I challenge.

"Yes, Reid." She stands and crosses her arms in front of her. It's a protective move, not a defensive one. "I wasn't trying to hide anything from you. We've never talked about the people we've been with, with the exception—"

"I don't consider someone who raped you a sexual partner, Elise." I bristle at her implication.

"That is not what I meant and you know it," she fires back. "The fact remains, he is the only one I've told you about. I didn't think who I've slept with was a big deal. I assumed by your own admission of being a player that you've had a more active lifestyle than I have."

"I don't care about the number of people you've slept with, Elise, I care that you slept with Theo."

"Why? We were both virgins. We both wanted our first time to be with someone we trusted and knew it would be safe with. Theo wasn't sure how he really felt. It was experimental. A means to an end."

"So it was one clumsy time and that was it?"

"Not exactly." She bites her lip. "It was a weekend at the Ritz. We checked in on a Friday and checked out on a Monday. But that was the intention all along. Learning what we liked and didn't like. What we would and wouldn't do."

"Did you enjoy it?"

"What do you mean?" She has the grace to look truly confused.

"Did you enjoy the sex?"

"What does that have to do with anything?"

"Answer the question."

"It's a ridiculous question. It was sex with someone I love and trusted. It wasn't a drunken one-night stand. It was planned. We both went into with a list, and we kept going until we got it right. It wasn't what sex is like when you are in love with someone. It was doing what Theo and I do. We worked out a problem. I introduced him to Ross the very next week. What he has with Ross is different than what he had with me."

"Seeing as how you don't have a dick I would imagine it would be."

"You know what I mean, jackass. It was different because they love each other. What I did that weekend with Theo in no way compares to what we have. I've never had the sexual connection with anyone that I have with you. I don't understand why you are bothered by this."

"Theo knows," I yell, losing the last of my composure. I hate myself when I see her flinch. "He knows all your stories. All your tells. Your cues. He knows everything."

"We've known each other for more than twenty years. Of course he knows. It still doesn't compare to what I feel for you."

"No matter how much of you belonged to Theo, I took, I don't know...*solace*, in the fact that he might have your heart, but I'm the one that knows what it feels like to be inside of you. Knows what you taste like. Knows the sweet little moans you make before you really let yourself lose control. I'm the one that knows what it feels like to have your body quiver under mine. But I don't even get that part of you." I run my hand through my hair. "He knows what you look like when you come. I love to watch you fall apart beneath me. He *knows* what that looks like. That kills me, Elise."

"I can't change the past, Reid. And to be honest I wouldn't if I could. I'm not ashamed that I slept with Theo. It was safe. And I'm not going to sugarcoat it for you, there were times it was hot, but he never got from me what you get from me. He doesn't know what you know. What is this really about,

Reid?"

"I just told you."

"Bullshit. This isn't about Theo getting me off. This isn't about sex, and you know it."

"I want all of you, Elise. I refuse to settle for less."

"You have all of me." She picks up a messenger bag and throws it across her shoulder. "Whether you keep all of me is entirely up to you."

chapter fifteen

Elise

"**Y**ou two need therapy," Ross says into the camera, pointing to me and Theo.

I'm by myself on the plane to Memphis. Ryan didn't meet me at the airport. I didn't expect him to feel differently than he did yesterday, but I was surprised he didn't show for the flight. I conferenced Theo once we were in the air. He and Ross were still at home.

"Why? Because we won't apologize for being best friends?" I don't hide my bad temper.

"Because as good as you are for each other, you also use each other as a crutch."

"I resent that," Theo says.

"Only because you know I'm right. Look, Elise, it took a while for me to get used to sharing Theo's heart with you. It wasn't until I came to understand that he has the capacity to love more than one person. But it was also because he worked hard to make sure I knew that, no matter how much he loved you, I am the love of his life. He did that by sharing parts of himself with you, but not letting you have the only access to those parts."

"But you had to let him show you that Ross. Reid won't let me show him."

"It's because you are showing him sweetheart. Just not the way you think you are."

"I swear you are talking in circles."

"What happened yesterday with Ryan?"

"Didn't Theo fill you in?"

"He did. I mean what happened afterwards. Who did you turn to? Who was the one you talked to about it? Who was the one you let comfort you?"

"In all fairness, Theo called me."

"I know. And I had a discussion with him about that last night. He's having a hard time letting you go. But those are his issues and not yours. Answer my questions, Elise."

"I can't help that Theo has the advantage of knowing Ryan."

"Reid doesn't have to know Ryan. His role is not to take care of Ryan, his role was to take care of you. Let me finish," he says when I start to interrupt him. "I heard Theo's side of the conversation yesterday. While he does care for Ryan and what he and his family is going through, that was not his focus. He talked to you about how you were feeling. He walked you back from thinking you had made a mistake. He helped you problem-solve and work out what the next steps would be. He made sure your heart would survive the fallout of losing a dear friend, if that is what ends up happening."

It's quiet for a minute while I think through mine and Theo's conversation yesterday.

"Reid is your person now. He needs to be the one that does all those things for you. Theo is the backup, or the person you complain to when Reid is making you crazy. Reid is your Sunday love. Not Theo."

"Sunday love?"

"You know, the person you want to make love to on Saturday night but instead of sending them home you want them to stay. To work Times crossword puzzles with on a Sunday morning. The one you want to make waffles with, stay in bed all day and read with. A Sunday love."

He turns to look at Theo. "You aren't her soft place to land anymore. You have to let her go."

"What if—"

Ross plants a soft kiss to Theo's temple, holding his face next to his. "You can't stop life from happening. You have to let her go."

"But the last time—"

"You can't stop bad things from happening to her, Theo. Elise is not responsible for what happened to her. Neither are you. No matter how much we protect those we love, life and bad things happen. It's time, babe."

The hum of the engines is all I hear for a long minute.

"He's right." Theo clears his throat. "I shouldn't have called you yesterday. I should have trusted Reid to be the one to be there for you."

"I admit that I should have handled that differently. What I can't change is the fact that Theo and I slept together. I know Reid's reputation. I know he laps my number like an Indy car."

"This one wasn't as hard for me," Ross says. "I didn't have the feeling of competition with you. I could give him things you couldn't."

"Dick." Theo deadpans and I see his hand disappear beneath the table.

"Stop that." Ross swats at him. "It's more than that and you know it. Sex with a man is never going to be the same as sex with a woman. That's a given. But that isn't why it wasn't an issue for me. It wasn't an issue, because, like I said a few minutes ago, Theo made sure I knew I had his heart. If Reid knew he had yours, he wouldn't care who you slept with. My guess is he loves you enough to take what he could get. And that was your body. When he found out even that wasn't his, he let it get the best of him."

"When did you get so smart?" I ask.

"I was wondering the same thing, Elise." Theo puts his arm around Ross. "He's right, though. If the ship goes down and I can only save one person—"

"I'm fish food," I finish for him.

"But you would be tasty fish food. Make sure you know how you really feel, then call him and work it out. Keep me up to speed on Ryan and his family. I'll have hospice set up by this afternoon. Ross is already working with Dr. Davis and the hospital."

"I love you. Both of you."

"We love you, too, sweetheart."

Theo disconnects the call, and I lean back in Reid's oversized desk chair. Being in his office makes me miss him. I think back to our previous conversations. Ross is right. I did say Theo was my heart, but that was before I knew I was in love with Reid. Goes to show you, "I love you" can't replace a real conversation.

On a whim, I call Reid's office and can't hold back my smile when his surly face pops up on the screen.

"Is everything okay?" Reid's response is short.

"Yes. I wanted to see if you had a minute to talk."

"Sir," his assistant says in the background, "you have to leave now if you are going to make your flight."

"Where are you going?"

"I have a deal going sour. I have to go to LA. I'll be back in time for the benefit on Monday."

"Do you need your plane? I can charter a medical flight."

"Of course not. That's more important. I'll fly out commercial. I have to go, Elise. I'll call you as soon as I can."

The screen goes black. Fine. I'll fix this later. Obviously he needs a little more time.

Shawn has breakfast ready for me when I come out of the office. I ask him to eat with me and we spend the remainder of the flight talking. I learn he is Reid's go-to attendant. The pilot and copilot are also the only ones that fly for him. We talk about the trip to Indiana, what he should expect, and who will be on the flight.

Just before we land, Shawn informs me that Reid has a car waiting to pick me up. I was just going to Uber it, so I appreciate the sweet gesture.

When I am settled in the car, I text him, "Thank you for having a car for me. I hope you made your flight."

I wait to see if he is going to respond but put my phone away when I realize his is more than likely off for his flight.

The driver pulls up to the set of pink buildings that make up the St. Jude campus. The driver and I exchange phone numbers, and he explains I am to call him when I am ready to leave. He is on standby while I am in Memphis.

There aren't words to describe appropriately this hospital and its staff. These people give so much of themselves to care for children and their families who are facing the worst thing they will ever face. I respect them so much.

I recognize Emily's nurse who gives me a soft smile. "They're expecting you."

I knock softly and enter the room that has been Emily's for more months than any of us could have ever imagined.

"Elise," Ryan's mom greets me affectionately. Her fierce hug is almost my undoing, and I have to remind myself that I am the one that is here to offer them comfort, not the other way around.

"You came," Emily says.

"You called didn't you?" I smile. "You call, I come. That's how this works." I lean down to kiss and hug her. She wraps her hand around mine.

"I told mom," she says weakly.

"Janice, I made her a promise. I wasn't coming to push you into something you aren't ready for. I just came to help her put a voice to her wishes. I came to be here for her."

She laughs. "Of course. That's why you're Elise." She moves to stand beside Emily. "Ryan got here last night a couple of hours after Emily talked to me about her wishes." She looks at her daughter and rubs her cheek. "It was a long night for the four of us. Ryan Sr. called from the farm. Emily explained what she wants. Dr. Davis came by to see us and gave us as much information as he could."

She turns and faces me. "I'm taking my daughter home." Her eyes fill with tears. "She's earned the right to say enough is enough."

I take Janice's hand, and the three of us stand connected to each other, not speaking.

"Will you come to visit me on the farm?" Emily asks.

"No." Ryan's angry answer cuts mine off.

"Ryan," Janice says sternly, shocked by the disdain in his tone.

"Elise, you need to leave."

"Ryan, she's my friend and I want her here," Emily protests.

"I might have to live with your choice, but you don't get to choose this, Emily. Elise." He holds the door open for me.

"I actually only came to make sure you're okay, Emily. I have to fly back this afternoon to New York," I lie. "I'm so proud of you. I will be checking on you though, and sending plenty of glitter and tiaras."

"Every girl needs a tiara," she smiles timidly.

"Janice." I hug her.

"Give him time," she whispers in my ear.

"I love you, kiddo," I say to Emily. "Make sure they make you those chocolate chip cookies I love, and if you walk around naked, make sure the pastor isn't there." I wink at her, and her giggle is enough to shatter my heart into a million pieces. I disguise the quiver in my voice with a chuckle.

"I love you, Elise." She reaches for me, and I lean over for a hug.

I leave the room, and Ryan follows me into the hall.

"Do not come to the farm."

My emotions are raw with the knowledge that I just said my last goodbye to Emily.

"Ryan," I choke.

"Don't act like you have a heart now, Elise." He turns and leaves me standing in the hallway.

I don't know how long I stood there before an assistant asks me if I am okay. I nod my answer and take the elevator down.

I have the driver take me to the Memphis airport. There's only one more flight to New York and it's not for another four hours. Once I make it through security, I send Ryan an email with the specifics he needs for the flight tomorrow. My call to Reid goes straight to voicemail. My thumb hovers over Theo's number, but it just doesn't feel right. After the conversation with Ross this morning, I find that the only person I really want to talk to is Reid.

I hit Knox's number and push send.

"My baby sister is in New York for three days before she finally calls me?"

"I'm actually in Memphis, but I will be back in New York tonight. Since Bren is still out of town, I thought maybe I could stay with you till Reid comes back."

"Ah, yes. Mom told me you were dating Reid Beckett. Why aren't you staying with them?"

"They don't get back until Monday."

"What's wrong?"

"Nothing is wrong. They're calling my flight. I'll take a cab and see you tonight."

"Okay. Love you."

"You too."

I still have plenty of time before they call my flight, but I'm too emotional to go into it in front of a terminal full of people.

It's 8:30 by the time I greet Knox's doorman. He informs me that Knox is in the restaurant located in the lobby. I'm dressed a little too causally, but they don't seem to mind. Knox is already walking towards me when the host escorts me to the table.

"Hey, sis." Knox pulls me into a tight hug lifting my feet of the ground. "Man, have I missed you. He kisses my cheek, and I squeeze my arms around him. "What's with the vice hug?"

"One of my team's little sister is dying with cancer. I was

in Memphis visiting her. It's just hard, you know."

"I know." He doesn't push me to talk about it, he just hugs me until I finally let go. Knox was eight when I came to live with my family. Bren was only a month old. He never once made me feel like I was any less his little sister.

I loved my new parents the minute I met them. Our father owns his own advertising business and has always been big on giving back to the community. He grew up poor and has never forgotten what it's like to live in poverty. I was with my foster mom at the adoption offices having my annual picture and information updated in the system when he toured the facilities to get a sense of the work they do. He was doing some pro-bono work to devise a campaign to increase adoption awareness. They introduced me to him and explained what I was doing there and how important it is to have updated systems and how they were using the internet to help. That was the day Miller and Julia Donovan began the process to become my parents.

It was unusual at the time for an African-American family to adopt a white child. It didn't matter to them. They saw a child who needed love, and they knew they had love to give. Everything I am today is because of them.

After dinner, Knox gets me situated before heading out to meet someone I am sure won't be around tomorrow. Knox is a serial dater.

I try Reid again. It's only seven o'clock on the east coast. It doesn't go straight to voicemail, but it also goes unanswered.

The next day, I have lunch with my team and update them on how the trip to Memphis went. None of them have heard from Reid, but I play it off, suggesting to them that he must be trying to beat the deadline before he loses the deal.

Blake and I wrap up our case on the Speaker. We were

able to eliminate all evidence of his daughter's abortion and take care of the person attempting to blackmail him. Nothing keeps someone from exposing dirt on you like having dirt on them. Seems like Senator Blackwell had some skeletons in his closet that were enough to make him forget what he had learned about the Speaker's daughter. The video I found of his wife's brother fucking him gagged and bound while other men urinated on him was enough. Blake took care of the heavy-hitter Blackwell had working for him. I don't know how and I don't need to know. Blake would bring me in if he thought he needed to. Thankfully the need to wear a gun on my person is gone, and the security detail has been released.

Life is back to normal, only there's no Reid, no Ryan, and no Theo. Well, Theo would be here, but other than checking in on work cases, I've been distancing myself. I just don't want to talk to anyone but Reid. It was like a switch flipped inside me, and Reid is the only one who can calm my spirit.

I spent the day with Knox on Sunday. Knox is a creature of habit and eats Sunday brunch at the same place every week. We were waiting our turn in line with our arms wrapped around each other. I had just finished telling him about how angry Ryan was and how his words had affected me. When he tried to comfort me with a kiss on the forehead, some woman walked up and caused a scene. It was clearly one of Knox's many dates. Her behavior was so crazy, that he went ahead and let her believe we were a couple. After she left, I tried to remind him that when you stick your pecker in crazy, this is what you get.

I had stopped trying to call Reid on Friday. He wasn't answering my calls or returning any of my text messages. He clearly needed the time to himself and that was something I could give him. He said he would be back in time for the benefit. I could wait until then.

It's Monday morning and I pass through the security of Taylor Organization. I am escorted to a private elevator that takes me to the 43rd floor where Emme's assistant, Cassie, has me wait for her in her office. A large glass door slides open and Graham Taylor steps through. I hear a slight whimper, and I'm not sure if it came from me or my Roxy, because holy fuck this man is magnificent in person.

"I'm sorry, I was looking for my wife. Graham Taylor." He extends his hand in introduction.

I shake his hand and am thankful I can remember my own name.

"Elise Donovan."

"Are you here to see me?"

"That's funny, he was just here," we hear someone say from the other room. "There you are. Your appointment is here."

"Thank you, George. Show him in." Graham turns to me and raises his brow.

"I like what you've done with the place," Reid says looking around. He stumbles slightly when he sees me.

"What are you doing here?" Reid asks.

"That is what I was just wondering," Graham answers before I can. "I thought you sent her in your place, but that can't be it since you are here." He folds his arms across his chest, waiting for a response.

"She's not here as representation for BE. Elise?" Reid put his hands in his pockets.

"I'm waiting for Emme."

"We established that. What I want to know is why?"

"I have some connections in Paris. She and Jules are headhunting an executive to run the Paris side of the business.

I'm here to help build a profile."

"She's good. I'll give her that." He looks to Reid. "You already merged with Theo right?"

"Last week."

"Your main asset is already going rogue. You don't know where she is or who she's meeting with."

"Fuck off, Graham," Reid says back.

"I'm not his asset."

"Elise, don't start. What?"

"Nothing. Just having flashbacks," Graham chuckles. "Sorry, buddy. I wasn't aware."

"Fuck off, Graham," Reid says again, which only makes him laugh harder.

Emme comes around the corner like she's on two wheels. She is strikingly beautiful. Her rounded stomach enters the room before she does. Her cheeks have filled out since the last time I saw her, somehow making her look even more endearing. She's wearing a low V-neck black shirt, which perfectly displays her full breasts, over a pair of fitted black leather pants. She looks killer.

"Off. I need them off. Now."

"Emelia, what are you talking about?"

Cassie flies in and hands her a pair of scissors.

"Hey," Adam says, entering the office, "Jules is coming for lunch. You guys want to...my God, Emme. Your boobs are, Ow!" he exclaims, rubbing his shoulder where Graham punched him.

"Graham," Emme yells through a door off the office. The desperation in her voice has her husband increasing his pace.

"One day you're going to learn, Adam," Reid says with a smile.

"Damn. I swear he's getting stronger. That one really did

hurt." He's still rubbing his shoulder. "Adam Taylor," he says to me, reaching his hand toward me.

"Elise Donovan."

"Why is Elise Donovan here?" Adam asks. Reid shrugs.

"Isn't she your employee?"

"Oh my God. Why do all the men talk over you in this office? You do realize I am standing right here." I ask them.

"What are you laughing about?" Graham comes out of a hidden panel in the wall.

"Reid. And glass houses." Adam says with a smirk.

"Fuck off both of you," Reid says.

"Sorry about that." Emme emerges from the same panel, only now she's wearing a little swing dress that falls softly over her stomach. "You know the *Friends* episode where Ross can't get his leather pants back on? Well, I couldn't get mine off. They were sticking to me and I was having a pregnancy hot flash."

"Did you all meet?"

"Elise Donovan," Graham and Adam say in unison.

"I see your reputation proceeds you," she smiles.

"Why is she here, Emelia? What's going on that I don't know about?" Graham surveys his wife.

"She's here to talk about the Paris position."

"You don't call in a fixer like Elise Donovan to headhunt a fashion position."

"You do if she's your friend."

"You know Elise?"

"Yes. She and I worked on a couple of projects together when I worked with Jackson." Graham's hand idly rubs Emme's stomach as she stands next to him.

"I call bullshit," Adam says.

"Me too. This conversation isn't over. Adam come in

here. I want you in on my meeting with Reid," Graham says. "Nice to meet you, Elise. Emelia," he looks hard into her eyes. "Behave," he insists before leaving her with a kiss.

Reid retreats before I can say anything. He won't meet my eyes.

"So. You and Reid Beckett," Emme says sitting on the couch, curling her legs under her.

"We're trying. I'm experiencing a few learning curves." I sit across from her.

"I had those, too. So did Graham. It gets easier. Just stay the course."

"If you say so. So...why am I really here? Nice job on coming up with the same reason as me."

"Great minds think alike," she smiles. "I want to talk to you about a cause I am thinking of taking on. I need your opinion."

"Okay. Shoot."

"I want to start a national conversation about rape. A conversation that influences change."

"I heard you finally closed the case on your sister's rape. I assume this is personal for you."

"It is. And I know it's personal for you, too. You know the Vice-President is hosting a women's summit. He's about to bring rape front and center. I want to take that momentum and effect change."

"To what level?" I ask.

"I want to focus on campus assaults and sexual violence in the work place."

"Why all the cloak and dagger."

"I just like to keep Graham on his toes," she waves dismissively and winks. "Give him something to punish me for. Mostly I didn't want to tell your story. I know you are very open and public about what happened to you, but you are more than your experiences and I didn't want to introduce you to the guys that way. You're kick-ass Elise Donovan. That is how you should be introduced."

"So you want me to get it off the ground for you?"

"The Foundation will be funding a not-for-profit called the Addison Foundation. I want you to run it. You'll have a healthy budget to manage. With your political and legal connections, I think you are the right person. Also, I heard you speak. I snuck in the back when you spoke at NYU a few months ago. You have a way of making people connect and talk. More than half the battle is getting people to have the conversation."

"What's your timeline?"

"I'd like an answer next week."

We say our goodbyes, and I'm already thinking about it on the elevator ride down.

"Hey," I say, surprised to see Reid waiting for me in the lobby. "I was hoping to get to talk to you before the benefit tonight." Standing this close to him, I'm reminded of what it feels like to be in love with this man. I think about how I haven't spoken to him in five days, and I reach for him. My hand falls back to my side when he speaks.

"Elise, you're fired."

"What?"

"You refuse to acknowledge my role in this company. In your life. This isn't going to work."

"What are you talking about, Reid? I've been trying to reach you to talk."

"Elise, I'm not willing to share you. I want your all. You, however, want to give it to Theo, to the team, to any case that is urgent. To the man you were with yesterday."

"What man?"

"I saw you, Elise. I came home early. Only you didn't stay at my place at all while I was gone, and then I see you in front of the restaurant."

"I can explain."

"I heard it. I heard you both when you were explaining it to that girl. You have a four-week clause during which you will continue to work and appropriately hand off your cases. I received a request for a consultation that you will handle tomorrow. Other than that, you won't be assigned any new cases. Ryan will take the lead when he returns from leave."

"Reid." I take a step towards him.

"Goodbye, Elise." He turns and walks away.

chapter sixteen

Reid

How can my place feel empty when she was only here a couple of nights? I pick up the strawberry chapstick still on the bathroom counter and run it over my lips. It tastes of her. *Christ. Pull it together man.* I toss the tube back onto the counter next to her things. There's not much, but I guess I should have Coop send them back to her.

It's only been a couple of hours since I left Elise standing in the lobby of Taylor Organization. I release the towel around my waist and drop it in the laundry basket inside my closet. I have no desire to go to this benefit tonight. The last thing I want to do is put on a tux and talk with anyone. The reminder of Elise on my lips is enough to have my dick at full staff. *Traitor.* I ignore it and dress for the event.

I know it was childish not to answer her calls, but I was frustrated. And angry. And childish. I've never wanted someone more than they want me. I mean, I've chased pussy before, but only as a means to an end. With Elise, I want her. All of her.

When I saw her yesterday looking at that fucking guy like he hung the moon and stars, it took all I had in me not to pummel his ass. And even though that girl seemed totally crazy, neither one of them denied her accusations. I know Elise. I know she didn't turn off her feelings for me and move on to someone else that soon, but the fact remains, I need her heart and she wants to fill it with everyone she meets.

It takes me three attempts to finally get my bowtie looking halfway decent. Coop is waiting for me when I get into the car.

"Would you like me to take care of getting Miss Donovan's suitcases to her, sir? They're still in the trunk," he asks as he pulls into traffic.

"I suppose so, yes."

The glance he gives in the mirror lets me know he thinks I'm a dumb fuck, but I don't care. He pulls up to the red carpet, and I steel myself to make the walk alone. This is an event that Taylor Organization throws each year. Last year's was cancelled at the last minute after a devastating loss to the organization, and to Graham and Emme, specifically, when Emme's first intern Reggie, was shot and killed on the way to the event. Her bodyguard and friend were hit in the crossfire. I was surprised they were doing it this year, but Graham said Emme was insistent on following through with the program Reggie championed.

Flashbulbs blind me, and I compose a fake smile that I'm sure is fooling no one.

Graham and Emme are just inside the door greeting guests. I have to admit, I never thought Graham Taylor would settle down. But I understand what finally drove him to it. Emme Taylor is a sight to behold. She's wearing a back-less gold dress that leaves nothing to the imagination in the front. Her pregnant body is on full display. I don't make a habit at looking at another man's woman, but Adam is right. Her breasts are magnificent in that dress. She's made more beautiful by her smile and cheeks so round, if she were a five-year-old you wouldn't be able to keep yourself from pinching them.

"Reid." She greets me with a hug. I return her hug, my hand touching her bare back. I pointedly make a "this is heaven face" over her shoulder just to piss Graham off.

"Oh my God. Don't get him started," Jules, Adam Taylor's wife, catches my smile and laughs, pulling me into another hug. "I've already heard it from him a hundred times tonight."

"I'm not crazy about this dress," Graham mumbles.

"So you've said." Emme rolls her eyes.

"I think you look magnificent. It actually feels wrong to think a pregnant woman can look this sexy."

"Reid," Graham growls. An actual growl. It would cower a regular man. But I grew up with this silly fucker and am not intimidated in the least.

"It's silk," Jules says. "It's meant to show every dip and curve. You did that to her boobs. Not me."

"This is what happens when you knock me up, honey." Emme places a soft kiss to his cheek, and I suddenly think of Elise. Graham wraps his arm possessively around Emme, his hand resting protectively on her bump.

"I hear congratulations are in order." Jules pulls the conversation back to me. "Elise Donovan," she clarifies. "I hear you two are an item."

"Emelia," Graham reproves.

"I know what I saw, Graham. So, are you going to pursue

it?" she asks me, dismissing her husband.

Adam's shoulders slouch when I don't answer. "Dude. You fucked it up already." He shakes his head.

"Maybe she fucked it up," I suggest.

"Not possible and watch your language," Ruth Taylor says, hugging me. "Reid, how are you? I had lunch with your mother when I was at a conference in Boston a few months ago."

"Graham, my water broke!" Emme says in a rushed breath. We turn to her as one and see the bottom of her dress is a darker shade of gold.

"Mom!" Graham lifts Emme into his arms.

"Women have babies all the time dear," Ruth reassures him.

"Graham, put me down. I can walk."

"I'm surprised he doesn't have an ambulance following her wherever she goes," Patrick says, coming to stand next to me. Jackson Hollingsworth, Emme's best friend, laughs, pulling his husband's body to his. "She's three weeks early. I don't think he had that on the plan until two weeks out."

Within seconds there's an entire entourage surrounding us: Graham's security team, a couple that appears to be Emme's parents, four men that Graham keeps calling "dwarfs" for some reason, and several others I don't recognize.

"Looks like it will be a full waiting room."

"That's Emme. Heart so big people can't help but love her." Patrick smiles and Jackson places a kiss of adoration to his temple.

I excuse myself from the commotion and find Dean and a couple of our buddies drinking near the bar. Word has spread that the hosts are making a rather interesting exit. Maybe I can sneak out, too.

"Were you able to save the deal?" Dean asks when I set my drink on the tall table.

"I was. It'll wrap next week." I take a long sip of whiskey. It provides just the right amount of burn.

"Holy shit," one of the guys says, looking across the room. When I turn in that direction, there she is. Elise. She's walking this way, and she looks like the fuck of a lifetime on legs. How is it possible for a dress to be that revealing, but not showing any skin at the same time? It's a deep green, high-neck gown that looks like it was sculpted to her body. I can see the curve of her breast and her nipples. I shift my stance in an attempt to reposition my now-hard cock.

"Dean," she smiles and reaches up to kiss his cheek. Her dress is cut deep on her back, and I've run my tongue up her ass enough to know it's an inch away from being exposed. My fingers grip my drink so tight, I fear it might shatter in my hand.

"You look edible," he purrs, and suddenly I understand Graham's need to punch Adam all the time. Fucking brothers and their fucking warped sense of humor.

"You look handsome." She straightens his tie.

"Elise Donovan." She greets our friends when we fail to introduce her. I glare at them in a way that lets them know I will cut their balls off if they don't stop looking at her that way.

"Elise." Gabby comes up and hugs her friend. "You look... well, you look fuckable."

"Gabby." Elise raises a brow as a warning to her friend. "Reid."

It takes me a minute to realize I am being spoken to. She waits until I acknowledge her. "I wanted to introduce you to—"

"Babe, you'll never guess who was in L.A. while we were," Amber says as she walks up and slides her arm around my waist, kissing my jaw. I want to cringe at how wrong it feels, but because I see the guy Elise came with walking up, I make no move to stop her.

"Amber." I say her name in an attempt to get her to stop talking.

I want to kick my own ass for the look on Elise's face right now. Dean's isn't too far off, and I'm pretty sure Gabby is one breath away from taking my last one.

"Sorry, I saw someone I know." The man she came with walks up and plants a kiss to her temple.

"No worries." She smiles at him, but it doesn't reach her eyes. When his hand falls to rest on her hips, I want to break his fingers. "Ready?" she asks him.

"Didn't you want to intro—"

"Another time." Elise cuts him off and shakes her head at Gabby, who promptly halts whatever she was about to say.

"Nice meeting you," she says to the guys and takes the man's hand to leave.

"You were in L.A. *with her*?" Dean asks through clenched teeth.

"Amber, we were not in L.A. together. We were on the same flight."

"Reid." She seems actually shocked by my version of the story.

"Amber, I told you then and I'm telling you now, we're over." Her face turns crimson to match her dress, and a second later I'm wearing my whiskey.

"Well that seems fitting." Ross walks up and pins me with a stare.

"Would you all excuse us, please?" He asks. While

everyone walks away, an image of my balls hanging on their Christmas tree comes to mind.

"What the hell are you doing man?" Ross takes a drink from a waiter.

"Where's Theo?"

"Schmoozing. Want to talk about it?"

"No."

"Fine. I'll talk, you listen. Theo has the capacity to love more than one person, but his sun rises and sets with me. He is a better man because of Elise. She has known him since he was five. She readied him for me, and for that I couldn't be more grateful for her. The man I love and who loves me with all his heart is protective, wonderful, kind, and stubborn as hell, and I have her to thank for it. So, no. I've never felt threatened enough to push him away. I felt blessed and held him closer."

He places his hand on my shoulder as a sign of support. Or pity. Or both. "You're too good of a guy for me to not tell you, you're fucking this up."

I wake up with yet another hangover. After Ross' words of wisdom, I left the benefit and came home to an empty house and a full bottle of bourbon.

I try to stop the pounding in my head and kick the empty bottle on the way to the bathroom. Jesus, I haven't drunk like this since college.

A shower and strong toothpaste finally abate me of the smell of alcohol. My housekeeper takes pity on me and fixes me a home remedy that strips the enamel off my teeth, but I finally feel like I am back in the land of the living.

When I get to work, I see that the team seems to be settling into their office space well. Today is Elise's first day in our actual office, but my excitement to show her the office I had designed for her has dissipated. I spoke with Ryan on the way in. His sister is home and resting. He sounds miserable, like he hasn't slept in days. I, of course, have no words to offer in support, but I feel obligated to check on him every couple of days. I know it would be important to Elise. A knot forms in the bottom of my stomach. It's not that I was a complete and utter asshole before Elise, but I doubt I would have taken the time to involve myself before her.

Elise is waiting by the elevator when I walk up. Before she sees me, the guy I've seen her with twice now comes through the revolving door and calls her name. He lifts a scarf in the air and I hear him tell her she left it at his place last night. I'm certain I only have myself to be mad at that Elise went home with that guy last night. The thought that anyone else got to peel her out of that dress drenches my mood faster than an ice bath.

I leave them talking in the lobby and take the next elevator up, ignoring everyone who speaks to me along the way.

"I was hoping you had a minute," Elise states, entering my office several minutes later.

"You're late. Your first appointment is in the conference room."

"I didn't have anything on my calendar. Remind me why I am taking on a new client? I thought I was to start closing them out?" She looks startled by the shift in conversation. I hand her the file.

"He wouldn't take no for an answer, and he asked for you specifically. Brooks Anniston is high profile and knows a lot of people." Her silence brings my focus from my computer back to her. She looks … small.

"Reid, I can't take this case. I need you to assign it to someone else," she pushes back.

I don't yield. "I'm not Theo, Elise. You don't have a problem understanding that any other time." A childish dig, I know. "This isn't a 'pick the ones you want to work' and 'pass off the ones you don't' kind of place. I'm not going to baby you."

"Reid, you don't understand."

"Elise, you're late." I cut her off before she can elaborate. Her face displays an internal battle I don't understand. She turns and leaves me in the office.

I'm pissed at myself for thinking this day was going to go differently. I had resolved to listen to Ross and try to talk with Elise today. Clearly that is no longer a viable option.

Thirty minutes later I'm coming back from my main office on the top floor, and Elise's guy is in the front lobby. I have no idea where the receptionist is.

"Could you tell me where I can find Elise?"

"You'll need to wait for the receptionist. I don't make a habit of knowing my employees' locations."

"I'll do that. I don't know why my sister can't send a simple text when she's running late. An unfortunate habit she learned from our mom, I guess. I'm Knox by the way." He extends his hand and I take it out of engrained politeness. "It's a pleasure to meet you. Elise has told us all about working for you. She speaks highly of you. You've earned her respect. That's not always the easiest thing to do. She's a fixer. Cautious by trade." He smiles and rocks on his heels. "She also told me about your relationship. I assume this is where I have the big brother talk with you, ask you about your intentions with my little sister." His smile is wide and inviting.

"Would you excuse me, please?"

I leave him standing there to go in search of Elise. The conference room is empty as is her office. The assistant has unpacked her things already. I glance at the pictures. Besides the ones with her team and Theo, they are all of Elise with an African American family. One of her on her graduation day. One on New Year's 2013 with the family of five holding up sticks with mustaches, oversized glasses, and lips attached to them. One with a beautiful girl that, based on the age, I assume is her sister, Bren. And one on a beach with Knox. He is flexing his muscles, and Elise and her sister are faking a yawn of indifference.

My pace increases on the way to my office to see if she is waiting for me there. I pull my phone out of my pocket to dial her number.

"Who the fuck let Brooks Anniston in here?" Theo thunders in a tone I've never heard before.

"I don't have the time to argue with you, Theo. He needed a team and I took him on as a client. I had Elise meet with him earlier. I'll fill you in later, but right now I need to talk to Elise."

Theo puts a hand to my chest. "Elise met with Brooks Anniston? And she was okay with that?"

"What is the problem with Brooks Anniston?"

"Where is she?" Gabby bursts into the office.

"Who?"

"Elise. She told her assistant she was coming to your office. I want to know who the hell this Anniston guy is and why he put his hands on her."

"What are you talking about?" Theo and I both question her.

"Her assistant said she came back to her office with a

handprint on her face. When she asked her what happened, Elise left saying she was coming to your office."

"What the fuck was Dylan Richman doing here?" Blake barrels in with a look of a man intending to do harm. His hands are full of pictures. They're of Elise. I snatch them out of his hand. They're of Elise in a hospital. She has bruises on her mouth and neck in the outline of a hand. There are bite marks on her breasts and legs, and bruising and dried blood on her thighs. I can hear the blood whooshing in my ears. My whole body begins to violently shake as I register what the pictures mean.

"You let Dylan Richman in here?" Theo's eyes narrow on me and his voice is an eerie whisper.

"Everyone stop." My hands bring everyone to a halt. "Let's work the problem, people. What's wrong with this Anniston guy and who is Dylan Richman?'

"Anniston is Elise's biological father," Theo says.

"And Dylan is the asshole who raped her," Blake finishes.

"Her father?" Gabby asks.

"Coop, I need the last hour from conference room 4," I say into the phone. A ping announces the video has landed in my email. Fast-forwarding, I see Elise entering the conference room. Theo is enraged by the guy on the screen.

I recognize Brooks Anniston. We all listen as he speaks.

"I've paid a small fortune for your services, Elise."

"What is he doing here?" Elise asks.

"You will fix the mess you made. I am grooming Dylan to be a partner in my firm and that can't happen when you have an active civil litigation against him."

"He raped me and he will answer for it in court." She crosses her arms.

"Stop being petty, Elise. Dylan already explained how

you wanted more from him and he didn't want you. I expect you to clean up the mess you made. The next time you decide to smear a good man's name," he drops the photos on the table, "don't have pictures of you whoring it up."

She locks eyes with him. "Go to hell, Brooks."

"That's no way to address your father. You will drop the charges against him."

"No. I won't. And you were never my father."

"You were evil from the minute you came into this world. You stole your mother's life, the only woman I've ever loved. Now, you're going to keep this man from a partnership because he won't put his dick back in you? You are good for nothing."

Elise attempts to leave the room and Dylan blocks her path. For the first time, I see a flicker of fear flicker in her eyes, and I mentally add another name to my list of people to destroy.

"Get out of my way, Dylan. I'm not incapacitated this time, and I'm not afraid of you."

"Make me," he challenges with a leer and licks his lips as his eyes move over her body. He reaches out to touch her, and she steps out of the way of his advances. He laughs, enjoying her torment.

"Elise, I'm growing tired of this." Anniston moves to stand beside Dylan. "I heard you were spreading your legs for Reid Beckett. He won't want you either. You know you have a knack for choosing men who see your true value. You're worthless. It's why I gave you away. It's why Reid will if he hasn't already seen the light. Men like us—"

"Don't you dare put your name in the same sentence as Reid Beckett's. You're not even a tenth of the man he is."

Before she can even see it coming, he slaps her so hard

across the face she has to catch herself from going down. I swear to God if it's the last thing I do, I'll ruin Brooks Anniston.

"I'll expect to see the charges dropped by end of day," he says, straightening his shirtsleeve under his jacket. Without another word, he and Dylan leave Elise standing in the conference room.

I pick up an object and hurl it across the room. It hits one of the glass walls encasing my office, shattering it into a million pieces.

"Reid." Theo attempts to calm me, but I am so far past my control that I don't even register his words.

"Where's Knox?" I ask running to the front office. Maybe Elise is with him. He's not there. I hit the stairwell, run the flights down at breakneck speed, and burst through the stationary door. The sun stuns my eyes for a minute, my chest pounding, Elise is nowhere to be found. I circle the block. When I come back around, I see her exiting the building. She appears dazed. I call her name, and when she turns toward me, I can still see a vivid imprint of a hand on her face.

Before I can make a move, Miller Donovan folds his daughter in his arms, and escorts her to his waiting car and pulls away.

"Reid, I'm telling you, man, I don't know where she is. You need to be patient. I know Elise. She needs time to herself," Blake explains.

"She needs her friends and family."

"The Donovan's aren't sweating it."

"Because they know where she is."

"They don't."

"Have they heard from her?"

"Only in the group email. Like you. Like Emily."

It's been two weeks. Two weeks of emails with the same two words: "I'm okay."

I was able to ascertain that Miller and the family are getting the same group emails. Emily appears to be the only one getting a daily email that has a copious amount of communication.

"What Emily needs is Elise." I reply.

"Ryan still won't allow it at this point, but if she did, Elise would know."

"How would she know? Are you telling her? Do you know where she is?"

Blake exhales a frustrated breath. "You're making your-self crazy, man. There is nothing you can do. I know it feels helpless, but you have to give Elise the time she needs. And stop trying to pinpoint her emails. I know your guys try to trace it every time she sends one. Elise hides people for a liv-ing. She won't be found until she's ready."

"Bullshit, Blake. No one plays this better than you. One million dollars in your account before noon if you tell me where she is. Two million." I up the ante when he doesn't jump at the offer.

"Breathe, man. You can do this."

"I wish I had your confidence," I admit unashamedly.

"Elise loves you. With everything she has. I've seen it with my own eyes. She'll come back to you. You might have to fight for it. She can be stubborn," he smiles. "I came in to talk to you about Brooks Anniston and Dylan Richmond."

"No. You are too close to this, Blake. I have someone else working it."

"Who? I don't trust just anyone."

"Trust me."

"Does this have something to do with that 2:00 appointment you had today?"

"Just trust me."

Graham Taylor has been working from home since the birth of his daughter. I hated to bother him, but his assistant assured me he was taking calls and would be more than happy for me to meet him at his home office.

His security man greets me as I step off the elevator. It sounds like a family reunion is going on.

"Reid." Graham comes down a hallway and shakes my hand before guiding me to his office.

"Graham, I hate to bother you at home."

"It's no problem. I'm working from my home office while Emme takes maternity leave. I'm only going in for meetings I can't do via conferencing. Have a seat." He offers me a chair and takes the one across from it. Adam is sitting behind Graham's desk.

"What's going on? I take it this is not a casual visit."

I spend the next thirty minutes filling them in on Elise's assault at school, who her birth father is, and repeat what happened in the conference room. By the time I'm done, Graham is no longer sitting but walking back in forth in what appears to be an attempt to stay calm. I get the last word out and he hits an intercom. "George I need Harry and my wife. Now."

"You beckoned, sire." Emme arrives a couple of minutes later, with a smile on her face. Graham levels her with a kiss that only men deeply in love can give. When he comes up for air he runs his hands over her arms, almost as if he's reassuring himself that she's okay.

"The last time you did that, you got this." A man enters the room carrying a swaddled baby.

"Dad. You know it takes more than a kiss. See, the man has to—"

"Fine, fine! Stop. You win. Stop."

"She's beautiful." I stand and look at the baby in his arms. Emme greets me with a kiss.

"Ah. Makes sense now. This explains your sudden spurt of protectiveness." She hugs her husband. "How's Elise."

"She's traveling."

"Is that what we're calling it?" She lifts a knowing brow.

"What do you know?" I ask.

"Yes, sweetheart. What do you know?" Graham studies his wife.

"There is a whole list of what I know."

"Do you know where she is?" I ask hopeful.

"Do you?" She counters.

"No," I answer.

"Then I don't either. I do know that she will be starting her position with The Foundation in the next several weeks. A position she took *after* you fired her."

"When you get it wrong, you go balls to the wall don't you?" Adam chuckles, still sitting behind the desk.

"You have no idea."

"I'll leave you gentlemen to talk. I better not read about accidental deaths in the paper." She glares at her father on her way out.

"Reid, I'd like to introduce you to my father-in-law, Harry Forrester. This is the man you need." Graham takes his newborn in his arms and motions for us to sit. Harry listens to the story and crosses a knee over his leg before sitting back.

"I'm already working on Brooks Anniston. By this time next week his firm will be dismantled, he will be disbarred and bankrupt."

"How?" I ask in disbelief. This is exactly what I wanted to happen.

"Miller Donovan and I are close friends. He's a couple of weeks ahead of you. I got a phone call the very day he picked Elise up from your office."

"In fairness to me, I was trying to give Graham some time with his family."

"It wouldn't have mattered. You'll understand when you have kids. Fathers have a means of accelerating things when it comes to the well-being of our children. Especially our little girls."

"Thank you, sir."

"No problem, son. Dylan Richmond proved to be a little more difficult, but not impossible. We were able to track down some cases he was able to make disappear. Three of the eight women have agreed to join Elise's civil suit. Miller is funding the legal expenses. Two of the eight never pressed charges, and there is a possibility they will. We aren't pushing anyone. It is their choice. If they choose to move forward, they will have the best attorneys on retainer. Dylan has been disbarred for conduct unbecoming. We have men following him and will continue to follow his whereabouts at all times to ensure the safety of the women testifying."

"You really have thought of everything."

"I'm the dad of two daughters. One that was sexually assaulted. Miller and I understand each other." He stands and walks over to Graham. "Now if you'll excuse me, I'll let you all finish while I move on to happier things." He extracts his granddaughter from his son-in-law.

"So, how are you going to fix your mess?" Graham sits back down.

"Sounds like your father-in-law did it for me."

"I meant with Elise. Sounds like she needs to be reminded who's in charge."

"Oh my God." Adam runs his hand over his face. "Not this same ole nut."

"It's fine if she needs time, but she wouldn't leave again for weeks at a time with no communication. Not without a strong conversation of expectations."

"I hurt her," I admit, the words leaving a metallic taste in my mouth.

"Fix it," they reply in unison.

"I take it you're getting the 'who's in charge' speech." Emme walks in with a gorgeous little girl on her hip. She has coppery brown skin and a three-inch halo of curls. Emme bypasses Graham and hands her off to Adam.

"Ollie." Adam snuggles her and peppers her face with kisses that make the little girl giggle.

"Olivia has a soft spot for Adam," she says, writing something down. I laugh at Graham's sullen look.

"I'll pay for this later," she mumbles under her breath.

"Emelia, what did you do?" Graham gives his wife a look that reminds me how I feel about Elise.

"You can contact her at this email." She hands me a piece of paper. "My advice, communicate with her before you go get her. She's staying at our guesthouse in the Hamptons."

"Emelia."

"I like her. When I heard dad talking with Mr. Donovan, I called her and offered her a place to get a way for a while." She sits on his lap, placing a gentle kiss to his lips.

"You're not sorry at all are you?"

"Not even a little bit." She kisses his nose. "Seriously, Reid. I've been getting to know Elise over the last couple of weeks. We're similar in a lot of ways. Give her some time."

Graham looks at her with a heat that would peel paint.

"Reid," he says to me. "Go get your girl."

chapter seventeen

Reid

"**I**'m going to get her."

"You can't do that."

"I'm sick of this shit, Dean."

"What I mean is you can't go to Elise. You have to go to Ryan. The team will meet you at the airport. His sister isn't expected to make it through the night."

"What? Does Elise know?"

"You need to think like a boss right now, Reid. Your team needs you. Blake talked with Ryan. He doesn't want her there."

"That will crush Elise."

"He's losing his sister. Elise will have to wait."

"It's not that simple. She's my priority."

"Since when?"

"Since now. Since I got my shit together. Since always."

"Go to Ryan. Gabby said his sister wants to be buried on the farm the day after she passes away. She doesn't want her family to suffer by having to wait and mourn."

"Jesus. Where does a thirteen-year-old get that kind of insight from?"

"It's a shitty hand, no matter how it's dealt," Dean says.

"Blake has already talked to Elise. She wants everyone there for Ryan. I'll be in the city until you get back. If she needs anything, I'll make sure she's taken care of. Just call me."

"I don't know, Dean. I don't know this team like Theo and Elise do. I don't want to intrude on a family in their worst hours. I just want Ryan to know I'm here for him if he needs anything."

"And you do that by going. Trust me. You need to go. Plus, you're their ride."

"I need to swing by and get my things."

"You don't have time. You have plenty of things on the plane. Just pack a bag from them. Wheels up in an hour."

I try Elise again. Straight to voicemail. Blake and I are going to have a serious conversation when I see him.

Traffic is heavy and it takes me the full hour to make it to the airport. Shawn, my steward, greets me as I climb the stairs.

"You're the last one to board, sir. We're ready for takeoff."

"Thanks, Shawn. And thanks for the last minute change in plans."

"It's my pleasure."

I greet the pilots and make my way to the main cabin. The team is seated around a table. I want to go into my office and work, but I know I need to engage. I take a seat next to Fran.

"Hello, everyone."

"Boss," they reply. They seem tried. Off their mark.

"Thanks for flying us," Fran says. "Commercial wouldn't

get us there until later tonight, and I think Ryan could really use us there as soon as possible."

"Of course," I nod and offer her a small smile. "Did I interrupt something?" They were talking before I sat and now there is just awkward silence.

"No," Blake says. "I was just telling the girls that Theo is flying in from Chicago and should already be there when we arrive."

"I came straight from a meeting and didn't have the chance to ask, do I need to have my office make arrangements for us?"

"I took care of it already," Gabby says. "There will be a car waiting for us when we land. There is a small motel that a family friend runs. They have rooms held for us."

"I have to admit, it feels a little intrusive for me to be there during such a personal time for his family."

"Ryan says you have been checking on him every day. He would want you there," Fran assures me.

More silence. I'm contemplating an excuse to move to my office when Gabby starts.

"You've been working on him?" she asks Fran.

"Everyday. He's not budging."

"And what about you?" she asks me. "What has he said to you? About Elise," she clarifies.

"We haven't talked about Elise."

"Why not?" She says this a bit too forcefully and doesn't back down when I give her a stern look.

I release a breath of agitation. "Gabby, the man's sister is dying. He and I are just getting to know each other. I don't think it's my place to tell him how I feel."

"Exactly," Blake agrees.

"He has to be pushed. He is going to need Elise."

"I agree," Blake says, "but we can't fix this for him. There are some things we have to do by ourselves."

"Bullshit," Gabby counters. "Ryan is grieving. He doesn't know what he needs. Of course he's not going to make the right decision."

"We have to respect his wishes," I say in an attempt to end this line of discussion. "I would, however, like to talk with you." I stare hard in Blake's direction.

"I was just following orders," Blake says, obviously not needing any explanation.

"I knew you knew." Gabby hits Blake in the arm.

"I'm your boss. You follow my orders."

"Sorry, man. If it's a work thing, I'm your guy. In this, my loyalty is to Elise."

"You could have told *us*," Gabby hisses.

"If Elise wanted you all to know, she would have told you. Besides, she didn't tell me where she was staying."

"How did you know then? I'm pissed Elise didn't trust me enough to tell me." Gabby crosses her arms, flopping back in her seat.

"I outfit her with her burner phones. Of course I know how to find her. I've talked to her. She needs time. It's not my place to tell anyone where she is." He gives all of us a hard stare. "And I won't apologize for it. I would do it for any of you."

"Until Elise asked, and then you would tell her."

"Gabs." Blake shakes his head in frustration. "You know Elise doesn't need me to tell her things. She can find the answers all on her own."

"I know. Her ninja skills seriously piss me off." Blake playfully pats her on her head. "Did it feel good to beat the shit out of Dylan?" she asks him.

"I haven't touched him. Reid handled it all."

"Actually, Miller Donovan had it all handled before I was able to." I fill the team in on what happened. I don't think Elise would mind.

"We don't think they would try to go after Elise, do we?" Fran asks.

"No. They are being watched, and even though Blake won't admit it, I know he has someone on Elise."

"I don't, actually. Whoever she is staying with has their own team watching her," Blake says before thanking Shawn for the meal he's setting in front of us. "How did you find her?" Blake shifts the conversation to me.

"I have my ways."

"Emme told you," Blake says, not withholding his smile.

"Yep."

"Emme hid Elise. I love her," Gabby says peppering her fish. "She seems like a really fun person to hang with. I forget Elise helped her when Blaine Moore was being accused of stealing from his production team."

"I think Elise also worked with her when Theo helped with the video."

More pieces of the puzzle about Elise fall into place as I listen to them talk over dinner.

We touch down a little after two in the afternoon. Blake helps the girls load their suitcases into the back of the Tahoe while I attempt to call Elise again. Straight to voice mail and Blake still refuses to give me the number to the phone he gave her.

"You want to drive, boss?" Fran reigns in my attention.

"How far to the farm?" I look around. We are definitely in bum-fuck Indiana. I have no idea where we are going.

"About a 60-minute drive."

"Nah. I'm going to do some work. One of you can drive."

"Gabs, you're shotgun," Fran says, climbing behind the wheel.

"I'm going to nap," Blake announces, sliding the last of the bags in place.

"I'll take the third row. You can stretch out," I offer. I want to have some distance between me and the girls, so I can think about what I want to say to Elsie. I wanted to email her from the plane, but knew I needed to participate in the conversation.

Cocooned into the last row, I prop my laptop on my knees and open my email. I have about a thousand from being out of pocket today, but those will have to wait.

I watch acre after acre of corn stream past the window as I write, delete, and rewrite the email.

"Grow some balls and just do it," I mumble to myself. I decide to just say what I really want to tell her: "Dove, I love you. I'm sorry. Please call me. R."

"We're here." Fran announces pulling me out of my reverie. One hour and I have eight words to show for it. I hit send.

We enter under an iron arch that announces we are on the farm. Fran drives another five or so miles before we pull up to a classic white farmhouse with a large wrap around porch and green shutters.

There are a few cars already here, and there appears to be at least a couple dozen people milling about. When I climb out of the car, I move over to Fran whose eyes are wet and brimming. I squeeze her shoulder in support and step to the back of the SUV. Theo greets me with a handshake and a one-armed hug.

"Thanks for coming, man. I know it will mean a lot to

Ryan and the team."

"When did you get here?"

"About an hour ago."

"How is he?" Gabby asks, coming around the side.

"Struggling," Theo says.

The girls head into the house.It's strange. Men are the one's designed to be tough, but the women are the ones going straight to Ryan while the rest of us hang back, not really sure what to say or how to offer comfort.

"Has he said anything?" Blake asks.

"Nothing," Theo replies. "His mom told me he hasn't eaten in days. He won't say more than three words to anyone. He's completely shut down. The only time he has something to say is when his mom makes him leave the room so Emily can FaceTime with Elise. He gets so angry about it that she insists he leave."

"Everyone here family?" I ask, nodding a hello to someone greeting us.

"A couple of siblings on their parent's side. Other than that I think it's mostly people from church."

"Let's go," Blake says softly. The three of us climb the steps to porch. Theo opens the screen door. The entryway and main room feel like a home, like love lives here.

Theo guides us to the back, through the dining room and into the kitchen. Ryan is pouring the girls a glass of lemonade. Every available counter space is covered in food. There must be enough food here to feed a hundred people.

"I'm Janice, Ryan's mom." A pretty brunette woman introduces herself to me.

"Nice to meet you. Reid Beckett. I hope I'm not intruding. I wish we were meeting under different circumstances."

"You aren't intruding at all. Emily wants Ryan to have his

family around him and that is what you all are to him." She hugs Fran and introduces us to her husband. Ryan bears his father's name and they are spitting images of each other.

"Thanks for coming, boss," Ryan says when he enters the kitchen. He shakes my hand and then Blake's. He gives a half-hearted hug to the girls, but when Fran and Gabby both try to force him into a deeper one, he isn't having it. It's clear he doesn't want to be consoled or comforted.

"Uncle Paul and Aunt Mary just went in," he tells his mom.

"Why don't you get some fresh air? Show your friends the farm. Then they can start setting up some tables to feed everyone."

"We're on it," Gabby tells Fran. Both of the girls grab aprons. Before we've even stepped out onto the back porch, Gabby has four men moving picnic tables closer to the house.

The farm is large, I suppose. I have to admit I know nothing about farming. There's corn as far as the eye can see. I can see the barns and the areas the animals are kept. I can't help but to think of Elise. I imagine her stripping down and running into the kitchen only to be greeted by Ryan and his preacher. The image curls my lips slightly.

Ryan rattles off a bunch of facts about that farm that no one really seems interested in, when Blake interrupts him. "I wish I had words to make this better, Ryan."

Ryan stops, looks through him, not at him, and turns to leave. Blake reaches out to stop him, placing a hold on his arm. Ryan doesn't say anything, but his eyes move from his arm where Blake's hand is up to Blake's face.

"Fine," Blake concedes and drops his hand. "What the fuck? How long has he been like this?" Blake asks after Ryan walks away.

"Since we brought her home." The voice from behind startles us.

"Sorry about the language, sir," Blake says to Ryan, Sr.

"Janice and I thought he might settle down once we were back on the farm, but nothing has seemed to work. We're worried about him. He hasn't slept in days. He won't accept anyone's touch other than to hold Emily's hand. It's like he wants to crawl out of his own skin. We should have insisted he call you all sooner. He needs you. My son is as stubborn as that mule I have in the barn." He squeezes Blake's shoulder.

"What can we do?" Theo asks.

"Just be here. Elise is taking the brunt of it. I trust her. She knows."

"Knows what?" Blake asks.

Ryan, Sr. looks at us like he's a little surprised we haven't put the pieces together already. "Elise knows he would never forgive himself for being angry with Emily for not wanting to fight the last weeks of her life. She's protecting him from himself."

The girls have the tables draped in checkered cloths and wildflowers on the table.

"It looks like a shindig," Blake says with furrowed brows.

"It's a celebration of all Emily is," Fran says. "Now, move the tables back under the overhang. It looks like rain."

We run food to the tables, making sure everyone is fed. Ryan and his parents are back upstairs. Once everyone is situated and eating, the skies open up. The heavens seem to be mourning with the family.

The rain and the late hour push some of the folks on home, and by the time we have everything cleaned up it's close to seven.

We sit on the front porch, giving polite goodbyes to

those leaving. The rain is steadily coming down in sheets, and I wonder how anyone can see to leave this place. I guess when you live here you know where you are going.

"My sister is with Emily right now, but I know Emily will want to see you girls," Janice says to Fran and Gabby. Ryan steps out onto the porch and flinches when his mom touches his arm. I stand and offer her my seat. We all sit in silence and listen to the rain.

A large pickup truck pulls up, and Janice stands to greet more church people. My heart skips a beat when I see Elise standing in the pouring rain. Her hair is in short braids. She has on a raincoat and yellow rain boots that come up to her knees, and she's more beautiful than I have ever seen her. I move away from the pole I was leaning against and take a step toward her, but Theo's arm wraps around me holding me in place.

"What the fuck are you doing here?" Ryan takes three steps down. Elise stays frozen in her spot, not moving, not saying a word. The porch light is shining on her face. The rain pours over her as she steels herself against Ryan's tirade. "I told you I don't want you here."

Janice starts to say something, but Ryan, Sr. stops her. Ryan takes more steps towards Elise. She takes four big ones without an ounce of hesitation at Ryan's anger.

"This is your fault. I'll never forgive you. She would still be fighting."

Theo vibrates a little, and I realize he still has his arm wrapped around me. I'm not sure if he's holding me in place or if I'm holding him.

"You aren't welcomed here. Go the fuck home, Elise," Ryan howls, moving his finger out of her face to grab her by her open raincoat, pulling her slightly off the ground to his eye-level. "Leave or I'll make you leave."

Janice's soft gasp is enough to move me, and this time Theo doesn't stop me. Elise wraps her arms around Ryan before I make it down the porch steps. As the rain pours over them, Ryan's resolve breaks, and he wraps himself around Elise, falling to his knees. His sobs are audible even from the porch. Her hand rests at the back of his head, buried in her neck.

"I don't know how to live in a world without my sister."

"I know sweetheart." She kisses his forehead, wrapping her arms tighter around him.

"I'm sorry for the things I said."

"I know that, too."

I close my eyes and release a breath I didn't realize I was holding, praying Elise didn't use all her forgiveness on Ryan.

"Walk with me," Theo says, nodding to his left. "Let's go," he says when I don't immediately follow.

We walk around the porch to the back of the house. The rain is now a light mist, and I follow Theo out to the barn. It's lit and filled with a variety of farm animals. Theo picks up some pails and hands them to me.

"You know how to feed farm animals?" I ask.

"Yep. His parents taught us when we came out here to visit. Everyone pulls their weight." He runs a bucket of corn down a feeding trough for the chickens, nodding for me to do the same for the goats. Afterward, we lay hay in the furrows for the cows.

"I was mad at Elise," he says, leaning against the pitch fork handle.

"Why? I was mad at Ryan," I admit.

"Not now. In college. The night Elise was raped, we were supposed to go out." He clears his throat. It's clear it's still hard for him to talk about. "We had a fight. She said I was pushing Ross too hard and was going to lose him if I didn't figure it out. I lost it. I let my anger get the best of me and didn't show for our plans. Didn't call her. Nothing. Just didn't show. It was the only time in my life Elise and I weren't on the same side of things. She texted me and called me. Tried to fix it. She came by Ross' and I wouldn't answer." He fidgets. "She texted me several more times. Told me she was going out with Gabby and that she hoped I would meet them. I was still mad, so I didn't go. Then she stopped texting me. For Elise that is unusual. She's like a dog with a bone until she gets a response from you. Then I actually got mad that she gave up that easily. That she didn't try to reach me again. That I didn't hear from her for several hours. I was such an asshole. I wanted to make her sweat it out. To have to work for it. It wasn't until I got a 911 text from Gabby that morning that I actually returned a call. When I got there," a tear drops down his face, "and I saw what she had been through. What that bastard had done to her. And I knew. Knew I had fucked up and Elise had paid the price.

"I'm telling you this because you fucked up, Reid. You didn't trust Elise to do what she does best, to run this team and this company. You didn't trust her decisions when it came to her own safety. You didn't trust her. You fucked up, and Elise paid the price."

"Christ man. Don't you think I know that? Every fucking day she's been gone, I've known that." I kick a pail and chickens scatter.

"Then fix it. Elise doesn't need to be coddled or protected from doing what she does best. She needs someone who will take charge and fix things so she doesn't have to always be that person. You're that person for her, Reid. I saw it the first time she was upset and she went to you over me. I know you thought I was mad or upset by that, but I wasn't. I was just waiting for you to understand. When all that happened with Elise, I was a mess. Ross never left me. He healed me from the inside out. Yes, Elise and I slept together. Yes, we will each have a part of each other's heart, but she doesn't look to me to fix things. Not like she does you. That's a part of her I've never had. Not on this level. My point is, you're fucking this up thinking it has to be all or nothing when it comes to Elise's heart."

We finish in the barn and head into the house. Most everyone is gone. We find Ryan's parents and the girls talking softly.

"Finally he ate," Janice says, placing a plate in the sink.

"Why don't you all head to the hotel and get some rest. We'll call you if anything changes. Emily's resting. I know my daughter. She isn't going anywhere tonight."

"We'll go around the porch," Theo says pointing to our muddy feet.

As we all walk around the side of the house, my heart races at the thought that I'm finally going to get to wrap Elise in my arms. We turn the corner to see Ryan asleep on the swinging bed, his arms wrapped around Elise like she is an anchor holding him in place. And for once, I don't feel envious about it, because even though she's giving herself to Ryan, I know her heart is mine.

The rain begins to fall a little heavier again. The wind lends a soft sway to the swing. Janice hands me a quilt with a wink and continues saying her goodbyes. I lay the quilt over them and place a soft kiss to Elise's temple. She doesn't wake but her hand comes up to softly pat my cheek, and in that moment, I know this is the love of my life.

chapter eighteen

Elise

"I knew you'd come," Emily says, with her eyes still closed, when I climb in bed next to her.

"Where else would I be."

"You're the one person Ryan depends on."

"I'll let you in on a little secret."

"Do tell." She pulls on me, and I help turn her on her side so that she's facing me. She's weak and has been in and out of it since I arrived a few hours ago. Janice had told me Ryan hadn't been eating or sleeping. I knew it was time to come. As soon as he let go of his emotions, the exhaustion bore in and he finally slept. I've been sitting with Emily for the last hour or so, giving Janice time to rest, too.

"I'm not the person Ryan depends on."

"Yes you are. He lets himself relax around you."

"He's not as serious around me, but he's in love with Fran. She is the rock he depends on."

"What?" her eyes shoot open. "How did I not know that and why are you just now telling me?"

"Wasn't my story to tell."

"I'd promise you I'd take it to my grave, but I can't pass up one last time to tease my brother." She giggles, but I see the resolve in her face. She's ready.

"Are you scared?" I ask her, a tear falling down my face. We've talked twice a day since she's been home, but it's been about thirteen-year-old girl things. Things to make her laugh or dream. Things to help her forget, even if just for a minute.

"I'm not scared for me. I was scared that Ryan wasn't going to get where he needed to be before I left."

"You know you are my little sister, and I have loved every conversation these last several years."

"I know, Elise." Her eyes close. "Thank you for giving me friends. Without you and Gabby and Fran I would never know what it was like to have a boyfriend or fall in love or have sleepovers in high school. You let me live through you guys."

"Maybe that is how you are so wise. You're beyond your years. I'm going to miss you so much. You may only be thirteen, but you have given me more than I could ever give you." I kiss her forehead.

"So if he's in love with Fran, why didn't she make him better?"

"Well, love can be hard to explain. Ryan has known this was your decision and that it was the right decision since you made it. He just wasn't ready. This wasn't about him needing me and not Fran. It was about him protecting her from himself. He was too angry. And he is too protective of his love for Fran. He would never put this on her. He hasn't even told her he loves her."

"He is so lame. Has he kissed her?"

"Do not answer that question, Elise." Ryan's voice comes from the chair next to the bed. "And what do you know about kissing?" He lays on the other side of Emily.

"My brother is finally back." Emily turns over on her back and looks at him. "Are you going to tell Fran you love her?"

"Thanks a lot, Elise." Ryan sighs. Emily laughs knowing she has gotten me in trouble.

"Stop deflecting and answer her question," I cajole.

"While you're answering," Emily adds, "are you going to tell us if you've kissed her?"

"I already know the answer," I say.

"There's no way you know that answer, Elise," Ryan retorts.

"The night at our retreat, when Gabby stayed with me, I ran to the cabin to get something she needed."

"You mean the night she had sex with Owen against the tree?" Emily asks.

"She's thirteen, Elise. You told her about Gabby having sex?"

"Hush. I'm living vicariously through them."

"She's thirteen going on twenty," I remind him.

"I should have never introduced you two. You're a bad influence on each other."

"Leave us alone, Ryan. I won't get to experience this for myself. Elise is just helping me live. Go on, Elise." Her comment sends a wave of sadness through both of us that Ryan and I ignore. He winks at me and I continue.

"Anyways, I came by the cabin that night..." I pause to see if he remembers what night I'm talking about.

"How about you don't finish this story, and I won't tell Gabby that I know she had sex with Owen against a tree."

"Deal." We pinky promise. Our hands fall to a rest on top of Emily's.

"Do you love her?" Emily asks Ryan.

"Okay, so I've kissed her." Ryan feigns frustration.

"See, you have to ask bigger questions for him to avoid so you can get the answer your looking for," Emily tells me.

We spend the next hour laughing and talking about things that have nothing to do with Emily's condition. Emily and Ryan eventually fall asleep.

I slide out of bed and make my way downstairs. The house is quiet. Most everyone is home or at the hotel. It's almost four and I know the men will be here soon to start the farm chores. The girls did a good job of putting some of the food away. I rearrange the fridge to hold more of the containers left on the counter.

By the time the sun is coming over the ridge, I have breakfast ready and the screen door has opened and closed about a dozen times. People are back. I let one of the church ladies take over breakfast so that I can run to the motel to shower and change.

Theo is sitting in a rocking chair in front of his hotel room when I pull up.

"Ross coming?" I ask.

"He will when it's time. He's covering for another doctor, so he didn't feel like he could take more than a couple of days." He stands, wrapping me in an embrace. "You look good, sweetheart. Time away agrees with you."

"Thanks." I hug him back. "I need to get a room. I want to shower. What time are you all headed over?"

"They're all finishing breakfast in the diner. We should be leaving in about twenty minutes."

"I need more time than that. I'll meet you guys at the

house. The men were there to start the chores around the farm when I left, so I think the only thing needed is to keep people fed and be there for Ryan."

"How's Emily?"

"As expected. When I get there, I'll wrap up the service arrangements. I don't want them to have to worry with it."

"Okay. Shower. Maybe sleep an hour or two, if you can. I know you didn't get much last night. Take my room."

The room is open. There's something quaint and refreshing about being in a clean, bare-bones motel. I leave my muddy boots outside the door. The bed is unmade and I have to talk myself out of climbing into it. Dropping my clothes as I go, I walk the short steps to the shower and let the water run over me. The emotions I've held at bay since I got here are overwhelming. I knew that Ryan needed someone to place his anger on, but it's been hard to not be here for him. Hard knowing if I was making the right call. Hard knowing there was a chance he would never forgive me. Hard knowing this will be the last of my story with Emily. It's just a matter of time now, and the thought of losing her is more than I can handle.

The curtain slides open and Reid turns and pulls me to his chest. His arms encase me. The dam that I've had neatly holding everything into place breaks. Reid tightens his hold as the sobs escape me.

"This isn't something you can fix, Dove," Reid whispers into my hair. And in one statement, he has drilled to the core of what I am feeling. Helpless. This truly is not something I can fix.

"I don't know what to do with that. I don't know if I've lost my love for fixing things for people, or if it just filled a part of me that doesn't need filled anymore because I have you to fill it with."

"Whatever it is, Dove, we'll figure it out. Together. You can't run when it gets tough."

"I didn't run," I say with sudden irritation.

"You were AWOL for two weeks, and I didn't know where you were."

"I didn't run, Reid. I wasn't AWOL. I left. There's a difference."

I can see the stubbornness setting in his brow.

"Elise, I had no idea where you were."

"You left me, Reid. You were upset that I slept with Theo and ended it. Without a conversation. Without working through it. Then I tried again and you made assumptions about Knox. I tried a third time when I attempted to tell you about Brooks Anniston and you wouldn't listen. You don't trust me, Reid. It's clear to me. Why isn't it clear to you?"

He bites his lip, contemplating something. I can feel his erection against my stomach.

"I wasn't with Amber in LA. It was a coincidence that we were on the same flight."

"I know."

"You know?"

"Yes, Reid. I know. I told you, I hate drama. And I know you. I know your character. I know you wouldn't tell me you love me one day and sleep with someone else the next."

"I'm sorry."

"I accept your apology." I kiss his lips.

"You aren't going to make me grovel."

"No. These last couple of weeks haven't been about making you grovel. They've been about me. Deciding what I want. Who I want."

"I love you, Dove."

"I love you, too."

"We should get out. The water is starting to get cold."

I lean up on my toes to kiss his chin but he pulls back, cutting his eyes down to me.

"Elise."

"Reid?"

"Don't you have an apology to make?"

"No."

"No?"

"Did I stutter?"

Everything happens so fast that I can't process what order they happen in. All I know is the water is off, and we're in the bedroom at the foot of the bed.

"You don't think you owe me an apology?"

"Nope." My face is the picture of defiance.

He grabs a towel and places it on the end of the bed before motioning me to sit. He takes a step back and crosses his arms.

"I found out yesterday where you were staying."

"I know. Emme told me. You don't think she would tell you without giving me a heads up, do you?"

"Emme told me to give you space and to send you an email. Graham told me to go get you."

"That sounds like Graham," I smile.

"You might want to reconsider the smile when I tell you what he said before that. He suggested I should remind you who's in charge." He begins to pace back and forth. His erect cock sways slightly with the movement. "I've thought about this a lot, actually, since boarding the plane yesterday. And I think he makes a very valid point, Elise. When we started this, did I or did I not tell you that I run this?" He stops pacing and gestures between us.

"You did." I lean back on my hands and watch him.

"Why are you smiling?"

"You're cute."

"I'm serious, Elise. I never thought I was into spanking outside of sex, but I'm having second thoughts." He lifts me and lays me across his lap in one motion. "If you and I are going to be married, you need to understand that you don't leave. Ever. Do you understand?" He smacks my ass.

"Married?"

Another smack. "Of course we're going to marry. You're the love of my life."

"Did you plan on asking me?"

Another smack. "Are you going to say what I want to hear?"

"What do you want to hear, Reid? That you're in charge or that I will marry you?"

Another smack.

"I don't know what your intention is, but that's just making me hotter. Can I have a few more?" I giggle with the sole intention of getting a rise out of him, and I don't mean just his blood pressure.

"Satan suck a dick, you are the most frustrating woman I know," he growls, throwing me through the air. I land with my back on the bed. Reid lays on top of me, his weight holding me to the bed. His lips find mine and he kisses the giggle out of me. When he stops for air, the intensity of his gaze crashes into me.

"Elise, I really am sorry. I do trust you. I promise to do my best to balance my need to protect you and your need to do your job well."

"So, I'm not fired?"

"No, you're not fired."

"What if I quit?"

His raises my hands above my head. His eyes sparkle, and he runs his nose down mine before placing a light kiss to my lips.

"Are you ever going to make this easy?" he chuckles. "I promise I'll fuck up, but I promise I will always love you and I will never leave you. Marry me, Dove," he says sinking into me.

"Yes."

Elise

"What the fuck is that?" Gabby expels in a sleep deprived growl, attempting to turn off an alarm that is not even in the room. "Is there a fucking rooster in here?"

"The only animal in here is OctoElise." Fran answers.

"How can she sleep through that?"

"I never thought I could hate a cock." I say gravelly, letting Gabby know I'm not sleeping *through the siren ringing in my head*.

"Elise, you have your hand on my boob."

"She had her foot inside the back of my underwear earlier." Fran says rolling on her back.

"My feet were hot. And?"

"And your ass is like a butterball. It cooled them off."

"How small is this bed?" Gabby asks.

"How much did we drink last night?" I ask in total

disbelief of how I am feeling. I know better.

"Enough that the three of you had to be carried home." The male voice has the three of us lifting our heads to find Reid laying on the chaise lounge in the corner of the room at the farmhouse.

"Oh my god. It's coming back to me now. Did we re-enact all the best singing movies?"

"Yes." A smirk rises on Reid's lips at Fran's question, but he still has his eyes closed. "It started going off the rails by the time you all got to Wayne's World Bohmeian Rhapsody scene."

"Total classic." Fran rolls towards me snuggling into my side.

"Did I take my top off?" Gabby asks.

"Yep." Reid doesn't give her a reprieve.

"You had a camisole on underneath." I reassure her.

"There better not be video." Fran warns.

"I can hack into it if there is." Gabby reassures as there's a light knock at the door.

"Breakfast is ready." Ryan whispers entering wearing dark shades. He jumps a foot in the air when his mom speaks loudly over his shoulder.

"Good Morning Sunshines." Janice enters. "Everyone up."

"Chores to do." Ryan Sr. booms from the hallway and our groans and discontent makes them smile more.

"Where are the others?" Fran whispers standing and having to sit back on the edge of the bed before Ryan comes to help her to her feet.

"Why are you screaming?" Gabby throws a pillow over her head and hides.

"Gabriella Jane. Up." Janice stands in the room until we are all standing and giving her our best 'Yes Ma'am.'

"Why didn't she make Reid stand?" Gabby asks pulling on her pants and falling on her ass.

"Parents like me." Again, he doesn't open his eyes to respond.

"My parents don't." I mean mug him.

"They like me better than you." He pulls more covers over him and attempts to drift off.

"We should have gone back to the hotel with Theo and Ross."

"They were short rooms. Pipe busted." Gabby pulls on a beanie and we both throw on extra layers. "It's colder than a donkey's ass out there."

"All I know is, you don't work, you don't eat. And I'm not sharing my food. I don't care if we are engaged to be married." I run a finger over my 3-carat cushion cut diamond set in a diamond band. Simple but beautiful.

"I gave you a company, you would think you could give me a piece of bacon."

"Oh my god. Please don't get her started again." Gabby moans grabbing her scarf and heading out the door.

"You didn't give me shit. I started *my* company with *my* own money and *my* own reputation."

"But I didn't make you follow through on your non-compete clause."

"Because there wasn't one."

He slides to the end of the lounger and grabs my thighs pulling me into him. His head rests against my pelvis as he runs his hands up my legs.

"You still smell like the sex we had before we went to the bar."

"Nasty. I need a shower." I run my hands through his brown curls. I love his hair.

"I think it's hot. Kept me hard all night. Knowing you were covered in me." He says trailing light kisses across the skin he's exposed above my waistband. "Especially when that guy started to dance with you."

"I don't think it works like you think it does. No way…"

"Trust me. Men know."

"Cause you pee on things to mark them? Not sure I understand the thinking."

"You don't need to. I understand it. That's all that matters." His mouth starts to climb higher, pulling my shirt up, revealing my sans covered breast. I pull away to protests.

"We gotta go. I want to eat, so we gotta put in the work. Life on a farm."

"Why I live in the city." He begrudges standing.

It's been a little more than a month since we were here for Emily's funeral. Ryan took a leave of absence and stayed here with his parents until he felt like they were in an okay enough place for him to leave. He'll be headed back to the Chicago office next week. From there he and Reid are working out where he will be logistically. Chicago or Manhattan.

Theo and Ross arrive to help with chores, looking no worse for the wear. Feeding the animals works off the hangovers we're sporting and by the time we are done we are more than ready for the breakfast Janice has prepared.

We squeeze the ten of us around a table meant for eight. Everything is fresh and I swear there isn't a restaurant in New York that could hold a candle to our breakfast this morning.

"So, what's the schedule?" Janice asks passing the freshly squeezed OJ.

"We fly out tonight around dinner time. We'll drop the Chicago group off then fly to New York." I answer. "Then I'm headed to D.C. tomorrow."

"Don't feel like you have to stay here for us." She passes the eggs.

"There's snow in Chicago. They aren't expecting the airports to open until later this afternoon." Reid takes more bacon. "If we wait until dinner we're less likely to have delays and be forced to take these jokers to the city with us."

"Well then, I'll make sure lunch is ready around noon." Janice says.

"Ooh. Is there any of the potato salad left from yesterday? Can we have that today too?" Blake asks.

"Of course," Janice winks at him. "We've really loved the noise in the house the last couple of days."

"We'll be back in the summer." Gabby says breaking the silence that fell as we all reflect on why the house is quieter now.

"I want to meet with everyone for a couple of hours while we're all together." I say.

"Do I need to remind you this isn't your team anymore?" Ryan says with a mouth full of biscuit. "I know this because they are now my team. You are just a consultant."

"Ryan." I give him the evil eye. "Don't make me embarrass you in front of your parents."

"Boss, I recall you said you could control her."

I raise a brow to Reid at Ryan's comment.

"Elise. It's Ryan's team now. You consult when needed."

"Fine." I reply sourly, eating more bacon.

No one says anything for a beat waiting for more of a fight and I think they are a little surprised when it doesn't come.

"Elise?" A large smile spreads across Ryan's face as he says my name. "Since you're a consultant and I've been gone for a while, I was wondering if you could meet with the team today for me. You know, go over a few things." His eyes finally reach mine, filled with mirth and a hint of mischief, and I know then he's going to be ok. I throw a blueberry. "It'll cost you the last of your bacon."

Janice has lunch ready by the time everyone is showered, changed and at the table to meet. I take a minute to really reflect on the role each of these people have played in my life. For the last few years they have been every part of what I do. With me every step of the way.

I watch Fran and Ryan steal looks when they think no one else is watching. Both have been constants for me. Even. Steady. Gabby and Blake are alternating telling a story from the bar, making Janice and Ryan Sr. laugh. These two are loyal to the core. If I were to kill someone these are the friends that show up with a shovel and body bag. No questions asked and a bottle of red to drink afterwards. Both willing to step outside the lines if need be to get the job done. Both will be working directly with Reid in New York.

Theo and Ross as planned will stay in Chicago until the time is right for Ross to leave. Ross taught Reid and me both a great deal of what it means to trust the person you are in a relationship with. Theo. What can I say? He's my Theo. Reid wraps his arms around me and places a soft kiss to my temple, pulling his mouth to my ear.

"I promise to always be your person and make sure you are loved."

"It's just a lot of change."

"Yep. Exciting isn't it." He challenges me and pulls away just enough to get a read on my expression. He's right. It should be exciting. It is exciting. I realize then that slowly over the last few months he has been helping me transition without me even realizing it.

"I love you." I kiss his nose and finish my lunch.

It doesn't take long to clean up and only a couple of hours to make sure we have all the accounts covered and know what direction we want them to go in.

Reid has taken over three other companies that are keeping Ryan and Fran busy with the Chicago team. Gabby is hiring and building the New York office and Blake is working mostly for me and some for Reid. As usual, what I have him doing is to stay under the radar. Just by the nature of today's environment we've been using Gabby's hacking skills more and more. We are also considering hiring one of the world's most feared hackers, known to everyone simply as Mask. Blake and I know her by her given name, Charlotte.

"Done?" Fran asks recording the last of the notes on her laptop.

"We're done." Ryan says, slapping a deck of cards on the table.

"I'll get the snacks." Gabby says headed to the kitchen.

"I'll grab the beers." Ryan follows her as the rest of us clear our spaces. Reid continues to work on his laptop. Theo and Ross have moved to laying on the couch and watching the game while they rest.

"What's the score?" I ask.

"We're still ahead by like 1200." Blake says shuffling and dealing out hands as everyone takes their seats.

"So. You and Dean?" Ryan asks Gabby looking at Fran's hand.

"For now." Gabby answers non-committedly.

"That sounds promising?" Ryan questions.

"We're just enjoying each other right now. No stress."

"You guys enjoyed the hell out of something last week. That headboard was beating my wall harder than a choir boy in a porn shop."

We all turn to Fran and she shrugs her shoulders, "It's an expression. Either way," she continues, "there's a difference. You were just enjoying that John guy last summer. This is different."

"Of course, this is different. John was Rumpleforeskin. It's just not my thing." Gabby says.

"Cut or uncut. It's never been a deal breaker for me." I put in my two cents.

"I just can't. My grandad used to play with this gel filled tube thing. Said it was a stress reliever. When I slept with that guy in college that was uncut all I could see was that toy." She shivers. "It freaked me out. The eye goes in, the eye pokes out."

"What the hell are you even talking about?" Ross asks and Theo tries to persuade him to stay out of the conversation and not give Gabby any reason to expand.

"Now Dean. His is cut…"

"Finish that sentence and become unemployed." Reid threatens. "I do not want to talk about my brother. Actually I'm not comfortable with this conversation at all."

"Of course you aren't honey." I kiss his shoulder.

"But you understand what I'm saying right Elise?" Gabby winks at me.

"Hella smooth Gabs." Blake shakes his head.

"Gabrielle Jane." Reid gives her a chastising look and I know he acts mad but he can't resist Gabby. I think ever since he pulled wood out of her ass, he's had a soft spot for her.

"So Blake. How's it going with you?" Gabby asks and I

give her a death stare to be quiet.

"Good. I just wish we could get somewhere with the community center."

"How's West?"

"Gabby." I warn and she shrugs.

"I'm just saying. We still aren't talking about it?"

"No. We aren't." Blake shoots an eye at her.

"Whatever tickles your pickle." She winks then adds softly. "When you're ready." And Blake acknowledges her with a nod.

A week later

"Gentlemen." I say my goodbyes.

I was hesitant to be a part of this summit. There were no women in this group. I wasn't sure how a group of men can tell rape victims how to feel. I quickly realized that to call out rape in the country, it is going to take a group of men to stand up and say— This is wrong and we won't tolerate it. Just like women needed men to help them get the vote and will continue to need men to help in reaching equality in pay. Is it right? No. Is it true? I think so.

"Walk you out?" Pierce asks me closing his briefcase. We've been working together since I started consulting. Emme's offer was hard to refuse, but I felt like there were too many things I wanted to be a part of to be tied down to a singular focus. Emme agreed and I started my own consulting firm. Of one. Just me. I will still be the lead in the Addison Movement that Emme founded. So far business has been non-stop and I'm well on my way to adding another person. I'm not sure yet if it will be someone from my team or if I will bring in new blood. Reid and I are still discussing it.

We agreed, well I felt strongly, and Reid finally gave in, that we shouldn't work together. It was too hard for him to separate Elise the fixer from Elise his soon-to-be-wife. It took a while for me to decide. A part of me loves that he wants to look after me, make sure that I'm always safe. Loves that I am his priority. The business woman in me wanted the freedom to do as I wanted and to choose the clients I wanted. So, we compromised. Something he isn't used to doing.

"You heading back to the city today?" Pierce asks, escorting me off the elevator.

"I am. I have a friend coming home tomorrow and I want to be there when he arrives."

Ryan is back.

"I won't keep you long." He helps me into my coat when we stop in the lobby. It's the beginning of the year and it's freezing in D.C. Snow and ice are expected later today. I'm really hoping my flight isn't cancelled this afternoon. It's the earliest they have.

"I'd like to solicit your services." Something in his voice and his expression seem distant. Almost hollow. He runs a fierce law-firm in the city and has been serving as our legal counsel in writing the laws we are hoping to push through congress.

"What's up?" I study him and for a man as powerful as he is, he has trouble meeting my eyes.

"I need help finding someone. She's been eluding the people I've had searching for her. I'm wondering if you might have better fortune than they are."

"Who is she?"

His jaw ticks. "A friend."

"Pierce. You know once I start poking around, I will find

out everything anyways. You might as well tell me."

"She's my sister. She got mixed up into some things and ran away."

"Is she a minor?'

"No. She's 22."

"Okay. Send me what you have so far. I'll get started on it. I assume there's no limit?" Financially Pierce is set. He's heir to a large fortune and is one of the contributors to The Foundation that Graham and Emme are part of with 9 other billionaires.

"Yes. I don't care what it costs. If I have to utilize my other assets, I will."

"Other assets?"

"I choose to live off what I earn with my firm. It's more than enough for several families to be comfortable. The money I inherited I access only for the Foundation."

"I'll take care of it."

"I know it goes without saying, but I'd like this to remain between us."

"Of course."

"Would you like a lift to the city?" He asks escorting me from the building into the freezing air. "I'm flying back today."

"That would be…"

"She has a ride." A sultry voice that is directly connected to all the delicious feelings I have, sends me into overdrive.

"Reid? What are you doing here?"

"I came to get you. I didn't want you getting snowed in. Thought we could leave before the storm hits." His eyes fall to where Pierce's hand is resting on my lower back. He placed it there when guiding me through the door before him.

"Pierce." Reid greets him coolly and he laughs, removing his hand to shake Reid's.

"Hey man. I was just offering Elise a ride."

"Like I'd let her ride with you. You're a handsy mother-fucker."

"Ignore him."

"Trust me." Pierce says. "I learned a long time ago how to tune him out."

"You're welcome to ride back with us." Reid offers.

"Nah. The plane has to be back for a company flight tomorrow anyways. I'll go back with it."

They shake and I offer a hug to Pierce before he leaves.

Reid shows me back into the building and we take the elevator to the roof. There's a helicopter waiting for us.

"When did you get a helicopter?"

"I didn't. Graham let me use his. I didn't want us to get delayed. Already there's a back log of flights. Pierce should have ridden with us. I'm not sure he'll get out of here. Even with his private flight."

My arm shoots out to brace myself against Reid. I don't like being this high up, not to mention it is freezing up here.

We are secured into the back of the copter. I've ridden in it once with Emme. There's reclining seats and a large in-wall television as the main seating. There's a bench along the back of the wall where the bar is housed.

"How long is this flight?"

"Ninety minutes." We sit in two of the reclining chairs.

"What did Pierce want?"

"He needs me to work on a case."

"Anything you can discuss?"

"I honestly won't know until I get the file, but it doesn't look like a case that we will be able to discuss."

"Just so long as you remember our agreement." He gives me a pointed stare as our flight home begins.

"I remember Reid."

As part of our agreement when we got engaged, any case I sign on to that requires me to have security or to be armed, then Reid and I discuss it before I give final sign-off. Not the specifics if it's sensitive information, but at least the parameters. As my soon to be husband, I understand and respect of his need to make sure I am safe. And as his soon to be wife, he respects that I make educated decisions about what I should and should not be involved in.

"I hope Ryan and Fran make it in."

"They're here already."

"They are?" I can't keep the excitement out of my voice.

"He and Fran came in early to get ahead of the storm."

"They seemed excited to be staying at the house with us."

"Elise?"

"Yes?" I look up from my magazine when he doesn't answer right away. When my eyes meet his, there's a heat in them I've never seen from anyone before.

"Strip."

"Reid. I don't think this is the…"

"I said strip. Now." He adds after I hesitate.

Slowly, I peel myself out of my clothes while my fiancé's eyes feast over me. When I don't receive the next directive, I take matters into my own hands and straddle my knees on each side of his hips, massaging my clit as he runs his hands up and down my thighs, his aroused gaze directly on my face. As I continue to take my own pleasure, Reid undoes his buckle and lowers his waistband. His hands find my hips as he guides me down his rigid cock. He runs his tongue up my sternum and across my throat. When he clears the underside of my chin his eyes pierce mine and he issues his command.

"Go."

acknowledgements

I cannot believe I am three books into this crazy ride. Who would think people would want to read what I write? Crazy. CRAZY!

I was taking my niece somewhere the other day. She was in the backseat with her friends and they were singing to songs on the radio while talking about this cute guy at the basketball game we just left. It got me thinking about time and how quickly it moves. (Sentimental I know. Not my usual forte.) It was two years ago I wrote Taylor Made and less than a year ago since I published it. It seems like yesterday.

There are so many people who made a book happen. Who made *this* book happen. From the ones who work on the book to the reader who encourages an author with a simple message or share of a post. Each one giving up a portion of one of our most precious commodities. Time.

Everything we do is based around time. What time do the kids need to be there? What time does my next meeting start? What time are mom and dad getting here? What time does our flight leave? What time does the wedding start? What time is the funeral?

One commonality that we all share, no matter race, sex, creed, nationality or who you love— is time.

Every day I interact with readers and bloggers I am reminded what an honor it is to be given your time. What a gift that is to me. I never want to take for granted the time you give from schedules, families and friends to stop and enter a world I have created. The time to become a part of my characters' lives. The time to invest in me as a writer.

Thank you so much. I am grateful.

about the author

Stay up-to-date on upcoming releases and free reads by KJ Lewis by joining my newsletter

Newsletter bit.ly/kjLewisNewsletter

Keep in touch!
Website www.kjLewisBooks.com/